COURTNEY MILAN

Once upon a Marquess

For Thwee
who taught me to literally hold my tongue.

I ate your lip gloss the first time because
I thought I would like the taste. (I didn't.)
I ate your lip gloss the second time
because I was your younger sister.
Really not sure about all the other times.
Probably just poor life choices.

Chapter One

London, England, 1866

If it could have spoken, the tea table would have groaned. Biscuits, oranges, cordial, and two sorts of preserves were only the beginning of the burdens that Judith had forced the poor furniture to carry. Sandwiches and scones were still to come. The sugar bowl was filled; the teakettle stood ready to do justice to the small quantity of Darjeeling that she had purchased at far too high a price. The paper in the front parlor had been scrubbed clean, and a cheery bouquet of violets, obtained from the girl down by the market, decorated the side table.

It had been three months since Judith Worth had last seen her younger brother, and nothing—*nothing*—would stand in the way of his homecoming. Everything was finally turning out right. Almost everything, that was. But so long as she figured out that last unfortunate bit of business with her sisters, it would be everything in truth.

"There." Judith scooped the orange cat off the table.

Caramel had jumped up to investigate this strange and no doubt interesting collection of things to push onto the floor, and she meowed in protest at having her purpose frustrated. Judith set the sandwiches in her place. That left only…

"Theresa," Judith called, "where did you put the scones?"

No answer. Judith peered down the hall; nobody looked back at her except Squid, another one of Theresa's cats. He licked a paw and regarded Judith with suspicion and a swishing tail.

"Theresa!" she called.

"What?" Her youngest sister was not in the kitchen plating pastries. She stood at the window in the front room, her willowy figure half-hidden by the curtains that Judith had so painstakingly sent out for washing.

Judith sighed. "Ladies don't say 'what.' They say 'your pardon,' or 'yes, Judith.'"

"But I said 'what.'" Theresa puzzled this over with a frown. "So either ladies *do* say what, in which case you stand corrected, or I am not a lady, and I don't need to say 'your pardon.'"

Someone else would think her sister was sassing her. But no; that was just Theresa. And there were more pressing matters.

"What did you do with the scones?" Judith asked.

"Your pardon?"

"What did you do with the scones?" Judith repeated.

"Your pardon," Theresa shot back.

"For the love of mallards." Judith inhaled and made herself count. One mallard. Two mallards. Three… "I did not mean that you were *only* allowed to say 'your pardon.'" Her patience felt like an act of heroism. "Simply that it was a preferable response to shouting 'what?' like a common scullion. Please answer my question."

"Oh, I understood what you meant," Theresa said. "But you said 'what,' and I know *you* consider yourself a lady. I was just correcting you."

"I said 'what'? No, I didn't."

"*What* did you do with the scones," Theresa repeated. "Although I have to admit that 'your pardon did you do with the scones' sounds extremely strange. It can't be proper English."

One mallard. Two—no. Never mind the mallards. No amount of mallard-counting was going to help. She'd given her sister one solitary task the entire morning: Take care of the scones. How hard could it be?

She took a deep breath. "Theresa. Where are the scones?"

Theresa frowned and looked around, as if trying to figure out where she'd set them. The small front parlor wasn't what their family had once had. Once, Judith wouldn't have had to make the sandwiches herself, nor even place them on the table. Once, the dishes would have been porcelain and her younger brother would have been escorted by a pair of footmen in a coach instead of making his way home from the station on foot.

But there was no point counting once-upon-a-times. Once was not now. *Now* there were sandwiches and there was a table, and while Judith still had breath in her body, there would always be a welcome home.

Assuming, of course, that she ever found the scones.

Despite Judith's haphazard efforts to teach her sister deportment, Theresa always seemed to need something in her hands. Her fingers, seemingly of their own accord, pulled a bit of hair loose from the coronet of blond braids arranged on her head.

"Scones." Judith tapped the single empty spot on the table with her finger.

"Right." Theresa slowly nibbled that strand of hair. "Those. I got distracted."

Some people thought Theresa stupid. She wasn't, not remotely. She was just the kind of clever that cared so little for what others thought that it was often mistaken for stupidity. When she could make herself sit still long enough to read, she understood everything. But she was always distracted—or, at least, she was always distracting herself. She'd been difficult from the moment she was born.

"Concentrate," Judith said. "Start from the beginning. You took the scones from the oven. Then what happened?"

"No, before that," Theresa corrected. "I got distracted by the body on the front stoop."

Judith winced. "Drat. Not another dead rat. At least tell me it's in one piece. Or did Squid get at this one, too?"

Theresa turned back to the window. "I don't think we should blame Squid for this body. It looks human; that sort of prey is rather out of his league."

Judith's mind went blank. Slowly—because someone had to do something—she crept forward and looked through the curtains. "Oh," she heard herself say, as if from a very great distance. "You're right. I don't think Squid is at fault..."

"Of course not," Theresa said. "He is really an excellent cat."

Judith's eyes didn't seem capable of focusing. Once upon a time, there had never been bodies, not anywhere on the family properties.

She had, in fact, believed that time included the present. The neighborhood they lived in was cramped and crowded, but it was at least safe. Or so she'd thought. It—she found it easier to think of the thing before her front door as an *it*—lay, limbs splayed at odd angles, all awkward turns and disjointed twists. Ragged hair—possibly blond beneath the cap—obscured the face. A scarf in a fluttering greenish-blue wound around the neck.

Eton blue. Her heart came to a standstill. But this...*thing* was too small to be her brother. Her pulse started again with a painful thud as she recognized one last detail: A knife handle protruded from the chest.

"Wait here," she said sharply.

Once upon a time, she might have screamed, but she was beyond an attack of the vapors. Lady Judith Worth—that poor specimen of belabored femininity who might once have collapsed in a swoon—had been through too much to hesitate now. She turned the key in the front lock and thrust the door open.

A breeze, scented with smoke from the factory three streets down, wafted in. The street was mostly empty, the day uncharacteristically gray and cold for summer. Little curls of fog greeted her, flirting with bits of rubbish that had collected in the gutter. Thirty yards down, almost hidden by the mist, Old Mother Lamprey stirred a common pot by the side of the street. A man passed by her, clutching a coat around him and looking warily from side to side. Alas, nobody looked as if they'd just left a corpse behind.

Speaking of corpses. Judith took a step forward, squinted at the thing, and let out a sigh of relief. No wonder the limbs had seemed so unnatural. It wasn't a body—at least, this thing had never been living. It was a set of clothes stuffed with hay, the sort of straw guy that might be burned in a glorious bonfire in early November.

But it was July. Guy Fawkes Day was a distant memory. And this was not just any set of clothes; it was the blue-fabric uniform that an Eton boy would wear, complete with insignia. Whoever had left this grotesque thing here had thrust a knife through what would have been the heart of the corpse, spearing it to the top post of the railing. It was a rusted blade with a splintering handle, but a knife didn't have to be sharp to cut to the point.

Judith had seen the same tableau before. It had been in the caricatures of her father that had hung in all the gossip-shop windows: stabbed through the heart and buried at the crossroads, as all suicides had once been.

There was a reason she had no use for once-upon-a-times.

She walked up to the body and took hold of the knife. If she gripped it hard enough, her hands would stop shaking—just like that. She gave the handle a hard yank.

It resisted for a moment, sending splinters through her gloves. Then it came free of the wooden post with a jolt, one that sent her staggering back a pace.

A piece of paper, fashioned into a square and folded small enough that she'd not noticed it at first, remained speared on the blade. She slid it off and opened the missive.

To Benedict WorthLESS, the note read, *traitor's son and useless rat. We look forward to the next Half. Come prepared. Better yet, crawl away like the cowardly scum you are and don't come at all.*

It was signed simply: *You know who.*

Anger flooded her vision with red. *Her* little brother. This was *her* little brother they were talking about, her sweet twelve-year-old boy. She'd practically raised him herself. She'd fought for him. She'd scrimped and saved, and when even money hadn't opened doors, she had argued. She hadn't let up, not until the trustees had reluctantly agreed to let her brother come to Eton for the summer Half as a start. She'd worked for *years* so he could have a chance to take the place that should have been his.

And *you know who* had stuck a knife through his heart in effigy. They'd called him *Benedict Worthless.*

After the scandal with their father and their elder brother, she hadn't imagined that Benedict would be popular. Not at first. But she'd hoped that if only she managed to get Benedict off to school, his warm smile and his wry sense of humor would eventually win over the other boys.

Stupid. That was what came of once-upon-a-time thinking. Those wistful *if onlys* never happened, not to their family.

But it didn't matter. Eight years ago, Judith had promised that her brother and sister would have something like the life they had been born to, no matter what she had to do to see it through. She hadn't ground her way through impossible odds just so some bullying schoolboys could ruin Benedict's chances.

"It's not a very good body," Theresa said behind her. "The legs are too short in proportion to the torso. Don't you think?"

"Theresa," Judith said. "Do you think it's good manners to criticize bodies?"

"Probably not." Theresa shrugged. "But it is good fun."

Judith changed the subject. "I thought I told you to stay in the house."

"But I wanted to see."

Judith sighed. "A lady does as she's told."

Theresa shrugged this off. "That's a useless rule. What is the point in even articulating it? If I'm a lady, I shall simply tell myself to do as I please. That way, I can satisfy everyone."

Judith cast a glance at her sister, but there was no time to chop logic. First things first: She had to get rid of this thing before Benedict arrived home. If this was what greeted him upon his arrival, he'd likely suffered enough indignities the last few months. She would spare him this last one. She knelt in front of the makeshift corpse, gathered its limbs, and lifted.

The thing's behind slipped, sliding down her gown, spitting straw across the steps to the house.

Judith gritted her teeth, shifted her weight, and regathered the straw man in her arms. It was unwieldy and she couldn't see her footing, but she held on as best as she could. One step down. A second. She found the third with her toe, but as she moved forward, her shoe slipped on loose hay. She grabbed for the rail. As she did, one of the arms worked loose, smacking her with a cuff that spattered straw in her face.

She dropped the body and swiped at her stinging eyes. Either she'd have to take it in pieces—and there was no time for that—or...

The man who had passed by Mother Lamprey a few minutes back hadn't taken any soup from her. Instead, he'd continued down the street, headed toward Judith. He frowned at the house two doors down from her and took a piece of paper from his pocket, peering at it suspiciously.

Judith made a snap decision. She straightened her spine and marched toward him.

"Ahoy there," she called. "My good man."

The man straightened and half-turned his head to her.

"Yes," she said, a little more loudly. "You there. I have a task for you, if you care to earn a shilling. It won't take but five minutes."

He turned all the way toward her, and in that moment, Judith realized her mistake. She knew this man, and he didn't need her shilling. In her mind, she'd thought of him as an unpleasant person. She'd let her feelings alter her memory, stooping his straight back, narrowing those wide, laughing eyes.

The reality of him was all too different. Little curls of black hair peeked out from under his hat. His trousers were crisply ironed and clean; his coat was tailored to the precise fit of his shoulders. Beneath the new mud he'd acquired on this street, his boots were the deep, glossy black that only the most dedicated valet could achieve. His eyes met hers. Dark, thick eyebrows shielded mobile eyes of a lighter brown. They were smiling eyes, mischievous eyes, eyes that said that this man knew a good joke, and if you leaned in, he'd tell you the punch line.

Those eyes lied. She knew them all too well.

He took a step toward her. "There you are, Judith. Of course I'll help." His lip quirked. "And there's no need to pay me. We're old friends, are we not?"

It had been eight years since she'd last seen him in the flesh. The sight of him froze her in place, robbing her momentarily of speech. Speak of once-upon-a-times gone awry. Once upon a time, there had been a marquess, and Lady Judith Worth had thought that he would conquer the world.

He had. She just hadn't realized at the time that he meant to take it from her.

"Well." She swallowed. "Lord Ashford. I didn't expect to see you here, but I suppose you'll have to do."

For a moment, that eternal smile of his faltered. He looked into her eyes, and she felt a cold wind sweep over her.

"Yes," he finally said. "I suppose I will."

Chapter Two

A military strategist had once told Christian Trent, the fifth Marquess of Ashford, that no battle plan survived contact with the enemy.

He had not, he reflected, truly understood what the man had meant until the moment he saw Lady Judith marching up to him for the first time in eight years. Her chin was raised a good two inches; her eyes snapped a brilliant, vivid brown. She was bristling with anger, and she was everything he remembered—vibrant, lovely, and stubborn. All the plans and lists that Christian had made in advance of this meeting drained right out of his head.

She gave him a cutting look from head to toe.

She had asked *him* to render assistance, he reminded himself. *She* needed *him*, for some reason. She was the one who had treated him as if he were a pariah and a monster these past eight years. Yet when he saw her for the first time, his heart still gave a glad, traitorous skip of recognition.

Here, it whispered. *You've finally come home.*

"I suppose you will have to do," she said.

The things he had done because he was *supposed* to do them. No doubt she still thought him the villain in her life.

"Yes," he said. "I suppose I will."

She gave her head a little shake, as if she could slough off the sight of him. "What are you *doing* here? I said—no, never mind what I said. There's no time for argument. We have a body to dispose of."

He'd considered a number of possibilities when Judith sent a note requesting his assistance. *Help me hide a corpse* had not been on that list.

He blinked down at her. "I beg your pardon? I don't believe I heard you correctly."

"We have a body to dispose of," she repeated, enunciating the words, as if saying them more slowly would make them more socially acceptable. "Now are you going to help me, or must I drag it to the midden myself?" She didn't wait for his answer; she turned and walked a few paces down the street toward a house where there was indeed a bodylike heap on the porch.

He had no doubts that after all was said and done, she'd still cast him as the villain of her life in her head. But he wasn't a mustachioed, plotting malefactor, bent on destroying everything good. He wasn't a blackguard. He wasn't an evildoer. He was the sort of villain who made jokes and tried to do the right thing, damn it.

No battle plan survived first contact with the enemy, so it was imperative that Christian kept his objectives in mind. He had just one: If she was going to hate him, the least she could do was hate him accurately.

"How exciting," he said to her back. "Hiding corpses. My favorite activity; how did you ever know? I always said that if I wanted to become an accomplice to murder, I'd do it on a public street in broad daylight. How kind you are to oblige me in this."

She looked upward, raising her hands in supplication. "I don't have time for explanation. There isn't a minute to spare."

"Of course not," Christian said. "If you wait too long, your next victim might get away. By all means, let me not delay my initiation into a life of crime."

She turned to him. "Oh, for the sake of cygnets."

Christian blinked for a moment at that turn of phrase until he remembered that Judith had started swearing on waterfowl at the age of eleven. He was never exactly sure how that had started, but now that he'd heard her say it, he couldn't imagine how he'd forgotten.

"If I had killed anyone," she went on, "do you think I would tell *you,* of all people? Have you eyes in your head? I'm talking about that." She gestured at an indistinct lump lying on the somewhat rickety steps leading up to a dismal-appearing house.

He squinted and let out a covert breath. It was not, thank God, a *real* body. It was a set of clothes stuffed with straw, a beige-ish-something-colored scarf trailing behind it.

"Here," she said. "Help me with it, and quickly."

"It's lovely to see you, too," he said dryly. "My, it has been years since we last spoke."

"Goodness." She pronounced that word with a hint of venom, touching her fingers to her forehead.

For a moment—just a moment—he had the sense of how much must have changed in the years since he'd seen her. For that second, Judith looked…

Old was not the right word. Neither was *haggard*; that last implied a loss of beauty, and he did not think that Judith could ever be anything but beautiful. But she was no longer a young girl on the verge of her first Season. She would have been…he subtracted from his own age…twenty-six last March, on the fifteenth, and the fact that he still recalled the date of her birth was not lost on him. But for one second, there was something about the way her lips pressed together, the way her eyes shivered shut, that made him think that Judith had very clearly become an adult, and not just because of the passage of time. She had responsibilities. She was, perhaps, weighed down by them.

She shook her head. "Might we defer the social niceties, if you please?"

He'd prepared himself for this. There was enough history between the two of them that given the opportunity, they'd descend into mutual sniping. He'd steeled himself to rise above the fray. He was not going to snap at her. He was going to be polite and kind. He was going to be himself, and if part of him thought that being kind was a weapon—a weapon of the *see what you're missing* variety—then, well, all the better.

"Body or no," Christian heard himself say with all the stiff, kind politeness he could muster, "I do not consider myself to be a complete savage."

"There is no time to not be savage," Judith said.

While he was working out that double negative, she bulled on.

"I promise you, in ten minutes, we shall go in the house and I shall make tea and we will ask after each other's families. We shall stare at each other with all the awkwardness that our situation entails, and if you like, we shall call that being civilized. But we haven't time for this now."

"You know," Christian said, "one of the reasons we always did get on so smashingly well is that we were both utter shite at etiquette. Very well. We can pretend later."

"This particular situation is difficult." She glanced at him. "Can you carry the entire…thing…or must I assist?"

Standing that close to Judith? He was too aware of her as it was. He looked over at her. He thought of her hands overlapping his, her body pressing against his.

"That would be entirely unnecessary," he said on a growl. Christian leaned down and gathered the straw figure in his arms. It was awkward and ungainly; the limbs kept trying to straighten. Judith was smaller than he was, and she'd likely not had the arm span to encompass the thing. He barely managed.

"I have it." He lifted. "When you say this particular situation is difficult, did you mean needing to dispose of this fellow here, or were you referring to the fact that we were going to get married until I proved your father and brother were traitors?"

She looked up at him with wide, outraged eyes, and stared ahead with compressed lips.

Better. If she was going to hate him, she'd best do so for the right reasons. "I see we're not discussing that," he said. "Never fear. Let's talk about…" He rustled the thing in his arms. Little bits of straw poked out from the clothing. "…George here. Thank you for him. This is an extremely convenient gift on your part. A straw man? For *me?* With Parliament sitting next month? I always say the House of Lords can never have too many."

She gave him a pointed look. "This way."

He followed her down the street. "Technically," he explained as they walked, "that's untrue. One *can* have too many straw men. 'Try another logical fallacy,' I'm always saying. 'Exclude more middles. Go for the *ad hominem* attack—I'm always hoping for some real insults, you know. But alas. It's straw men, straw men, straw men, nothing but straw men all session long."

Once, that would have made her laugh. Now her eyes flicked to him briefly. "I understood your jest the first time," she said. "There was no need to explain it."

"Right." He wasn't going to stop being himself simply because she hated him. "Uncomfortable silence it is, then. Don't mind me; I'm used to uncomfortable silences. Why, I annoy my mother twice daily, just so she can look at me reproachfully."

"The refuse heap is just ahead," she said. "To the right, and then turn into the alley immediately on your left after that."

"Just think," he continued. "If you'd married me after all, you, too, could be an expert in uncomfortable silences."

Judith inhaled sharply.

Good. He'd come all this way because she'd asked for his help—well, and technically, because he wanted something in return. If *he* was going to be made to feel uncomfortable, she should have to as well.

"If I'd married you after all," she said, "I would have had a real body to dispose of before now."

"How sweet." Christian hoisted the straw man higher onto his shoulder. "I knew you cared."

They turned the corner and found themselves standing almost face to face with a boy.

No. Not just *a* boy. For a moment, Christian felt light-headed. The boy was maybe twelve years old; his hair, somewhere between a dirty blond and a sandy brown, was badly in need of cutting. His hands were in fists at his side, and he looked down as he strode ahead.

The boy paid so little attention to his surroundings that he almost walked headfirst into Christian.

Christian almost let him do it. For one second, Christian thought he was looking at Anthony—at his onetime best friend, the boy with whom he had climbed trees and argued Aristotle and spent all his summers.

It was almost as if he had walked into one of his own nightmares. He couldn't breathe. God, he missed Anthony. Nothing in the world had gone right since his friend had been transported. Nothing.

But this boy was not Anthony. He was too young, and Anthony was too dead.

This must be...

"Benedict," Judith said, moving forward.

Benedict. The youngest child in the Worth family. He'd known Benedict first as a squalling baby, then as a precocious toddler, and finally, eight years ago, as a cherubic child with fat cheeks, dimples, and an eternal smile.

Benedict had neither dimples nor smiles now. Once Christian's mind was shaken of the terrible suggestion that Anthony had returned, he could see all the differences between this boy and his friend.

Benedict Worth was thin, too thin. His wrists were just bones underneath those wide cuffs. There were dark shadows under his eyes and a fading yellow bruise across his cheek. A scab across his lip spoke of more fights. He looked up at the two of them.

He didn't blink. He didn't frown in question. He simply saw the thing that Christian was carrying and he blew out a long, resigned breath.

Judith stepped in front of Christian. "Benedict," she repeated, reaching for him. "It's so good to see you."

He brushed off her embrace, stepped around her, and stared at the thing that Christian was carrying. He didn't say anything; he just quietly unknotted the scarf.

That was when Christian realized what he should have seen from the first. This was no straw man. It was a straw boy wearing an Eton uniform.

The scarf was likely that odd shade that everyone called Eton blue, claimed was green, and looked basically beige to him. Christian felt sick.

He'd given advice during her father's trial in the House of Lords. He had known when he uncovered the evidence that his best friend would be implicated in the process. But he'd been right, damn it. What was he supposed to have done? Looked the other way from their treason?

But in the aftermath, her family had lost its fortune. Her father had taken his life in the cell, and Anthony… God, Christian couldn't think of what had happened to his best friend.

He'd been right, but sometimes doing the right thing hurt people.

Benedict let out a long breath. "Well." His voice was high, on the verge of breaking. He didn't look at his sister. He didn't look at Christian, either. He simply shrugged his shoulders and looked away into the swirling fog. "I see there's no need to explain why I'm never going back."

Chapter Three

If the awkward nonconversation on the way to the midden had been uncomfortable, the discussion on the way back was downright disastrous. There had to be some way to negotiate the situation effectively, and Christian intended to find it.

Judith jerked her head in the direction of the heap just around the corner; Christian slipped past the two siblings to deposit the thing in the rubbish. But even following the two Worth siblings at a distance was awkward.

"Benedict," she was saying. "Sweetheart, I'm so glad you're back. There's scones. Currant scones. And sandwiches. And ginger-ginger biscuits."

Benedict stuffed his hands in his pockets. "Lay off, Judith. I'm not *eleven.*"

Judith's smile faded. "No," she said slowly. "You're twelve. A big—a man, I mean, and—"

"Stop patronizing me," Benedict snapped. "You think you can bribe me with sweets? I'm not going back."

For once, Christian decided to keep his mouth shut.

"Benny." She glanced behind them at Christian, and then back to her brother. "You know how important this is. How necessary."

At that age, Anthony had never looked so...old. Benedict's forehead wrinkled. His lip set. He shook his head and looked forward.

"See," she said, "you're obviously upset. Let's get you home, and…and…"

Home was on the horizon. Benedict didn't look at Judith as he trudged up the steps and opened the door.

"You'll see," Judith was saying behind him. "I'll make it work. I always do, don't I?"

Benedict stepped inside the house, and before Judith could follow behind him, he slammed the door in her face.

Judith swallowed. "Oh dear. That could have gone better."

Slowly, she ascended the stairs. Christian followed silently behind her. She opened the door and let out a gasp.

No wonder; Christian inhaled a lungful of smoke.

"Oh, for the love of geese," Judith swore. "Theresa! *Theresa!*"

"What?" A pale shadow in dark gray popped around the corner. Christian took a step back; Theresa Worth was almost as tall as Judith. She was blond and frowning and surprisingly pretty.

Judith faced her down. "Did you not take the scones from the oven? They're *burning.*"

"I like the smell of burnt scones." Theresa blinked rapidly at her sister. "I was playing Dante's Inferno. I was imagining that I was a heretic trapped in a flaming tomb. As the fire ate my limbs, I—"

"Tee." Judith set a hand on her hip. "You could have burned the house down, yes? Fire is not a playtoy. You are *fourteen,* for God's sake."

"I'm not stupid," Theresa said scornfully. "I was watching them. I had a bucket of water right here, just in case. Nothing was going to happen."

"At a minimum, you were *wasting* them."

"I was going to add salt! Everything is better with—"

"Not this," Judith said baldly. "Open the windows. Take the scones outside."

Tee blew out a breath. "I have to do *everything* around here. Benedict didn't do *anything* today. Why doesn't he have to help? Just because he's a boy and went to school— which *I'm* not allowed to do—he gets sandwiches and biscuits and fruit? All I wanted was scones my way. Why can't I have anything?"

"Your scones are scones of evil," Judith said. "And you're not doing *everything*. You're just cleaning up the mess you made. Now stop arguing and go do it."

Theresa made an enraged noise before stomping— loudly—down the hall.

Judith exhaled and shut her eyes.

If she didn't remember he was here in a moment, he was going to have to…

She didn't need reminding. She turned to him. That pasted-on smile of hers slipped at the edges.

"Civility," she said with a frazzled air. "Yes. I promised you civility when we returned." She bit her lip, as if puzzling out how to manage that. "How good to finally see you again, Lord Ashford." This was not accompanied by a smile. "And I did request your assistance, after all. Do make yourself at home in the parlor. Have a sc—no, not those. Have a biscuit. I need to, ah, go see how Benedict is…settling in." She turned away and then swiftly turned back. "No. I spend too much time around Theresa. I have to make myself clear. Forget what I just said. Do not literally make yourself at home."

"Figuratively will do," he agreed.

She nodded and dashed up the stairs, leaving Christian in a cloud of smoke.

"Benedict?" he heard her say. "Benedict?"

Civility. If they could agree on civility, they might be able to get through this.

Over the years, he had sent her a passel of notes. One, apologizing for raising the question he had at her father's funeral. Two, asking to see her. Three, several years ago, letting her know he was investigating her brother's disappearance. Four, informing her of the results of that investigation, and five, a few months ago, asking her for a favor.

He had not had a word of response from her. He'd heard nothing at all, in fact, until he'd received her letter this morning.

There is a matter of some delicacy before me, one that may require your particular reputation. If you're willing to help, send a man of business. In return, I'll consider the favor you asked of me.

He would solve whatever problem she presented, and she could easily solve his. He couldn't let himself care if she hated him at the end.

Although perhaps he could see why she might do so. He'd spent summers at her family's old house. It had been comfortable, clean, and spacious. This place? It was a hovel in comparison.

Mismatched cushions covered the chairs. There were no painted landscapes on the walls, just yellowing whitewash. A hutch sat against one wall. All the china, such as it was, was laid out on the table, and so there were empty shelves, with the occasional bit of thick crockery set in place with as much pride as if these dishes were the finest porcelain. It was all completely altered, all except...

Except, on the top shelf, there sat a familiar shepherdess. She was surrounded by three sheep. The shepherdess was china, as were the sheep. But the inner workings of the piece were clockwork. Christian should know; he'd given it to Judith almost ten years ago.

I don't want you to forget me, he had said. God, he'd been stupid then, thinking that his biggest worries were that he might miss Anthony—and that Judith Worth might fall in love with someone else.

He wasn't sure what it meant that she'd kept his clockwork shepherdess.

He could hear the indistinct murmur of Judith's voice from upstairs. Chipped china, threadbare cushions, and this rickety house in a neighborhood that could at best be called unfashionable. The shepherdess, looking over her shoulder, had once seemed serene and accepting. Now, that little arch of her eyebrow seemed mocking.

No, Judith hadn't forgotten him. That would have been too easy.

He sighed, picked up a plate, and served himself a biscuit.

Christian had ripped the pastry to pieces, and the smoke from the unfortunate scones had somewhat dissipated, by the time he heard Judith come down the stairs.

Technically, he reflected as he looked over his handiwork, "ripped to pieces" was a tolerably accurate description of the biscuit's demise. The part that would give anyone else pause was what he had done with the deceased baked item.

He had distracted himself.

He hadn't stood up and wandered around, poking into business that wasn't his. He had studiously ignored the roll-top desk he could see in the adjoining room, the papers neatly stacked in order. He hadn't questioned—much—whether the disturbingly rundown state of this home meant that creditors posed a problem for the Worth family, such as it now was. He hadn't even looked for Anthony's journals. He'd sat in one place and minded his business.

His business had been the demolition of pastry into its constituent crumbs. Demolition, then division: He'd separated the bits first by size, and when that seemed unsatisfying on some gut level, by deviation from roundness.

Then, he'd very carefully started eating—from the most irregularly shaped crumb toward the most symmetrical.

He was almost finished with the infuriatingly oblong bits when Judith came in.

She stared at him—and the four plates he'd laid end to end in order to sort the crumbs into place.

"Lord Ashford," she said. "What are you doing?"

He had been arranging crumbs. After a moment, he gestured at the plates. "Making myself at home. Figuratively speaking. Not literally."

She waved a dismissive hand in his direction, thank God, instead of saying something like *Is there something wrong with you?* or *Why is there a line of crumbs three-and-a-half plates long on my dining table?*

No. This was Judith. She'd never cared about his oddities.

"If you have to do that," she said, "next time use the big plates. Less washing up."

"Fewer gaps between crumbs," Christian agreed. "I didn't know where the large plates were, though. And it is doubtful there will be a next time."

Their eyes met, acknowledging the fact that he was unlikely to be in her home again. Not that he was unlikely to arrange crumbs when he was bored. Putting things in order was soothing. Some people found that odd—he'd heard various politely worded iterations of "Oh dear, Christian, what are you doing?" over the years.

But he wasn't *too* odd in that regard, he didn't think. After all, there was the phrase "out of sorts." Whoever had come up with that must have been something like Christian.

He'd assumed, for much of his young life, that the phrase described the peevishness of mind that one encountered when one had nothing to put in order. He'd always been confused when his compatriots used it to describe a mere lowness of spirits on account of not having had their favorite pudding at dinner. That had nothing to do with sorting at all.

It wasn't until Judith had walked away from him that he'd understood that *out of sorts* could also mean that you'd entered a state of mind where no sorting would help.

Judith was here now, but her presence didn't help. She sat across the table from him and took a biscuit of her own, which she placed on a plate. A single plate. She didn't meet his eyes. She picked up a knife and very, very deliberately, cut her biscuit in half. It crumbled, rather than slicing smoothly, little biscuit crumbs splattering about in an irregular pattern.

"Christian." She cut the biscuit in quarters. "I asked for your assistance on a delicate matter. You really ought to have sent a man of business, as I asked."

There was not an ice sculpture's chance in Hades's ballroom that he would have done so. "And as we both know," he said, "I am not much given to following orders."

She sniffed. "The matter is beneath you. I need someone to glower and look manly while I ask questions."

"I glower." Christian fixed her with his most intense gaze. "Behold this manly glowering."

She glanced up from her plate almost reluctantly.

He gave her his best glare: eyebrows drawn down, nose flared in distaste. "Answer the lady's questions," he growled, "or it will not go well with you." He glanced around the room and spotted a disappearing white tail. "You, or your cats."

Her lips pressed together, but she hadn't managed to hide her smile quite swiftly enough. He awarded himself a tentative point.

"You would ask too many questions yourself," Judith said. "And this, as I said, is a delicate matter."

Once, Christian had made the mistake of agreeing to watch over his second cousin at a musicale. Her mother had become ill halfway through, and his aunt—who was supposed to chaperone her—had been nowhere to be found. Lillian had run afoul of a "delicate matter," by which his cousin meant that she had started to menstruate while wearing a very white gown.

He'd sacrificed two handkerchiefs and a cravat in service of her dignity.

Christian looked over at Judith, who was subdividing her biscuit into indiscriminate crumbs. "Whatever delicate problem you are wrestling with, it is undoubtedly less delicate than some of the ones I have dealt with. I promise I'll keep anything you tell me in confidence."

Her chin went up. She looked off over his shoulder, as if seeing that unfortunate event eight years ago in the distance.

"If I have no other choice," Judith said. She tapped her fingers on the table. "Recently, and anonymously, I sent my sisters money to be held in trust for either their marriage or their majority—some four hundred pounds apiece. This was sent to our family solicitor."

Christian blinked at her. "Anonymously? You sent them? But—"

Her fingers stilled on the table, and she shook her head. "If I had wanted to explain myself on this matter, I would not have prefaced any of this with the comment that you ask too many questions. The money was not illegally obtained. I sent it. I don't wish to go into any further particulars. Might we continue?"

"I suppose," he said, looking up at the ceiling, "that this money was somehow derived from part of your father's fortune? Something that he managed to somehow hide?"

She sighed. "Those are questions. You are the worst nonquestioner I have ever met."

"True. But look at my glower." He demonstrated it for her again.

"Christian." She folded her hands on the table and looked in his eyes. "Lord Ashford. I know we were once on intimate terms. But you must get this into your head:

We are not friends. My father was convicted of treason. My brother was found guilty of abetting him. And the entire foolish investigation surrounding them would have come to nothing had it not been for you."

It was a good thing he was still glowering.

"We are not friends," she said. "My brother was transported. My father was sentenced to death, stripped of all the properties that he could be stripped of. The only things we had remaining were those few items that belonged to me and my brothers and sisters, alongside an ancient, moldering estate in the family name—and that's little more than a pile of rocks in the wilderness."

He knew all this.

"I need help," she said. "Because of you, my relations want nothing to do with me. I had nearly a thousand pounds set aside so my sisters might have a chance at a decent marriage. I know they won't find lords; I had hoped for vicars. Camilla will be coming out in a matter of months. I sent every spare penny I had to our family solicitor anonymously, and now he tells me he can't speak at all of their situation."

Christian slowly flattened his hands against the table.

"I need someone with some social clout to send the message that I'm not to be ignored. I have no one else to turn to. I need help. Not a joke. Not a laugh."

He waited for a moment, just to make sure that she was finished. "I could hardly forget that I figure as the villain in your piece, either. But you asked me for help. *Me.* Not anyone else."

"I had noticed."

He ignored this. "This is not about reminding you that we are familiar. This is who I am. I'm shite at etiquette. I make jokes. And despite everything that has passed between us, I still try to do what is right. That is why, after all these years, after telling me to my face that we are not friends—that is why you knew that if there was one person on this earth you could ask for help, it was me."

Her nostrils flared. "I thought I could ask you because you are in my family's debt."

Christian found himself smiling. He steepled his fingers. "Why yes, I am."

She shifted uneasily.

"I spent every summer with your family until I was eighteen years old," Christian said. "Your brother saved my life. You—" But he wasn't going to talk of her. He shook his head. "I *am* in your family's debt. That time meant more to me than I can ever say. But that isn't what you meant, was it?"

He didn't wait for an answer.

"Did I ask to provide counsel to the man who was presiding over your father's trial in the Lords? No. I did not. He came to me and asked me—*me*, a twenty-one-year-old boy, one who'd spent summers in the house of the man—to advise. He told me that I could ensure he had a fair trial. Of course, everyone in the House of Lords thought the whole thing was a joke and a farce at the time—something that they had to do to satisfy the public after those first rumors surfaced."

She shook her head.

"Talk of jokes. It was a great joke. An utterly hilarious joke. That's what trials in the House of Lords were, they told me. They were just there to meet the form of the law. That it was understood that nothing would happen."

He picked up another crumb.

"Or do you think I owe your family because the truth came out? They handed me a mess of financial evidence, all of it confusing. I thought, 'Well, here is something I can do—I can sort this out.' I thought I could be more than a useless block sitting to the side. I expected that once I cleared away the cobwebs and the tangles, everything would be put to rights." He looked at her. "What was I supposed to have done, Judith? Should I have realized that your father was *guilty,* and then hidden that fact? Is that why I owe you—because I assumed that should I find the truth, it would exonerate him completely?"

She leaned forward and practically spat at him. "You spent summers with my family. You should have known it wasn't true. He wasn't guilty. Anthony wasn't guilty."

She made no such impassioned defense of her father. Telling, that.

He simply shrugged. "I don't owe you your fantasies. I didn't ask for the rumors to be true. I didn't *want* proof your father had sent military secrets to Britain's enemies. It wasn't my fault the proof was there. It was your father's."

She flinched.

"We're not friends." They never would be. Not when she could scarcely look him in the eyes. Not when every time he looked at her, he remembered falling in love with her. Not when he still woke up in a cold sweat thinking of what had happened to Anthony. He was sure that he'd done the right thing, exposing the truth about her father and her brother. But he had never been able to quell that tiny whisper of doubt.

Judith was right. He wasn't here to make jokes. He was here to lay his final worries to rest.

"We're not friends," he repeated. "I'm not here to help you. You told me in your note you'd think about the favor I asked of you. I'm here because I want something in exchange. I want your brother's journals."

Her chin went up.

"*Anthony* was my friend," Christian said. "I miss him. It would be a comfort to have something of his." Not just a comfort; his way forward hinged upon those journals.

Judith's face was pinched. "My brother's journals are not for sale."

"Ah, well." He stood. "Then looking into your little problem is something that you can't purchase."

Her eyes flared in an almost-panic. "Please. There has to be something else you want."

Yes, he wanted to say. But he didn't speak, and he wouldn't let himself want. Judith felt like home to him in the way that only nostalgia and old memories could. He wasn't about to be tricked by that. He'd yearned for her too long, but no matter how much this woman looked like her, the Judith he wanted didn't exist. He wished for a world without complications, a world in which it didn't hurt to look at her. He wanted a world where he could laugh at how much her younger brother looked like his old friend.

He wasn't going to get any of that.

"I'll accompany you," he said. "While you ask your questions. Not my man of business. We'll agree that you don't have to like me, and I don't have to change. I'll borrow Anthony's journals for two weeks. I won't need them longer than that. That's my final offer."

He'd known that Judith had been shunned when her father was convicted. He could tell that she had nobody, truly nobody, to turn to now, because she actually considered his offer with a frown.

Her jaw worked. "You'll get the journals when I have confirmation the money has been credited to my sisters' accounts. And you won't ask questions."

"I won't ask *many* questions."

Her eyes narrowed and her nose wrinkled.

Christian simply shrugged. "We both know I'd be lying if I agreed not to ask any. If you ask for my help, you'll get help. My way." He held out his hand.

After a long moment, she took it, giving him a brief, firm handshake. She dropped his fingers almost immediately, pressing her hand to her skirt as if he'd burned her.

"When will you need me to do my glowering?"

She was still rubbing her hand against her skirt. "I'll make an appointment and send you word."

"Good." He stood, found his jacket. "Then I'll be going."

He gave her one last nod and took his leave. The stairs to the house creaked as he left. They were uneven; he hoped they were safe.

But the Worth family could not be his concern. He had to think of himself.

Once he had Anthony's journals, once he could make that list. Once he had given himself a target and a course of action, well… Surely then he would finally be able to sleep at night.

Chapter Four

udith made herself put away the feast she'd prepared. The chair where Christian had seated himself had been intended for her brother. She should have been in the midst of a happy celebration. Instead, the gloomy clouds outside seemed to have gathered inside the room. The oil lamp flickered; there was a new crack in the shade, and the light cast shadows on the remains of the feast laid out. Dark plates laden with what should have been a bounty stared back at her like ominous ruins.

It was a waste, a horrible waste. The biscuits would keep; the preserves, of course, wouldn't spoil. The expensive Darjeeling she folded up in a twist of paper. It might be useful on some other occasion.

The sandwiches, on the other hand...

That was what was left of her hopes. Stale bread, when she'd hoped for so much more. She piled sandwiches on a plate. By the time she'd cleaned up the remains of their noncelebration, night had fallen in earnest.

She headed upstairs with her plate.

The door to Benedict's room was still shut.

God, the memory of his face this afternoon still haunted her. He'd seemed closed and flattened. That delighted spark her little brother always had in his eyes had been absent.

Benedict had been five years old when their father's scandal had changed their lives forever. He scarcely remembered their old family home. He was the one who had first forgotten what should have been his due because of his birth. He'd been the first to adapt to their new surroundings, the first to stop complaining, the first to start laughing again.

She hated that someone had made him stop.

She raised her hand and knocked on the door.

Silence. More silence. Then, the shifting noise of furniture grating against the floor, and...

"What?" Benedict's voice.

"It's Judith. Can I come in?"

Yet more silence.

"I promise I won't lecture," she said. "But I have sandwiches. They're turnip. Your favorite."

Food had been a problem when she had first found herself here. They had sold everything they could— gowns, porcelain, jewels, toys. This property had come recommended by her solicitor. Not too unsafe, still in town, and there had even been a real oven in the kitchen for a cook. Too bad they'd been unable to afford a cook, but how difficult could it be to heat food?

Judith had quickly discovered the answer to that. It had been difficult. *Damned* difficult.

Benedict and Theresa had eaten almost nothing for what had felt like weeks. They hadn't started eating until Benedict had invented the turnip sandwich.

They were cheap, filling, and completely horrifying.

"Very well." A further scrape—as of her brother removing the chair from beneath the door handle—and the door swung open.

Her little brother, not so little anymore, looked up at her. "Good evening, Judith," he said politely.

Oh, his face. She could have cried. That bruise. The split lip. Up close, she could see the fading evidence of other injuries—tiny discolorations of his skin that said more about his Half at Eton than any of the complaints he had never made.

"Well," she said finally. "You look terrible."

That won her a cautious, tremulous turn of the lips.

"Here." She held out the plate. "You need a turnip sandwich."

He let out a long exhale and took one. He turned it in his hands, sniffing it, and then took a bite. "Mmm." His eyes shut. "Now that's a proper turnip sandwich. They don't make those at Eton, now. Never enough salt on anything. Salt makes everything better."

A turnip sandwich—a *proper* turnip sandwich—was made with two toasted slices of bread. One should be smeared liberally with brown gravy. The other bore a scrape of gooseberry preserves. Between these two disgustingly bedecked pieces of bread, there was a generous slice of roasted, peppered turnip. Liberal salting was the key.

A turnip sandwich, especially one made with such odd ingredients, should not have been *good*. It shouldn't even have been *edible*. But six-year-old Theresa had cried that she wasn't eating turnips, she *wasn't*, and that she wanted a proper sandwich. Benedict had invented this.

And when Theresa had still refused, Judith had salted the turnip.

"Salt makes everything better," she had said then. "Here. Try it now."

Amazingly, Theresa had eaten it. Ever since, it had been a household favorite. Which just went to show that children were disgusting.

But it didn't matter. If she could make Benedict's life better with turnip sandwiches, she'd spoon out all the salt in the world.

"You don't have to lecture me," he said, cramming a full quarter of the sandwich into his mouth and talking around it.

She hadn't lectured him, so she just waited.

"I know how important my role is. I'm to go to Eton. I'm to make friends and pave our way into society and take my place as earl one day, and...and..." He faltered. "I don't want to let you down, Judith. Nor Theresa, nor Camilla. But I can't go back. I can't."

"Here," Judith said as he bolted down the last bit of crusty bread. "Have another sandwich."

He took it.

"I know," he said through a mouthful of food. "I'm a Worth. Worths do impossible things."

She had told him that a thousand times.

He contemplated the toasted bread. "I tried. Really, I did. I tried being friendly, and they pummeled me. I tried being meek, and they pummeled me. I tried asserting myself, and they pummeled me. I offered them the ginger-ginger biscuits that you sent the first week as a peace offering. They took them. Then they pummeled me, and thereafter, they just stole them out of hand."

Her stomach hurt listening to this bare recital. Her fingers clenched around the sandwich plate. "Who are *they?*" Judith asked innocently.

Not innocently enough. He looked over at her. "I didn't try being a snitch, Judith," he said scornfully. "It's beneath me, and besides, it wouldn't work. They'd just pummel me again."

"You wouldn't be snitching," Judith said matter-of-factly. "Just disclosing a fact to your dear sister in confidence."

"Oh, well, in that case." Benedict shook his head. "Did you know I was born yesterday?"

Judith remained diplomatically silent.

"I know you, Judith," Benedict said. "You're imagining talking to them. You're thinking of how you can fix things, figuring out some way that you can make V—" He coughed. "Make them into my friends. But you can't fix this. You can't."

He did know her. He knew the precise direction of her thoughts, questing forward. She just wanted everything good for him.

But even before he'd been *pummeled,* as he put it, Benedict had always acted older than his physical age. He looked up at her with eyes that said he understood how things worked now, that he knew better than to try.

It broke her heart that he should think so. He'd been hurt, and he'd decided there was nothing to be done about it.

This isn't going to happen. Not this way. Not to my little brother, she promised him. *I will fix it. I will fix everything.*

She smoothed back the hair on his forehead. He looked up at her with wide, unblinking eyes, eyes that seemed like little oil lamps illuminating her.

Judith set her hand on his shoulder. "All right," she whispered to him. "We'll figure out something later. Sleep well." She leaned over and kissed his cheek.

"Did you have a sandwich?" he asked her. "You need to eat, too."

He was too young to be so old.

She crossed the hall to her next charge. Theresa, unlike Benedict, was sitting up in the bed that she shared with Judith. Her nightrail, a thick blue flannel, fanned out around her feet.

She was idly rubbing the cloth in her fingers. She was going to wear it out prematurely. She always did.

"Good night, Theresa." Judith might have scolded her for the cloth, but she'd scolded her enough as it was today. Any more, and she'd always be screaming at her sister. "Do you need anything?" she asked instead.

Theresa nodded. "I want you to tell me a bedtime story."

On another night, perhaps Judith might have obliged. Tonight, she wanted to go back to her desk. To look over her current project upstairs. She wanted to think of Anthony's journals—she had no idea why Christian really wanted them.

But when he had said they would be a comfort…

Up until that moment, he had looked precisely as she had expected Christian to look: confident, charismatic, and far too attractive. For a moment, though, he'd looked…weary. Bereft.

He should be bereft. He'd practically killed her brother.

She wanted to be able to feel all the things she hadn't let herself feel during the day, and she couldn't do it around her sister. She felt achy inside.

The novel from the lending library on Theresa's nightstand—something set in the time of Arthur—was the last thing she wanted to look at. Who wanted to read about courtly doings and brave deeds on a night like this?

She gave her sister a smile instead. "Theresa, I have so much to do. Do you really need me to read to you as if you were a child again?"

"Oh, no," Theresa said with a puzzled frown. "Of course not. I don't want you to read me a story. I want you to *tell* me a story."

Judith sighed. "Tee, none of the stories in my head are suitable for bedtime."

"I want you to tell me a story about Anthony."

The smile Judith had been keeping on her face froze.

Oh, God. She should never have told those stories in the first place. Years ago, when she'd believed Anthony was still alive, she'd brought out his journals to read to her siblings at night. But dry lists of men he'd encountered when he'd accompanied her father on that ill-fated ambassadorial trip to China, along with descriptions of the trade deals they'd made, had not made for good bedtime reading.

Judith had improvised. Instead of sitting in tents and reading reports, Anthony had fought off pirates. He'd caught sharks. He'd bargained for exotic trinkets and fought with swords.

Theresa knew that the stories had been stories. She had, after all, accompanied Anthony on that exceedingly boring trip. She had still adored Judith's tales, demanding they be told again and again.

"I scarcely remember him," her sister was saying. "I keep trying to hold onto the things I know. I know he loved me." She ticked these off on her fingers. "I know he called me 'Teaspoon.' I know when I used to fly into one of my rages that he was the only one who could calm me. I know he gave me the best hugs, like he was wrapping me up and squeezing me. He told me he would always be there for me when I needed him. I'm forgetting everything else." Theresa looked up at her sister. "I know I spent those two years on the ship with him and Father. I should remember him better than anyone. What if I don't remember him when he returns?"

Oh, God. The evening had wanted only this. Judith sat on the edge of her sister's bed and tried to stay calm and collected. "Theresa. Sweetheart. My memories can never be a substitute for yours."

Her memories were spiked, sharp things. She had watched her brother's trial. He'd not said a word in his defense. She'd watched his conviction, too. She'd ached as he sat in the dock, his face not changing as the evidence against him mounted. *Speak*, she had wanted to scream. *Speak*.

Anthony hadn't spoken. She wasn't sure who he had been protecting. Maybe her father, if she was being honest; when the evidence against her father had come out, the House of Lords had not yet convened. Anthony had stood trial first. He hadn't spoken at all. She'd watched him take his sentence of seven years' transportation without a hint of emotion. She'd traveled to Plymouth to watch him board the prison ship that was supposed to take him to Fremantle.

Judith had been the one to first read the newspaper report: His ship had encountered fierce weather. It had been blown off course, had landed not in Australia, as planned, but on the coast of Sumatra, of all places. When the population of prisoners was accounted for, Anthony had not been present.

"But at least you have real memories," Theresa said. "I don't trust mine. I remember—" She cut herself off with a sidelong glance at Judith. "I don't even remember what he looks like."

Judith had waited and waited to hear anything about her brother after that ship had sailed. A year had passed, then two. She had hoped and hoped. Back then, she'd had nothing but hope.

"Theresa," Judith said softly. "I want you to consider the very real possibility that…"

That our brother is dead.

"That I might lose *all* my memories?"

"No." Judith shook her head. "You won't. You're fourteen, now. You won't lose memories that easily. But it's not the memories that matter, darling. It's the feelings you have. What are the feelings you have for Anthony?"

Theresa looked upward. "I used to think that the world could not spin correctly on its axis if he were not present."

"I'm sure you've learned otherwise."

"Oh, no." Theresa shook her head. "I've just learned to walk off-center."

The world is never returning to center. He's not coming back.

She had never said those words to her sister.

She hadn't held anything back—she had told her sister the truth the day she learned it. Christian had her brother's whereabouts investigated; Anthony was nowhere to be found. Theresa knew that the prisoners on that ship had been decimated by disease and poor feeding by the time they arrived. The surgeon on board the ship had listed Anthony as ill. There were records of twenty-three men who had perished, and twelve more who were simply gone. During the worst of the storm, record-keeping had not been a priority on board. Anthony was one of those who had disappeared, and it was all too obvious what had happened to him. One of these days, Theresa would accept that her brother had been one of the dead, too.

But before Judith had known for sure, after they'd depleted the false tales from the journals, she'd invented stories about what might have happened on that ship. Anthony among the pirates. Anthony on a desert island. Anthony and the friendly dolphins. They'd been comforting tales of adventure, told to assuage the ache in her heart. They'd been comforting *then*.

They were soul-destroying now.

Anthony was dead. Their father was dead. Camilla was... Well, Camilla was not speaking to any of them. It was just the three of them, she and Theresa and Benedict, and it was Judith's responsibility to make sure that they were well. The earth hadn't spun correctly since she'd been placed so precariously in charge, but she'd kept it upright.

So she swallowed the lump in her throat and smiled at her sister. "You'll know," Judith said. "If you ever see him again, you'll know it's him because the world will right itself. If you don't want to lose your memories now, you might consider taking a moment every evening to go over the ones you have. Think of them every day, and you'll never forget."

Theresa nodded solemnly. "And one day," she said, "I'll be able to ask Anthony for the ones I've lost."

Tonight was not the night she would be able to make Theresa face the truth. That day would come, Judith was sure—but it wouldn't be tonight.

She fled before she broke down.

Up in her workroom, she surveyed the carnage. Bits and pieces of wire, coiled springs, and molded gears greeted her on the bench to the side. A sheaf of papers— her notes—sat on the table.

She was close, so close, to victory. Everyone had told her that her sisters would never have any real money of their own. That Benedict would never attend school. She should have run out of funds four years ago.

She'd managed it. It was the thing she told herself night after night when things got difficult, when all the worries she'd squelched during the day came back to revisit her. She'd managed.

By all the birds that had ever flown, she'd *won*.

Victory felt rather hollow tonight.

Her elder brother was dead. Her younger brother was being tormented. Theresa refused to face reality. And Camilla hadn't spoken to her in almost eight years. Judith had been proud, so proud of every evening she'd spent with her head bent over clockwork designs, every minute she'd wrangled through contracts with the man she worked with in Scotland. She'd planned it all so that

Camilla would get a little money a few months before she came out.

It wasn't the sort of inheritance they'd been raised to expect, but four hundred pounds was freedom. The freedom to marry for love—or to not marry at all.

Maybe she'd hoped that her next-youngest sister would know that it was from her. That it was her way of apologizing for that long-ago argument. *I'm sorry, Camilla. I love you. I want you back.*

She put her head in her hands, but she didn't let herself weep. Weeping was what one did when one ran out of options, and Judith wasn't finished. She was a Worth. She wasn't going to give up. Not now. Not *ever*.

When she was done not weeping, she raised her head and went back to fitting gears together in her mind. Dancing couples or gliding swans weren't going to be enough this time around. She needed a clockwork design that was simple, something that everyone would see and want.

She'd won before. She would just have to win again.

And if she had to bear Christian's presence to make sure that Camilla received that money before she debuted?

Well. She would do it. She would do anything to keep her family safe.

I n his dream, Christian was on a ship—not a steamship with smokestacks burning coal, but one of the older ships with big, billowing canvas sails. It was the kind of ship that a boy might receive as a toy on his birthday.

The ship felt a little like a toy, as if he were both standing on deck and holding it in his hand all at once. A storm raged around him. Dark clouds loomed overhead, and spikes of lightning stabbed out over him. Around him, waves rose like dark canyons and then crashed into valleys.

The deck of the ship had no rail. It was a dream so familiar that even in his sleep, he knew everything to be false. Nobody was on board except Christian—Christian, and the man he glimpsed across the deck, a dark figure obscured by sheeting rain. The man stood near the edge, near those dangerous waves.

Christian couldn't see the man's face, but he knew who it was. He'd had this dream before.

"Anthony," he called.

There was no answer.

"Anthony!" he shouted, but the wind whipped the words from his mouth, drowning them in the shrieks of the storm.

He made his way across the unsteady deck, groping, nearly losing his balance.

"Anthony," he said as he drew closer. "Anthony, get the hell inside. You're going to—"

As he spoke, a great wave of salt water crashed into Christian, rolling him, catching him up, filling his mouth so he couldn't scream. He grabbed wildly as he slid across rough wood. His hands found a rope; he held fast, choking, until the water passed over his head.

When he opened his eyes, Anthony was gone.

Christian scrambled to the edge of the careening ship. He was cold; his fingers seemed numb. There, he saw that familiar figure again, shrouded in the shifting shadows off the edge of the ship. Anthony was scarcely holding onto the side. His fingers slipped, grasping for purchase.

"Anthony."

The man's head tilted up.

Christian leaned down. "Take my hand." He reached down, stretching.

Christian had never managed to reach Anthony in any of his dreams yet, but still he kept trying. He had to.

The other man adjusted his precarious grip and reached up. His hand met Christian's with a solid shock. Their fingers slipped wetly, but Christian made himself keep hold of his friend's wrist. He held fast, even though the tossing of the boat threatened to yank his friend away.

"I have you," he said. "I have you. Hold on, damn you."

He braced himself to pull. This time, he'd save him. This time…

The man looked up. It wasn't Anthony. Christian had one shocked moment to look into his own eyes—light brown instead of blue. He had one moment to feel his own hand holding himself up in a weird, doubled dreaming way. Then he gave a great shout and let go in surprise.

The last thing he experienced was his stomach dropping as he fell into a great valley of water. He simultaneously watched himself slip from his own grasp.

"Shh," said a voice. A hand pressed against his forehead. A familiar taste, herbs and honey, bloomed on his tongue.

He woke gasping. Someone was holding his head up, tilting his chin so he could swallow.

Christian reacted without thinking, knocking the mug away, spitting the disgusting mess in his mouth out before he could think better of it.

"There, there," said a gentle voice. "You're only dreaming. I have more if you want it."

His mother. His gods-be-damned ever-loving mother. Christian inhaled, catching his breath. Waiting for his heart to stop racing.

"You were dreaming," she repeated. "It was just another night terror, Christian. I made you a little posset."

He could taste milk and spices and honey on his tongue. He could taste the laudanum, too. Bitter, ugly, and yet after all these years, it still curled around him, whispering that he could have peace. It would be the peace of utter surrender.

"No," he said hoarsely. "No possets."

"I heard you shouting three rooms over. You're not sleeping well, Christian. You're my son. I only want to take care of you, and I'm worried." She brushed her hand across his forehead.

His mother loved him. Christian had always known it. He owed her far more than he could say.

He had always had vivid dreams. They had been particularly bad when he was a child, and she hadn't fobbed him off on any nurses. She'd woken with him, soothing him, telling him it was all right. She'd saved him and damned him, all at the same time.

Just once wouldn't hurt. Just this once.

Laudanum lied. In the darkness, he could not see the bowl on the table to the side of his bed. He sat up and found it in the dark. There were a handful of beads in it, round little balls of all sizes jumbled together. His fingertips rolled over them in the dark.

One. That was the smallest, there, a hard nub scarcely the size of a pinhead. He captured it under his smallest finger. *Two.* Slightly larger. His heart began to slow. *Three,* a more imposing bulge, almost button-sized.

"No," Christian said. "I'm sorry, Mother. No possets. I've work to do tomorrow, and you know they always make me muzzy-headed."

His mother loved him; it was her only sin. He didn't want to hurt her. She didn't need to know everything.

Four. Five. Six. His breathing evened, his chest no longer ached.

His mother exhaled. "I heard you shouting," she said. "The servants must have as well. Servants talk. What do you think people will say?"

Seven was a gooseberry-sized bead under his left index finger.

"They'll say I don't sleep well."

She didn't say anything.

Eight. Nine.

"They could say nothing," she said. "And you could have a good night's rest for once."

Just this once. He could feel the tug of it. He could smell the laudanum, now that he'd calmed, that faint herbaceous sweetness in the dark. It whispered to him that *now* would pose no problem. Just a little. Just this once.

Laudanum lied.

Ten. The tenth bead was as big as an acorn. He held them all in place, ten beads, smallest to largest, one under each finger. If he could sort these, he could sort out his life.

"You can't go on like this," his mother was murmuring. "I worry for you. You need to sleep more."

It wasn't a posset he needed, and it wasn't a lack of laudanum that woke him up shouting. It was doubt. For a moment, he remembered Judith looking at him just this past afternoon, across a table laden with over-dry, over-spiced biscuits, and telling him that he should have known. He should have known Anthony wasn't guilty.

Christian pressed until those hard beads hurt his fingers. He'd never doubted Anthony's guilt. There was no question in his mind that Anthony had committed treason. Transportation had been too light a sentence.

He knew, after all, why Anthony had done it.

"Just this once," his mother said again.

It was never just once, but his mother didn't need to know. She loved him, that was all, and he loved her. She didn't need to know. "Not tonight, Mother," he said instead.

He had no doubt that Anthony was a traitor. No, the reason Christian woke at night was that he wasn't sure Anthony's treachery was *wrong*.

"I'll fix it," he said aloud. "I'm fixing it now." He wasn't sure whether he was talking to his mother or the long-dead friend who haunted his dreams. Christian lifted his hands and the beads rolled back to the center of the basin. "There's another way."

Something other than treason, something other than laudanum. He'd thought and thought. He'd made lists of lists. He was going to get Anthony's journals. He would identify the men who had so enraged his friend with their sins that Anthony had felt he had no choice but to commit treason.

Christian was going to find them, and he was going to bring them to justice.

Then he'd finally be able to sleep without dreaming.

His mother let out a disappointed sigh. "If you insist."

He patted her hand. "You've worried over me enough. Go get some sleep yourself, Mother."

He waited until she left, taking the laudanum-infused milk with her. When she had gone, he pulled the bowl onto his lap again. One bead. Two. Three. Ordering little pieces of the universe didn't bring him much peace, but it was some. He was going to solve this problem. He was going to solve it his way. But until he did...things were going to get worse, not better, because he was going to have to deal with Judith. He'd had little enough peace since the day that women had divided into *Judith* and *everyone else*.

Four. Five. Six.

He could still remember that day.

It had been a cold, gray, rainy day at the Worth household. He'd started it with no notion that his entire life would change over the course of an hour.

Seven. Eight. Beads didn't dispel the memory. Judith had been fifteen, and he'd been a year from starting at university. He'd felt his importance greatly. As befitted his new status as scholar, he had taken a book of Greek poetry to the blue parlor, ensconced himself behind the curtains, and started reading. A few hours into his studies, she had come into the room. He'd looked up with narrowed eyes, but she didn't see him in his comfortable window seat. She had looked down the hall furtively, and then, very carefully, she had shut the door.

On the one hand, being closed up in a room with a gently bred lady was not a good idea. On the other hand, *this* gently bred lady was Judith. He'd known her since the very first time he'd come for a visit with Anthony. He knew her from summers of play and picnics. He knew her mostly from trying to sneak away from her so he could go fishing with her brother.

Judith was *technically* a gently bred lady in the same way that Welsh corgis were *technically* herding dogs. Yes, the breed was supposedly used to handle sheep by other people—but one look at those ridiculous short legs and he could never take the dogs seriously.

He felt the same way about Judith. He'd dropped her in a lake once. After that, she simply didn't register as someone who needed to be handled with the kidgloves of propriety.

She seemed unaware of him. Instead, she'd gone to the clock on the mantel and had taken it down. It was a shelf clock, maybe two hands' height. She held it, turning it about, and then set it on the worktable.

He'd seen her there before, doing embroidery. She looked at the clock as if it were a French knot in need of unraveling. Then she had removed from her pocket a set of jeweler's tools.

That had riveted his attention. He'd watched as she removed the backing from the clock, and then—very methodically, very precisely—had begun to take the instrument apart. She had laid out the gears and springs, one by one. At first, he'd itched to arrange the pieces she removed by size or by function. By tensile strength. By any damned thing, instead of the bizarre ordering she made on the table.

She dismantled the entire thing, down to the minute hand.

He had wondered what she would do at that point. Would she walk out of the room, leaving behind this table covered with springs and gears? Would she attempt to put it all back, and then feign confusion when the clock no longer worked?

She did neither of those things. Instead, she took her father's heavy gold watch out of her pocket and set it on the table in front of her. Then, working just as methodically as she had done when she'd taken the thing apart, she'd put it back together again—piece by piece, no hesitation, reaching for each piece precisely as she had laid it down. The order he'd failed to comprehend before suddenly made sense. She'd set the parts out by order of assembly, the order in which you'd arrange these pieces if one cared not about their size or their color or their function, but about what they would become as a whole. Put together like this, they were not hunks of metal. They were a map to time itself.

Christian had spent his whole life sorting things. Watching Judith, he'd realized that the best order for things could mean something that made them more than the sum of their parts instead of reducing them to individual elements.

She snapped the back of the clock in place, consulted the pocket watch on the table, and smiled. "Fourteen minutes," she'd announced, seemingly to the room at large. Then she'd looked at him—directly at him, as if she had known he was there the entire time.

"That's a new record for me," she had told him.

While he was staring at her in disbelief, she had stood calmly, gathered her tools, and walked out of the room.

The Worth family had always been odd. It was why Anthony had adopted Christian without blinking at his more peculiar habits. But until that afternoon, he hadn't realized that Judith was *that* odd, and in that particular way.

After that he had tried—valiantly—to put this new, disturbing Judith out of his mind. She was his best friend's sister. She was supposed to be a Welsh corgi of a lady. And then he'd started noticing all the other things about her. Her smile. The fact that she'd developed breasts. He had tried not to notice her for two days before giving it up as a hopeless cause.

Wouldn't you know? It turned out that Welsh corgis were excellent sheepdogs.

Judith was still a hopeless cause. What did he want? He wanted to disassemble time itself. To go back to the point when the most difficult problem between the two of them was a thing of clockwork and gears, a machine to be disassembled and then put back together without any indication that anything had ever gone amiss.

Of all the people in the world, she was the one who had never made him feel odd or out of place. She'd never made his head itch by disturbing his orderings. She had been perfect, up until the point when he'd taught her to hate him.

Ever since then, his world had ceased to sort properly. Ever since then, he'd felt an itch in the back of his mind—the itch of a book out of place, a letter slid into the wrong file.

Eight years ago, he'd made a decision, and ever since then, it had eaten at him subtly, whispering that he'd put

Anthony in the wrong place, and that there was no way to correct his mistake.

He was never getting Judith back; he'd become inured to that fact by now. He'd settle for keeping hold of himself.

Ten.

He let the beads fall away and set the bowl back on his bedside table.

He lay back, adjusting his position on the pillow. Sleep came, eventually, and with it, dreams of clockwork ships sailing in storms.

Chapter Five

The good thing about sleep was that it wiped away the emotions of the prior day. One could wake refreshed, ready to take on the tasks of a new morning.

When Judith awoke in bed next to Theresa the morning after she saw Christian again, sun spilled through the curtains. She thought first of the tight clockwork turn she'd worked on last night—that quick reversal of figures, not so swift as to seem mechanical. If she could get that right, it might mean a little extra. Another thirty pounds, maybe.

She had hope again. There had been setbacks yesterday, but she was so close to her goal. The *hard* part had been earning the money to be held in trust for her sisters, to send Benedict off to school. From here on out, it was simply a matter of execution and making an appointment to accompany Christian to the family solicitor.

Not that she was worrying over that last task. Not at all. She wasn't thinking of him as she made a mental list of the things she needed to purchase. She had put him entirely—well, *mostly*—out of her mind as she got her shopping basket. She'd forgotten him—sort of, maybe—by the time she greeted her friend.

Daisy Whitlaw lived across the way, in one of the myriad flats that had been carved out of a larger house as the neighborhood fell into slow decay. They had made each other's acquaintance over the course of years of shopping. Daisy's father had once been a grocer—past tense both in the sense that he had lost his business years before, and that he'd passed away a year ago. Her mother had been a vicar's daughter. Daisy had never been a lady, not like Judith had, but she knew what it was like to fall slowly from grace. She'd understood Judith the moment they'd run into each other at the market.

Judith looked much the same as she always looked. She was wearing her favorite green dress, comfortable and clean, if faded; her shawl was looped over her shoulder, and her basket hung at her elbow, ready to receive that day's shopping.

Daisy was waiting in place, under the black painted pole of the street lamp. Her friend's day gown was faded blue, instead of faded green; her shawl was a dull gray instead of a dull blue. And she carried her basket—slightly misshapen and definitely aging—in her hands instead of hooked over her elbow.

They looked completely different. Daisy was tall and blond, where Judith was short and dark-haired. Still, everyone in this handful of streets knew them as an entity.

"Good morning, Daisy dearest," Judith called.

"Good morning, my lovely Judith." Daisy gestured her closer, and Judith crossed the street to her friend.

Daisy worked in a flower shop. She could put on her mother's accent when she wished, but most of the time, she spoke like the other residents nearby. She'd never asked where Judith had fallen *from*, a refreshing change of pace. Judith had been glad to have a friend who didn't ask her endless questions or who saw her as the traitor's daughter.

She and Daisy could be friends. A friend, one she could laugh and talk with, one who never reminded her of her past, had been as valuable as learning to make proper sandwiches. More, even.

Daisy hooked her arm through Judith's and they proceeded on their way. The market was four streets away, far enough to make the walk unpleasant on wet, drizzly days. Today, though, was glorious for once. The sky was clear, all the grime and muck washed away by last night's rains. The streets had been cleared by the same. The sun shone and the clouds—small, wispy, insubstantial things—hardly blocked its light.

"What shall you get at the market today?" Daisy asked after they'd gone about twenty yards.

This was the usual start of their game.

"Would you know," Judith said, "that we are fresh out of gold leaf in our household?"

She and Daisy had started the game years ago, when one of the local boys had accused them of thinking too highly of themselves.

"No!" Daisy turned to her in mock horror. "Not out of gold leaf! Why, however will you gild your beef?"

"I don't know," Judith said. "Why, just last night, with Benedict home for the first time in weeks, we had to have our filets seasoned with nothing but salt and pepper and a little rosemary."

"Oi." Daisy shook her head. "You ought to watch your stores with greater care. I find that a bit of gold leaf, laid on top of a fruit tart, aids the digestion. Without it, cream can upset the stomach."

"So true, Daisy dearest." Judith smiled and patted the other woman's hand where it laid on her elbow. "What is it that you are tasked with purchasing today?"

"Well." Daisy paused. She tilted her head up to the sky, so that sun spilled onto her face, as if thinking of something she needed. "I did need to stop by the glove-maker. Yesterday, when I was scrubbing the pots..." She stopped at this—manual labor didn't fit the game, after all—and finally shrugged. "Well, you know—I wore through my last pair of kidskin gloves with seed pearls."

In the game, one never pointed out that one didn't scrub pots wearing kidskin gloves. That would ruin the fun.

"Tsk, tsk," Judith said instead. "They simply don't make kidskin gloves with seed pearls the way they used to. Why, back when we were children, kidskin gloves—the normal sort, even before you added the seed pearls—could go through a year's worth of work in the grimiest scullery without falling to pieces."

"It's true," Daisy said mournfully. "Standards have fallen. We live in decrepit times."

"So," Judith said. "Gloves and gold leaf, then?"

This conversation had brought them from the relative quiet of their street to the market square. The stalls were bustling already. The greengrocer, in particular, would prove a bit of a fight. They'd have to go there first to lay claim to whatever decent vegetables remained.

Without discussing this, both women passed the glove-maker on the corner without a second glance and took their place in line. The summer harvest was delayed after a cold spring. The vegetables were still rather sparse: suspicious-looking turnips and last year's potatoes with little white sprouts growing out of the eyes made up the bulk of the bins. But there were some heads of lettuce and peas. And—wonder of wonders—a cache of oranges.

Oranges. They were dear, especially at this time of year, and who knew how far these particular ones had traveled. But an orange, peeled and split among three over breakfast... It would be a lovely treat.

Not a good choice, Judith warned herself. Not after she'd already splurged for Benedict's homecoming.

But the day was beautiful and Benedict was home, at least for now. An orange would make everything better. Judith mentally counted the coins in her pocket and those remaining in her dresser drawer.

One orange.

"I'll have twelve of the turnips," Daisy said as she came to the front of the line, "and sweet ones, too—none of the tough ones."

The grocer laid his grime-stained hands on the counter. "It's July," he said gruffly. "All the turnips are tough."

"Twelve of your best," Daisy said, with her head thrown a little higher. "And a good three pounds of potatoes. Smaller, please."

The man weighed these items out, and money changed hands.

It was a curious friendship, the one Judith had with Daisy, but that didn't make it any less dear. Theirs was not the sort of friendship where they told each other the truth. The truth was hard and nearly impossible to bear; talking about it would not make it any easier. When they did talk, it was as they had today—a conversation that centered on gold leaf and kidskin gloves, silk and strawberries, honey-wine and carriages. They talked as if they had no worries in the world.

And so, for the space of four streets, they could lay them down.

Doing your household shopping with another woman was an act of intimacy. Judith tried not to do the math. She tried not to divide those turnips by the two people in Daisy's household. Once, twelve would have seemed a great many turnips to her. Now, she knew that no matter how you mashed them, no matter how finely you chopped them or how large the quantity of water in the pot where the soup was made, twelve turnips divided by seven days and two mouths was not quite enough to fill the stomach.

These were the things they didn't talk about.

Judith got her own turnips, twice as many potatoes, a bunch of new peas, some lettuce that looked sweet, and her orange.

Daisy didn't blink at this, and Judith didn't offer any assistance. It was not how their friendship was constructed. She knew that Daisy noticed that she purchased a small sack of sugar, just as she could not help but be aware that Daisy asked for soup bones at the butcher, picking the meatiest ones because she could not afford chops.

There had been some months early in their friendship, before Judith had sold her first clockwork design, when their fortunes had been reversed. They were friends because they could show these things to each other. The shopping was simply the shopping: a voracious beast that must be fed, a thing that they did together because the only way to alleviate the dull reality of the world was to deny it its power.

Daisy didn't know any of the details of Judith's life. She'd never heard of the Worth family. Judith's father's suicide had never been a topic of conversation. With Daisy, she could be just another lady shifted by poor luck into this not-quite-respectable neighborhood, struggling to find the gentility in her poverty.

When the last of the bones had been wrapped in paper, Daisy raised her head and turned to Judith. "Well," she said, "I did not see any gloves that were worthy of my hands. My last pair had a matching set of diamonds right here." She pointed to the hollow of her wrist. "I find I can't accept anything less."

"No, dearest," Judith said. "Why should you settle? We never should."

"I've nothing else, then."

They had walked about halfway home when Daisy turned to Judith. "My mother says that you had a gentleman caller yesterday."

Ah. She *had* managed to forget that. Judith shut her eyes. "I did."

"Anyone of interest?" That was said a little more slyly.

Men, and their attentions, were not typically covered by the game. Men, unlike gloves, could be mocked or praised as the situation demanded.

"He was a marquess," Judith said simply. "We have known each other for years, and of course he was once in love with me. He asked me to marry him, but I didn't like the set of his chin, and so I told him no."

Daisy did not blink at this. Men were not typically covered by the game—but they both understood the game for what it was: a way to politely beg off a topic. And while she'd told Daisy nothing but the simple truth, she knew how the other girl would take it.

"A plague on those pushy marquesses," Daisy said with a toss of her head. "Once, I had a pair of dukes fighting over me. They were the most ridiculous things. One of them took a knife; the other grabbed a pistol. And, well, you know how those things work."

"No! Did they kill each other?"

"Certainly not," Daisy said. "But they lost all interest in me, because they were trying to determine whose weapon was larger."

Judith let out a laugh. "Isn't that always the way of it?"

Daisy let out a sigh, and then looked upward. "Isn't it, though. So you've sent him on his way?"

"As much as one ever can." Especially when she had an appointment to meet him as soon as her solicitor set the time.

Not for the first time in their friendship, Judith felt a twinge of regret. She and Daisy told each other horrible lies all the time; that was the point of their game. But they both knew that it was all falsehoods, and so in a way, those lies had more veracity and substance than many a whispered secret among friends. Telling her friend the bare truth and pretending it was a lie?

It wasn't right. It was the sort of thing that might hurt, if Daisy found out the truth later. Much like the facts of Judith's birth, the truth about Christian was not something she could admit.

But this was not the time for Judith to complain that the damned marquess who had once wanted to marry her had come to her assistance. Not when her best friend was squabbling over soup bones.

"They always do turn up again," Daisy said with a shake of her head. "I advise you to keep to viscounts. They at least know their place."

W ell," Christian said. "It has been rather a long time since we went on a drive together."

Drives in the summer were usually pleasant, the cool breeze making the heat bearable. But no breeze would cool the annoyance Judith felt at this remark.

She sat eighteen inches away from him on the single front-facing seat of Christian's curricle. She'd attempted to refuse his offer to drive her, but his return message had rightly noted that he could hardly claim to take a friendly interest in her family's affairs if he left her to arrive on foot.

He had been right.

She hated that he was right about anything, and hated that she was reasonable enough to admit it.

She glanced over at him on the bench. He held the reins loosely in his hands. His trousers were the kind of buff that attracted dirt: filthy paw prints, coal smears... She'd never thought about those things until she had to clean them. His boots glistened in the sunlight. He looked utterly at ease, smiling at her as if he'd forgotten the harsh words they'd exchanged a few days past.

Anyone who saw them together might imagine them a handsome couple enjoying a ride together. He was handsome enough with that little smile of his, that impish gleam in his eye tempting her to remember everything she'd tried to forget about him.

"Your memory is faulty," she informed him. "We never went on a drive together."

They'd only talked of it. That one summer after Anthony and Theresa and her father had returned home from China, they had talked about everything. She'd been unable to look at him without blushing, which meant that she'd spent a great many hours blushing. Their eyes had met at every opportunity, and they'd made excuses to spend time in each other's company. They'd been obvious, so damned obvious that even Anthony had noticed.

She glanced at him now. His eyes met hers; his twinkled in response, as if he were mocking her because she was still looking.

"You can court my sister when she comes out," Anthony had told Christian with Judith standing right beside him. "You can drive her in the park and all that other rigmarole. Until then, please refrain from making eyes at her when I'm around."

Judith had punched him in the shoulder for that one, but Anthony had shrugged it off.

"That's what elder brothers are for," he'd remarked with a grin. "Getting in your way, despite your own inclinations."

There had been no drives, no walks in the park, no courting, no coming out.

"There is nothing wrong with my memory," Christian said beside her. "I wasn't wrong. It has been a long time since we drove together. Infinity is a very long time. There aren't many times that are longer."

"Lord Ashford," Judith said. "We must pretend to be civil with one another for the next hour or so. Did you ever consider that there might be some danger in cracking jokes with a woman who would rather crack your head?"

He tilted his head to consider her. "No," he said slowly. "As a general proposition, I do not use humor to incite violence. I believe I am not abnormal in that regard."

On foot, the way to her solicitor's office would have wound through Hyde Park. In Christian's curricle, they merely skirted the edges. The park seemed an impossible haven of gentility to her right, a gathering of brightly colored parasols and lush green grass.

"You know what I meant," Judith said stiffly.

"Look! It's a joke! Kill it!" He raised one eyebrow at her in a superior expression. "Now there's a refrain heard in all the best drawing rooms."

Judith sniffed. "I see it more as: Look, someone is angry with me! Let me laugh at her."

He considered this as he directed the horses on to one of the driving paths through the park.

They were in his half of London, a part of the city where the houses were wide and the walls were kept ridiculously white. Here, streets were swept regularly and little flowerboxes adorned the windows.

Christian made an indignant noise. "You can't honestly believe I'm laughing at you."

Nobody here made pots of common stew containing don't-ask-what in the middle of narrow, cobbled streets. Even the sky seemed bluer here, closer somehow, as if the sun shone more warmly on the wealthy. Judith shifted in her seat, feeling out of place.

Everything felt hostile when her shoes pinched.

"No," she said. "Not precisely that."

The silver mirror of the Serpentine flashed at the edge of her vision. A pair of swans floated in the water, and another pair waddled on the grass next to the street. This was how everything always looked to Christian: cool, inviting, comfortable.

"It's not that you're laughing," Judith said. "Sometimes, it's downright cruel to crack jokes. People get upset for good reasons. Trying to cheer them up denies what is happening to them."

"No, it doesn't." Christian set a hand on the seat between them. "It's a way of recognizing their very legitimate feelings of distress and wishing that person well. You cannot reasonably think that it's cruel to hope that an unhappy person will feel better. It's like saying 'my sincerest condolences' at a funeral."

Once, they'd argued like this.

They'd sat on the grass in the country, very carefully not touching, and let all the heat they felt express itself in contradictions and laughter and careful innuendo. It had been as close as they could come to touching.

Now, they were still arguing. And he was looking at her with that gleam in his eye, the one that had always made her want to throw all caution to the wind.

Judith pointed at the packed dirt road ahead of them. "Watch where you're driving. That's the most ridiculous thing I've heard. You cannot honestly believe that offering gentle, appropriate sympathy to a bereaved woman at her husband's funeral is equivalent to asking her, 'Who is the greatest chicken-killer in English literature?' One of them supports her in her grief; the other attempts to cajole her out of her very real emotions because it's inconvenient for her to be glum."

Christian considered this. "I take your point. I agree that there is a time and a place for jocularity. I simply think that there are more times and places for humor than others care to admit." He glanced pointedly at her. "We are not presently at a funeral."

She couldn't think of him at her father's funeral. He shouldn't even have come, shouldn't have offered his support. He shouldn't have found her alone afterward. He shouldn't have asked her to marry him, as if marrying the man who was the cause of her grief would make it all better. He *shouldn't* have.

"By the by," he put in, "who *is* the greatest chicken-killer in English literature?"

"Hamlet's uncle." Judith shut her eyes. "He did murder most foul."

Christian looked over at her. His eyes widened. "Lady Judith, I am outraged. You dare take me to task when you were delivering a pun of that magnitude? There is no time, no place, for a joke like that. Ever." A smile indicated that he was joking. Of course; he was *always* joking.

"Only a mallard like you would say that," Judith said primly. "I find the murder of fowl extremely depraved."

The fowl were out in force in the park today. Ducks wandered the green, and another swan ahead was snapping at bread offered by a…well, that child was technically not *offering* the bread to the swan so much as holding it above his head and trying to fend the bird off.

Christian smiled at her, leaning an inch closer. "If I were a mallard, I'd think you would be more inclined to fowl-murder."

Once she'd loved this about him—that they could talk any subject upside down and inside out. Now, she could feel the pull of their old friendship, of that magical summer together, those hours spent wandering the apple orchard, "accidentally" running into each other day after day.

If she wasn't careful, she might fall into friendship with him again.

She looked straight ahead. "You're not a mallard. You're far worse. You're a...a..."

Ahead of them, the child panicked and threw his roll. The swan that had been on the grass darted into the driving path to snap it up. It happened so fast; the bird spread its wide, white wings and lowered its beak, a mere ten feet ahead of them. No, six. The distance between them was dropping all too fast.

And Christian was looking at her, not watching the road.

"Swan!" she said. "Swan!"

His grin broadened. "I'm a swan? That's utterly delightful!"

She grabbed his arm. "No! Swan! In the road!"

As she took hold of his wrist, the swan hissed, rising up and spreading its wings. One horse reared; the curricle rocked. Her stomach dropped, dizzyingly, and she held on tightly. The other horse whinnied in a panic and pawed the air. For a second, as the curricle tilted precariously,

Judith feared the conveyance would overturn. She braced herself, gritting her teeth, expecting the worst.

The bird took to wing at the last possible instant. Christian pulled on the reins, and after pawing the air one last time, the horses quieted.

Judith's pounding heart was left as the only evidence that anything had transpired. That, she realized, and her hands—both of which she'd clamped firmly around Christian's arm. She'd reached for him without thinking.

She could feel him through those layers of wool and linen—the curve of his arm, the tautness of muscle tensed from holding the horse back. Taking hold of him had brought her entire body next to his, and she felt the warmth of him now. He might have heard the beat of her heart, it was thumping so loudly.

He turned to her, looking into her eyes.

Her pulse was only pounding because the swan had given her a fright. That was it, surely. It had nothing to do with the sparkle of his eyes, the way his gaze dropped to her lips, briefly, before sliding back up to meet her gaze. Slowly, she unwound her hands from his sleeve and did her best to scoot—surreptitiously—a good six inches away.

He's not your friend.

Apparently, some dormant part of herself still hadn't comprehended that after eight years. She could just as easily have grabbed the edge of the seat instead of his arm.

She hadn't.

Christian knew now that her first reaction was to reach for him, and he was not the sort to let that sort of slip go by without a taunt or seven. Judith swallowed and clasped her hands together. He could taunt all he liked; if she pretended nothing had happened, he'd find no headway.

"Well." Her heart was still racing. "I suppose that swan will have a story to tell his friends tonight."

How could she tell he was smiling when she wasn't even looking at him? That mischievous look of his was detectable from the corner of her eyes. Oh, he knew that she was not entirely indifferent to him, no matter how she wished otherwise. He was laughing at her.

"You don't need to chortle at me," she snapped. "You need to pay more mind to where you're going."

"I wasn't laughing at you," he said. "Just imagining what sort of story that swan would tell, if it had friends."

She wasn't going to ask. She wasn't.

She resisted for four entire seconds. But that was the worst thing about Christian. He'd always roused her curiosity. He didn't need to taunt after all. He just smiled, and in the end, she could no more have kept silent than the horses could have stopped from rearing. She crossed her arms in front of her like a shield. "Very well. What would he say?"

"Well," Christian said, in an exaggerated Cockney accent. "You'll never guess what I did today, Fred."

Judith found herself blinking in confusion and turning to him. "What are you doing? Who is Fred?"

"I'm acting it out for you," Christian said, as if playing swans were a perfectly ordinary everyday event. "The story that swan there is going to tell his friend—that's Fred—tonight."

She shook her head. "Swans are regal birds. They're the property of the queen. So why would a swan have a Cockney accent?"

"Why, Judith. I never thought to hear such words from you. Accents aren't all that important. They're simply one way to separate out two groups on the basis of an irrelevant characteristic. Don't be so damned class-focused. Besides, it's irrational to object to the idea of swans speaking with a Cockney accent when swans have a limited English vocabulary to begin with."

"I—" She was unable to come up with a response that didn't involve pelting him with fruit. "That is the most ridiculous thing."

"What is ridiculous," he said piously, "is your attempt to import your limited local prejudice into the swan community. Swans have no care for such things. They're much more egalitarian than our species."

Judith sat back and gestured with an exaggerated motion. "I see. *Do* forgive me for that dreadful error. Please continue. What is our dear Cockney swan telling Fred?"

"You'll never guess what I did today, Fred!" Christian said in his Cockney accent. And then, supplying a different, somewhat lower voice, he answered himself. "What did you do, Bill? Pray tell."

"Stop." Judith held up a hand. "I can accept a Cockney swan, but why does Fred speak with a Liverpudlian accent? Should there not be some consistency in the swan community?"

"There's none in the human community," Christian pointed out. "Why should swans be less varied?"

It was on the tip of her tongue to object again—after all, if swans were not importing prejudice from humans, why would they import variety?—but from the gleam in his eye, she could tell he wanted her to argue. She bit her lip and folded her arms. "Very well, then," she said with poor grace. "Go on with your story."

"Well, Fred," Christian continued in his Bill-the-Cockney-Swan voice, "today, I ate a horse."

She could not have heard him correctly. "What did you just say?"

"Come now," Bill-the-Swan continued. "Don't look at me like that, all disbelieving-like. Would I be having you on, when it's a matter so closely touching my honor? You know I would never do that, my dearest darling."

Even in that put-on accent, even with that gleam in his eye, the words *dearest darling* sank into her skin. He was looking at her as he said it. It tripped off his tongue so easily, as if she *were* his darling. As if there were no swans, Cockney or otherwise, between them.

Judith dug her fingernails into her palm. "Why is Bill-the-Swan referring to Fred as his dearest darling? That seems inappropriately affectionate."

"Nothing inappropriate about it," Christian said with a shrug. "I already told you. Swans don't share our limited local prejudices."

She let out a long, careful breath. "I don't know why I bother to ask questions. Keep on; I couldn't stop you."

"So I was walking across the road," Bill-the-Swan said, "nice as you please, taking my time as a gentleswan does. And then, well. You'll never guess what happened."

Judith waited.

Christian waggled an eyebrow at her. "Come now, my savory algae patch. Give us a guess."

No. If she was going to play his game, she refused to play the way he intended.

"Bill," she said in what sounded to her mind like an extremely unsuccessful imitation of a Liverpudlian accent, "how many times do I have to tell you? You can't trust them roads, not with their horses and their carriages and their whatnots. One of these days, you're going to get run right over."

"Aw, my lovely great swath of duck weed." Christian winked at her. "I *knew* you cared. You just pretend like you don't. But I looked both ways, I did, and I didn't see nothing. Not until the great beast was fair upon me, lickety-split, charging at me with its hooves like dinner plates. Steam rose from its nostrils—"

"What a crock!" Judith interrupted in her best Fred voice. "I have seen many a horse on the path by Hyde Park, and not one has ever had steam coming from its nostrils."

"Am I telling this story or are you?"

Judith rolled her eyes. "Well, you're certainly telling a story, all right."

"Right, then. As I was saying: Steam rose from its nostrils in little wisps, like some kind of demon stallion. When it tossed its head, I saw fire in its eyes—that hint of flame, suggesting that the devil had put this beast on the road. That's when I knew. There were children in the park. I couldn't let that vile creature rend their flesh."

"Bill," Judith interrupted, "since when do you care about children? Nasty things, human children—noisy white wingless little grubs that they are."

"Human children?" Christian pulled back in surprise. "No, nobody said nothing about those awful things. No. I mean little fluffy cygnets, not yet feathered out. Whatever else would I be thinking of?"

"At this time of year? Who's nesting so late?"

"Am I telling this story," Bill-the-Swan said, "or are you?"

"Well," Judith huffed. "You're still telling a story, *that's* for sure."

"Right, then. I knew what I had to do. I puffed out my chest. I spread my wings. I brought my neck up like a giant snake, and I hissed at the beast from hell. It reared, flashing its daggered hooves at me." Christian demonstrated with exaggerated hand motions. "I saw those forelegs falling, and I was sure I was a dead swan. I had just enough time to launch myself at the beast."

Judith looked upward. "They call us mute swans. Clearly someone made an error when it came to you."

"God must have guided my beak," Christian continued piously. "I propelled myself at the thing's neck. I screamed in defiance—and next thing I knew, I'd pierced its jugular. It gurgled. It staggered. And then it dropped in a dead heap to the ground."

Judith turned to look at Christian. He sat back against the seat with a self-satisfied expression on his face.

"Really," she said in a disbelieving tone. "You killed it with your beak."

"I know." He settled against the seat, almost preening in misplaced swan pride. "I could scarce believe it myself."

"You know you have white feathers," she said. "There doesn't seem to be much blood on you."

Christian waved this off. "Demon blood. Demon horse. It smelled of sulfur. It burned like flame. But when the foul beast landed in a great thump on the ground in front of me, it disappeared in a cloud of smoke—hooves, carcass and all."

Judith let the silence stretch. She raised an eyebrow and looked at Christian. "So," she said. "If the horse disappeared, how on earth did you manage to eat it?"

There was a moment of silence. Christian caught her eye. His mouth quivered, as if he knew he'd been caught in a lie he couldn't talk his way out of, not with any number of accents. He shrugged nonchalantly. "Oh, well," he said. "That little detail. Once I knew I could slay horses, why would I stop with just the one?"

She couldn't help herself. She put a hand over her face and burst into laughter. She had no idea how he'd baited her into…oh, God, what had she just been doing? Talking to him in a Liverpudlian accent, pretending to be a *swan* of all things?

That was the way he was. You had to be careful of Christian. If you weren't, he'd have you playing his dubious Liverpudlian swan lover before you knew what he'd done.

He gave her a long, self-satisfied smile. One that said that he knew that she'd fallen into his trap. One that promised that she had only to do it again and again. That if she let herself, she could forget what he had done.

He'd made her forget for five entire minutes.

"And look," Christian said, in a tone so innocent that she knew that whatever he was about to say was going to be even worse than his Cockney accent. "I have the most dreadful sore throat to show for it."

She was almost afraid to ask. "From…the screaming?"

"No." He leaned in and dropped his voice to a low whisper. "I did murder most hoarse."

The pun was so appalling that Judith made a fist and hit her forehead. It was *her* pun, too; she couldn't even rightfully complain. She hit her forehead again. "Death is too good for you. Dismemberment is too good for you."

"You see," Christian said with a nod, "there we are. That's precisely what I wished to show you."

"Boiling in hot oil is too good for you," she said passionately. "Wait, what are you saying now?"

"We're not friends," he said. "But we could be excellent allies. Of a kind. We're working together, after all."

"What has that to do with your terrible sense of humor?"

"Just this: I think we're both happier when you're thinking of killing me than we were earlier. When you…" He paused.

When she'd grabbed hold of him. She'd remembered that she had once cared. She could still feel the echo of his arm against her gloves, if she let herself think about it. The feel of his muscle beneath her hand; the look in his eye. The memory of what they'd once been.

She strove for neutral wording. "When I braced myself using your arm?"

"Yes." He looked at her. "I know you'll never trust me, Judith. But that's precisely it. I trust you to never trust me, and in return, you can trust me to make sure you'll never trust me, even when we both stand in danger of forgetting. Alliances have been built on less."

She blinked, working that out. He *looked* sincere.

"You're proposing an armistice on the condition that I hate you," she said slowly, "and in return, you'll continue to make me hate you?"

"Precisely." He held out his hand. "We have things to do. This will be so much more effective than continually sniping at one another just so we can remember that we hate one another. Truce?"

She looked at his fingers. She looked at him. They *had* once been so much more. He was right; she was only sniping at him because she didn't want to remember how deep their friendship had run.

"Very well." She took his hand and gave it a firm shake. "Truce. I hate you."

"Excellent work," he said. "I'll keep your hatred stoked with swans and horses until we can part ways."

Chapter Six

"Christian Trent." Christian offered his hand as the solicitor entered the room. "Marquess of Ashford. I'm here with Lady Judith Worth as a friend of the family, to assist in her inquiries."

The man's handshake was almost perfunctory, his grip cool. Nothing like Judith's had been when they'd clasped hands to seal their alliance.

"Mr. Ennis," the little solicitor said, swiping at the thin row of white hairs that he'd carefully combed over his head. "Tea?"

"No, thank you." Christian sat on one side of the desk.

"We'd best get to business," Judith said.

"Business." Mr. Ennis sat down. "With the both of you?"

Christian had little doubt that his reputation preceded him, but normally, people tried to hide their reaction with greater success. He decided that a bit of a glower was in order, and so he narrowed his eyes at the man as if daring him to spell out why his accompanying Judith was so unlikely.

One. She hates you.

Two. You killed her brother.

Not much of a dare, with such easy choices.

"Yes," Judith said. "Business. With the both of us."

Mr. Ennis sighed. "Lord Ashford, you called yourself a family friend, did you?"

Christian added a mental heap of coal to the furnace of his glower, and growled a response. "Yes."

"That's what we're calling it these days, then." The man looked upward. "I see that standards of friendship have altered considerably in the last years." He didn't look at Judith. Instead, he gave Christian a pained smile. "I shall do my best to…what was it you wanted? Ah, yes. You wanted me to assist in some of your inquiries."

"I'm not making any inquiries," Christian said. "I'm here as a support to Lady Judith. She'll direct her questions to you."

Mr. Ennis let out a slow breath of air—not quite loudly enough to be a sigh—and pasted a false smile on his face. "Lady Judith knows I will answer any of her questions that I am capable of answering. Lord Ashford's presence is not required. In fact, one might call it downright counterproductive."

Judith smiled back, a curl of her lips as fake as the solicitor's. "How lovely to hear that. I'm here to inquire about my sister Camilla's—"

The solicitor raised a hand. "There we come to a grinding halt, Lady Judith. You are not your sister's legal guardian. I am not able to impart specific circumstances of her situation to anyone but the lady herself or someone charged with such power by her guardian."

"You once used to answer such questions."

"Matters change." The man looked off into the distance, his nose twitching.

"What matters have changed?"

"Er…" To Christian's eye, the man looked distinctly uncomfortable—like a fellow unused to telling lies suddenly having to invent a dying uncle on a moment's notice. "The ones that haven't stayed the same?"

"So," Christian said. "If we had Lady Camilla with us, you'd answer Judith's questions?"

"Assuming the lady was amenable and her guardian was amenable and that it didn't touch on any of the…other matters that I am unable to discuss? I don't see why not. I told Lady Judith as much last time."

Christian turned to Judith. "Why didn't we bring Camilla?"

He could tell it was absolutely the wrong question to ask the instant it came out of his mouth. The corners of Judith's mouth turned down. She sniffed, licked her lips, and folded her hands in her lap.

"Talk less," she whispered to him. "Glower more."

"Yes, of course," Mr. Ennis said to the room at large. "He is a dear family friend, indeed. One who knows all the relevant details."

Christian felt his cheeks heat.

"Did I not mention?" Judith spoke a little too brightly. "Camilla is not living with us at present. I have not precisely heard from her in something over a year."

Mr. Ennis's eyebrows rose. "Something?"

"Six and a half years is something," Judith replied with an overly false smile.

It was a good thing Judith wanted him to be quiet; he had nothing to say. He hadn't seen Camilla yesterday. But the household had been in an uproar. He could have missed an entire battalion practicing manuevers on the top floor.

He'd assumed that she'd been around somewhere, between the smoke and the strawmen. By the stuffed smile on the solicitor's face, this was a painful subject.

He winced. He couldn't imagine the Worth siblings divided any more than they were. *No wonder she still hates you,* his mind whispered. He brushed this away.

"Let us talk of Theresa," Judith said. "Theresa, in the past few months, ought to have received some notice—"

"My lady." The solicitor pinched the bridge of his nose. "You know I cannot talk to you of Lady Theresa."

"Whyever not? I *am* her legal guardian. And—"

"You are not her legal guardian," Mr. Ennis said.

Judith rubbed a gloved fist against her temple. "How can I not be? I'm her next of kin. There's no reason a female could not be her guardian; we had this out four years ago, you and I, and back then, you *agreed.* What has happened since? If it's not me, who is it?"

"This was not my idea," Mr. Ennis said, shaking his head. "I want you to know that."

"What was not your idea?"

"The idea that was had by the gentleman who is your sister's guardian," Mr. Ennis said slowly. "For reasons of client confidentiality, I cannot disclose his identity. He doesn't wish it, and under the circumstances, which are..." He searched for a word.

"Unusual?" Christian offered. "Unlikely?"

Judith leaned forward. "Unimaginable, maybe. Perhaps even *unbelievable.*"

Mr. Ennis just shook his head. "Let us just say they are unforgiving."

"You'll pardon me for saying so, but that sounds like balderdash." Christian tapped his fingers on the arm of his chair. "I have never heard of such a thing."

The solicitor ignored this. "He has, however, left explicit instructions empowering two other individuals to act in his absence. I am one of those individuals, and I have been directed to take orders from the other person."

"And that other person is?" Judith asked.

"Ah… That person has given me explicit, recent instructions not to tell you anything."

No wonder Judith had come to Christian. She absolutely needed someone to glower. He leaned forward.

"This is a sham," he announced. "It is utterly unreasonable."

Mr. Ennis made a pained noise. "Yes to the latter; to the former, I honestly have no idea. I've scoured the law books and I've come up utterly empty."

Clearly, more glowering was in order. Christian looked the man in the eyes. "How will it look when Lady Judith brings suit against you, claiming that you've defrauded her and her sisters? It would be exceedingly damaging to your reputation."

His glower bounced off the man entirely. Mr. Ennis wrinkled his nose and shrugged. "My lord, you will simply have to trust me on this. Lady Judith does *not* want to air any of this in public. To be quite frank, I'm not certain what *you* want. But I urge her, in the strongest terms, to consider other options. There are other ways to resolve this matter. But under the circumstances, which are…"

"Unforgiving?"

"Unbelievable," Mr. Ennis continued. "In any event, I cannot actually instruct you in any of those resolutions."

The whole affair was damned odd in the most peculiar possible way. Christian was pretty sure that he was holding onto some kind of a snake. Still, he couldn't shake the feeling that perhaps he was the proverbial blind man. Perhaps the thing in his hands might be attached to an entire elephant.

Christian tried once again. "We could fetch the person who sent the money in the first place. Surely you would have to answer to him."

Mr. Ennis frowned, tilting his head as he considered this. "Agh," he finally opined. "I…do not know if that would serve. You see… Agh."

"You call yourself a solicitor, when that's the sum total of the professional, legal opinion that you can offer? *Agh?*"

"Agh," the man repeated, more firmly. "I could repeat it, if you like, but for sterling advice such as that, I would have to charge by the quarter-hour. That would be in nobody's interest."

"Besides," Judith said, giving Christian a quelling look, "the funds were to have been sent anonymously. Identifying the individual who sent them might prove difficult."

"Agh," Christian said.

Mr. Ennis nodded. "You see? You're coming around to my point of view."

They had accomplished nothing, Judith realized on the ride back. Not with Christian's glowers. Not with her questions. She needed a new idea.

He sat next to her, looking forward, chewing his lip in contemplation. It was late enough in the afternoon that dark stubble dotted his cheeks, lending him even more of a roguish air. It didn't matter how he looked. She'd survived the encounter.

"I suppose it was pointless to have you along. But tha—"

"Ah, ah." He shook his head. "Allies, remember? It sounds like you were about to thank me. Don't. You hate me; we should avoid every mark of civility at all costs."

Ah. Yes.

He continued. "It also sounds as if you were about to send me off. That wasn't our agreement. I get the journals when you've received the money. We're not finished until we're finished."

"Yes, but—"

"As I see it, there are two possibilities. Number one, your solicitor is telling the truth about *agh*. Number two, he is lying."

Judith frowned at him. "Our agreement was that you wouldn't ask questions."

"I'm not asking questions," Christian said. "I'm doing precisely the thing you hate me for: I'm ferreting out the truth."

"You didn't—"

"The way I see it," Christian said, interrupting her again, "either your trusted family solicitor is a liar, and you can hate me for uncovering his perfidy, or some close family friend is a cheat, and you can despise me for demonstrating that he has embezzled funds. It's perfect. Our alliance is built upon precisely this sort of lose-lose scenario. Nothing could be better designed to foment distrust and dislike between us."

She wasn't going to speak. Not if he was going to continually talk over her. She folded her arms.

"Nothing," he said, "except my interrupting you. You hate that. Did I do it well?"

She sighed.

"Or," he offered, "if you hate me too much even for this discussion, you could just skip all the preliminary steps and give me your brother's journals."

Judith snorted. "There isn't the slightest chance of my offering you an unearned advantage of that magnitude."

"I thought as much." Christian shrugged. "In any event, if we are to find out where the money has gone—"

"Now it is my turn to interrupt you," Judith said. "The money was urgent because Camilla was on the verge of coming out. If I am not her legal guardian, the urgency intensifies. Who has charge of her? Will she still have a Season, or will that be blocked as well? The money is the least of our problems now."

He simply nodded. "So we must choose our next target. Do you think that Mr. Ennis is honest? If he is, who is this supposed legal guardian who has appeared out of nowhere to frustrate our purposes?"

"My purposes," Judith reminded him. "And... There is a possible answer. My uncle. Camilla's guardian. If it's anyone, it's him. He's the only other person I could imagine taking over the role."

"You haven't told me where the money came from in the first place." He raised an eyebrow at her. "You sent it anonymously, but how did you obtain it? Was he involved in some way?"

Judith turned to glare at him. "Those are questions. We agreed I wouldn't have to answer questions. He's not even technically my uncle by blood. He's uncle to the youngest three children. But we stayed with him during the years when my father and Anthony were away from England, and I've never lost the habit of calling him Uncle William."

Christian was frowning at her now. "Do I understand that correctly? Your uncle only offered to take in Camilla?"

Judith tasted a hint of bitterness on her tongue. "No. It was not like that. He offered me and Benedict a place as well. He said that if we came to live with him, we'd never want for anything. We'd have clothing, food, come-outs for the girls, schooling for the boys. We'd have everything, he said, as soon as the scandal died down. Camilla said yes."

"But you refused?"

Judith's fists clenched. "That's a question again."

"Of course you refused," he said on an intake of breath. "You, Camilla, and Benedict? What of Theresa?"

"She was difficult." She forced herself to stare straight ahead as she said those words. "Even more difficult when she was a child. After the thing with my father... She would scream for Anthony. And you know how some children have imaginary friends? Theresa invented an entire imaginary *sister* who she insisted was real despite all our attempts to reason with her. My uncle

thought she needed to be sent to a
actually referred to crushing her spir
There was a reason my father carted h
him when she was just three. He didn't
with Uncle William. He certainly didn't
Theresa's horizons."

Christian was looking at her with something like pity.
She didn't want his pity, damn it.

"So you said no," Christian said in a low voice.

"So I said no." Judith's voice broke despite herself.
"What else could I say? How could I accept comfort and
clothing at that cost?"

It had been the most difficult, exhausting *no* of her
life.

"You make it so easy." Christian's voice was a low
murmur beside her. "We're not friends. You hate me. This
entire mess is my fault. See how easy it is for me to remind
you?"

She examined her gloved hands. It had been difficult,
exhausting…and in its own way, in every small triumph
she had won, every barrier she had beaten down, utterly
exhilarating. It was one thing to hate him. It was quite
another to have him take pity on her for the very things
that had brought her pride.

"No," Judith said. "It was not all your fault."

He went very still next to her.

"We're not friends," she said, "but we are allies of a
sort. The truth has been bothering me since last we spoke.
My father was difficult; I never knew him well. Before he
inherited the earldom, he was in the army. After, he was
gone for years on end for his ambassadorial duties. When
he returned from his last stint in India, he was…odd. He

...ed some exceedingly strange notions." She ...uldn't look at him. "He served in too many wars before he inherited the earldom unexpectedly. I read all the evidence in the case, and I still have no idea what motivated him. I suppose Anthony might know, but…" She drew in a deep breath. "It took me years to admit it to myself, but…you could have been right about him."

"This is alarming." Christian pulled back from her. "We can't have you talking like that. It sounds like common ground."

"It isn't," Judith told him. "If my father was absent, Anthony was always there. It's Anthony I care about. You should have known that the evidence you found would unfairly implicate my brother. You should have spoken on his behalf at his trial. Yes, maybe our family would have lost everything. But I wouldn't have lost him. I wouldn't have had to do this alone."

He exhaled. "I see." He sounded as if he were poking needles into his thigh. His jaw worked for a moment as if he were trying to argue. Then he shook his head. "Good. Hatred is preserved. The alliance is safe." He looked away briefly before turning back to her and giving her a glower that could have incinerated her. "I could not have spoken on his behalf in any event. Your brother was guilty."

She exhaled.

He shook his head. "Make arrangements to visit your uncle."

"You make them." She didn't look at him. "He'll agree to a visit from you; you're in Parliament. I'm certain he won't answer my inquiry. He hasn't in years."

They'd reached her street. It was so narrow that if he drove down it, he'd not be able to turn the conveyance round at the end. There was no green grass near here, no cunning little parks, no swans floating on gentle manmade ponds. There was only the hard stone of the street, littered with little bits of paper.

He stopped the horses. "I'm going to get out and hand you down. It won't mean anything."

She let him do it. She let him come to her side, let him take her hands as she stepped down. Her hands in his didn't mean anything. It was a gesture as meaningless as his glowers.

His eyes seemed to track her so intently now.

She wouldn't look up into them. She wouldn't. She wouldn't think of his fingers curling around hers. Of the fabric of his jacket brushing her arm or her skirts against his legs.

Her slippers touched the ground; he let go, and she felt her lungs working again. She dared a glance up at him.

"Why are you doing this?"

"Because I want Anthony's journals."

"No. I mean, why are you trying to set me at ease?"

He didn't deny the claim. For a moment, he looked off down her street. Then he shrugged. "Because I want Anthony's journals," he repeated. "If you start forgetting you hate me, you'll panic and order me to stay away before we've resolved your little problem."

How well he knew her. She could feel that beat of panic now, a dull insistent thud in her chest.

"As for me?" He shrugged and looked her in the eyes. "I don't dare let myself forget you hate me. Not once. Without that, I might…"

He was standing next to her. She was bracketed between him and his curricle.

Once, she'd thought herself in love with him. With that pale scar on his cheek from the time he'd cracked his head on a rock. With the dark curl of his hair. With the way he could make her laugh despite herself.

She'd loved the way he looked at her—precisely like this. He had always sparked her imagination to a riot. She'd wanted more than his hand on hers, more than his lips on hers. He was the only person in the world who could make her feel both comfortable and uncomfortable all at the same time.

If she didn't hate him, she truly *would* panic.

She forced herself to look in his eyes. "You didn't say. What would you do if I didn't hate you?"

He met her gaze. Oh, she should never have looked at him. That spark of laughter in his eyes seemed to ignite into something heated. A thread of consternation coiled in her belly. It wound deep in her, threading through her heart, her breath, her wants.

Once upon a time, he had been all of her dreams. Somewhere, deep inside, some part of her believed that he still was.

He didn't answer her question. Instead, his hand made a fist at his side. "By all means," he said, "let us remember that you hate me."

Chapter Seven

The first thing Judith saw when she walked in her door was Theresa, sitting on a chair at the table, brushing her blond hair out of her eyes. Benedict sat across from her, watching intently.

"Will she be all right?" Benedict asked.

They were concentrating on the table where a small orange cat, wrapped in a blanket, lay mewing softly.

Theresa dabbed at the cat's leg with a small cloth. "It's just a little scratch, Caramel," she said in a soothing voice. "It will be all right."

Caramel was one of the four cats they already owned. Thank God.

"That cat that hurt you?" Theresa was explaining. "He was just hungry, not mean. With a little chicken—"

"No." Judith closed the door behind her.

Caramel jumped, wriggling in the blanket, freeing herself to escape down the hall.

"Judith." Theresa stood, brushing short, orange hairs from her bodice. "How good to have you home." She curtsied almost perfectly, proof that the deportment lessons had not been totally useless.

Judith had done an excellent job teaching her sister precisely how to manipulate her.

"One curtsy is appropriate at the beginning of a dance, or perhaps upon presentation to a social superior," Judith said. "Not when you're asking your sister to let you have another cat. Especially not when said cat is feral."

"Oh, please." Theresa gave up all pretense of manners. "Please, please. We don't have to *keep* him. Just *feed* him."

"Feeding is keeping." Judith spoke from long experience. "We can't feed every cat in London, you know. Four is enough."

Theresa switched smoothly to another tack. "You never let me do *anything.*"

"No," Judith said with a sigh, "I don't. It's because I'm a terrible ogre. I mean that literally. There's no point trying to keep you happy when I intend to grind your bones into flour in a week anyway."

Theresa's nose wrinkled. "Disgusting."

Judith rubbed her stomach and winked. "Delicious."

They both laughed at that, and Benedict managed a minuscule smile, too. Judith did her best not to pounce on him.

You smiled. Are you feeling better? Who hurt you, and how can I stop it? It had been scarcely three days since he'd come home. She had well over a month to solve the problem. The least she could do would be to wait until his lip was healed before probing painful wounds.

She settled for a simple inquiry. "And how was your day, Benedict?"

He shrugged. "Better. Theresa showed me how to hold a cat and give it stitches."

"Blankets," Theresa put in matter-of-factly. "Wrap anything in a blanket long enough and it will eventually feel better."

If only that would work for her. If only Judith could find a massive down comforter and hide from what she had to do. If she could cower under the covers and have her sisters' trusts appear as if by magic, there would be no need for Christian at all.

"How convenient that you should speak of blankets," Judith said. "It's time for bed. Go get ready."

Theresa was too sly to pout. She looked over at Judith and said, craftily, "I can't go. I haven't dusted yet."

"How surprising." Judith shook her head. "How convenient. The only time you mention unfinished chores is to avoid bedtime. Go; I'll take care of it. I'll be up in a few minutes to join you."

Her brother and sister made a show of grumbling, but eventually, she sent them up the stairs.

She wiped down the sideboard, the table. She stopped at the hutch. It contained all their china. Judith had purchased them, piece by piece. Those dishes represented hours of work on her part, trying to find sets that were mostly a little bit matched. If one squinted. They were a kind of promise to her brother and sister: Things were different, but they would survive.

But it wasn't the china that stopped her tonight. It was the shepherdess.

She'd sold everything she could after her father's conviction—everything that had belonged to her outright. Gowns for her upcoming season had gone first. Then jewelry. A carpet. The resulting funds had been enough to take this house for ten years with a scant fifty or so pounds left over.

She hadn't sold Christian's clockwork shepherdess, even though the figurine had been hers. It had been a gift, one she should never have accepted.

Judith's own mother had died when she was an infant. The second Countess of Linney had come into her life when she was four, and Judith had never known the difference.

The countess had been much given to laughing, even though—possibly even *especially because*—her husband was rarely in England. She'd adored bright colors. When she'd taught Judith to embroider, she had forever been encouraging her to add reds and yellows, bright blues and vibrant oranges.

Judith had been seventeen when she passed away. She'd fled the company that had gathered after the funeral, overwhelmed with sadness and fury. Her stepmother would never have wanted a sober, quiet gathering. She would have hated having the house draped in black crepe. If she had been alive, she would never have made Judith wear a black gown. And she would have winked at Judith and whispered that she should absolutely cheat with dark burgundies and welcoming browns.

But she was gone, and in a month's time, Anthony and her father would be gone, too. They were escaping the cloying black crepe that had been hung in the windows for a trip to China.

Judith had hidden in a curtained window seat, curling into a little ball. Her stepmother was gone; her father was leaving; Judith wasn't going to come out in society after all. Instead she'd have to go stay with her staid, sober uncle in the country for two years. Her entire life had altered in a blink, and it wasn't *fair*.

She had been seventeen; she was too old to feel sorry for herself. She was telling herself precisely that when Christian peered into the room. He'd looked about, left the door open, and come in. He'd had a box under one arm, and he had set this on the table.

She hadn't wanted to admit it to herself, but *he* was leaving, too. With Anthony gone, he'd have no reason to visit during the holidays.

They had talked, that summer. A few times a week.

Not that it meant anything. He was two years older than she was, and besides Judith wouldn't be out, not while she was still in mourning. They were friends. Just friends.

At least, they were friendly.

At least… At least, she recognized mockingly, he was friendly to her. She had too many friends who made the mistake of mooning after their brothers' acquaintances, only to have hopes dashed. No point in getting ideas herself.

"Judith," he had said. "I've been looking for you. How are you?"

She glared at him. "If you tell me that I'm a big, strong girl to be so stoic, I will tip a bookshelf on your head."

He touched his head. "Well. I'm not wearing any armor, and I'm not an idiot. So it looks like I'm safe on two counts." He shifted from foot to foot. "Would you be averse to a little discussion?"

"Please." Judith turned to him. "All these people here are so silent and grieving. The countess would be laughing at them all. She would *hate* this entire affair."

He nodded. "In that case, then, I've come to give you something."

She'd glanced at the hall. The low murmur of talk indicated that guests were still here. Her stepmother had been buried literally hours before. "*That* might not be appropriate."

He shut the door behind him, and she swallowed. That wasn't done, shutting the door. Not even for a boy— a man, really—who was a family friend. Not even one she had known since she was seven.

"Well," he said with a lopsided smile. "This would be inappropriate at any time, really. This gift falls on the wrong side of improper."

She hadn't known what to say. "Do you mean that in the sense of your arguments with Anthony? About how propriety is all useless claptrap?"

He looked upward. "Not all propriety is useless claptrap. Much of it serves a purpose. A prophylactic purpose."

She'd peered at him suspiciously. "Prophylactic? The last time you argued prophylactics with Anthony—"

His ears had turned red. "Did you overhear that? Ha, ha. Fancy that! Never mind. In this case, prophylactic means a rule that is designed to protect quite broadly. For instance, think of pistols."

"What sort of pistols?"

For some reason, this had made him blush even more. "Never mind the pistols. But if you're going to carry one, there's a rule you must learn—never point a gun at a man unless you wish him harm. It's one of the most important rules, even though most of the time, if you point that gun, nothing will happen. It's a rule that's meant to protect everyone for that one time out of a hundred when something horrible happens. Maybe you're jostled and you pull the trigger. Maybe that's the instant a spider drops on your head. Whatever it is, the only way to prevent horrible accidents is to never point a gun at a man in jest."

Judith had blinked at this. "You came here to point your pistol at me?"

He put one hand over his face. "In a sense," he'd muttered. "There's a rule that gentlemen ought not give ladies gifts that are too dear. Flowers, yes. Ribbons, maybe. But never anything particularly expensive or thoughtful."

"It will make the lady seem fast if she takes it," Judith had said with a nod.

"No," Christian said. "That's what they tell the young ladies. I don't think it's the true reason, though."

"No?"

"It's because some gentlemen aren't gentlemen. Sometimes, a man will *say* he's giving a gift, and then later, he'll ask for compensation in the form of attentions a lady does not wish to give."

Judith heard herself laughing. "Goose. Nobody will think *you're* seeking my attentions."

He hadn't laughed with her. He'd bit his lip instead and looked over at her. "Won't they?"

And then he handed her the box he was carrying.

It had been heavy. She'd needed two hands to steady it on her lap. Then she'd lifted the lid.

Inside that wooden box had been a brilliant tableau. A shepherdess sat in a field, her face upturned. She had been smiling. The painter had captured the look of sun kissing her lips.

But that had not been the best part. Around her, three clockwork sheep were arranged on a little track that wound round the figurine's skirts. And when she pulled the shepherdess out of the box, there was something underneath her—a thick volume, the spine stamped with the notation *Elements of Clockwork*.

"Oh, my." Judith had touched the figurine and then found the mechanism and wound it. The sheep danced, turned, and—one by one—leapt a tiny wooden fence.

She had turned to Christian. He was watching her with an unreadable expression on his face. Even if she couldn't read his expression, she could comprehend what he'd given her. This wasn't the sort of bauble one handed to one's best friend's younger sister on a whim.

She had been glad. "It's perfect."

He had scuffed his foot against the carpet. "If you flip it over, you'll discover that the clockwork can be accessed via a simple panel. You can completely disassemble it, if you wish."

That had been it: the moment she had known that he'd seen her, that he knew what she most desired, and that he'd wanted to give it to her. It was more intimate than a kiss. She was seventeen; he was nineteen. She was unlikely to see him at all in the next few years.

She had been old enough to think of boys, but not quite old enough to do so seriously. Up until that moment, she hadn't let herself dwell on the possibility of Christian. He spent summers in her house, for God's sake; there was no point working herself up to being nervous in his presence.

She was nervous now.

"It's extremely improper," he said. "Far too expensive. And I had it commissioned for you in particular, which makes it even worse. But I won't ever ask you for anything because of it. I won't even remind you I offered it."

"Won't you?" She felt almost wistful.

"No," he said. "While your father and your brother are gone, you are going to stay with your uncle three counties over. You'll be in mourning, not taking visitors. We won't have a chance to talk at breakfast. We shan't have any meetings in the orchards. You won't be out. So no, Judith. I won't have the opportunity to ask you for any attentions. Not for two years."

She nodded. "It's a farewell gift."

His eyes had held hers. "By the time I see you again, you'll be nineteen, and every inch the lady. I am not asking you to do anything improper, Judith. But I must admit that I'm hoping you will do me the honor of..."

She had waited in utter confusion.

"Of not forgetting me," he said.

She hadn't. She'd taken his shepherdess apart and reassembled it until she could see the gears in her sleep. She'd studied the book and saved her pin money so she could order the parts she needed to make the sheep leap backward, and when her first attempt had failed, she'd tried again.

She had never forgotten him. Not during those two years while her father was away and she was stranded in mourning at her uncle's. Not when she saw him again after all that time. Not after her father's trial.

She'd thought of him the day she sold her first design for a clockwork dancing couple.

She picked up the shepherdess now and gave it a perfunctory wipe.

Her memory was too good. She also couldn't forget Benedict's lip. She remembered that the little bits and pieces she'd scraped together for her sisters added up to a tiny fraction of what they would have had...and that it felt like she'd spent the last years of her life scrambling from one sinking ship to the next.

They should have had more. *She* should have had more.

"You're right," she told the shepherdess. "I can't let myself forget that I hate him."

ire ahead," Christian was saying to Mr. Lawrence, his man of business, as they walked in the front door of his house. "We'll need a conveyance of some sort when we arrive."

"Yes, my lord."

Beside him, the butler gave him a faint nod in greeting and tilted his head slightly to the right.

Christian turned back to his man of business. "Reschedule my meeting with Lord Grafton."

"Yes, my lord. Already accomplished."

The butler moved ten degrees, back into Christian's field of vision, and mildly cleared his throat.

"And find my notes from the Worth affair, if you will—there's one matter I must think about briefly."

"Of course, my lord. I'll have them brought right over."

The butler cleared his throat a little louder, and when that didn't work, coughed mildly into his fist.

"Good." Christian handed his hat and gloves to the butler, hoping that this was the source of the man's insistently putting himself forward. "Then we can knock off these last—" He stopped midsentence, looking into the front drawing room.

His mother sat, a stiff expression on her face. Next to her on the sofa was Lillian, his second cousin, and her husband, Viscount Stafford. They were staring at him with matching, pained looks that suggested he had either murdered a score of baby elephants in the public square and was still dripping blood, or he was guilty of some minor breach of etiquette.

For instance, not noticing that he had visitors when he walked into his house.

Also, possibly, not remembering that he had promised his mother that he'd be home to visitors today. Damn it.

He handed his hat and coat to the butler and walked through the doors. "Lillian," he said. "You look well. You're much recovered from your confinement."

"Thank you, Christian."

"And Stafford. How good of you to come by."

He reached for a biscuit; his mother frowned at him, and he left it on its platter.

"Do sit with us," his mother said coaxingly. "Talk."

Small talk was the last thing on his mind. He could have engaged Stafford on some of the little matters dithering about in Parliament if they'd been alone, but they were in mixed company. He might have enjoyed drawing Lillian out—he had never known what women talked about when they were alone until his cousin had begun to whisper details—but she'd never divulge her secrets with her husband present. Besides, he had a journey in the morning to plan.

Still. His mother handed him a cup of tea that she'd prepared, and he dutifully seated himself and set the cup on the little side table.

"Ashford." Lillian touched her fingers to the coiled plait of dark hair wound about her head. "We are here on a very serious matter. We request that you give this your utmost…ah…consideration."

He reached for a sandwich. "You perceive me all considering consideration."

"Something dire has happened." Lillian reached for her own teacup, as if it were filled with liquid consolation instead of just brown brewed water. "Something truly, dreadfully awful. Your reputation will never be the same."

"Oh my." Christian sat up straight. "They've found out about the elephants."

Lillian frowned at him. "The…*what?*"

"The baby elephants. In Trafalgar Square. With the guillotine…? Oh, you mean they haven't realized that was me? Good, good. Never mind. Carry on."

His cousin exhaled. "Christian. Do be serious. I am."

"Continue," Christian said. "You were saying that something truly awful has happened."

Lillian sniffed. His mother handed her a handkerchief, which she used to dab at her eyes.

"My dear Lord Ashford," Lillian said, "you know you're the dearest of my cousins. I care for you as if you were my own brother. Despite your terrible sense of— well, never mind that. I can't bear to see you suffer so. I would do anything to have you as happy as I am."

"How am I suffering?"

She dabbed at her eyes and looked at him. "Lady Cailing said that you should be struck from the list of eligible bachelors."

Christian took a bite of his sandwich. The bread was dry; the cucumber was limp. Clearly, he needed to discuss sandwiches with his cook. In fact…

No, no distracting himself with that now. His mother and cousin watched him expectantly, as if they'd disclosed all they had to say.

"That's it?" he finally asked.

"Christian, Lady Cailing is respected in the highest levels of society!"

He supposed she was. He sighed and tried to take the complaint seriously. "Why am I to be so censured? Am I accused of murder?"

Lillian dropped her handkerchief. "Is there any danger of that?"

"He's joking," his mother said with a shake of her head. "You know how he is—always joking about murdering people." She gave him a reproachful look.

"Not always," Christian put in unhelpfully. "Sometimes I joke about murdering baby elephants."

Three very proper people stared at him in utter horror.

"Although in my defense," Christian continued, "this time, they weren't really *baby* elephants, not by months. They were toddler elephants at the worst. I'm sure that makes you all feel better."

"Christian." Lillian put her face in her hands, and her husband patted her shoulder consolingly.

Christian sighed. "I never remember when it's appropriate to joke about baby elephants. Not over tea, apparently. Tell me—elephant death is more of a breakfast subject, isn't it?"

Lillian looked over at his mother. "Yes. I see what you mean. It's getting worse. Much worse."

Christian inhaled slowly. It was one thing to tweak his cousin and mother. With their long faces and dire pronouncements, he'd expected something that had actual consequences. But they cared about him, and he cared about them. "Very well. I'll do my best to behave. Why have I been subject to such blistering, terrifying censure? And why is Lady Cailing saying such terrible things to your face? Someone should speak to her about her dreadful manners."

"Of course she didn't tell me directly! How horrible that would be." Lillian sniffed. "She told Lady Whitford, who told Lady Dunworth, who told your aunt Madge, who told me."

Christian smiled. "Oh, that's good. You made it sound as if I were a total pariah. Instead, I'm the talk of the town."

"Christian." His mother glared at him across the table. "How can you jest so at a time like this? After all the work we did to make sure your image was so perfectly sustained, and now..." She shuddered. "I will admit that your somewhat peculiar sense of humor has not harmed your chances the way I thought it would. People seem to actually enjoy it."

"Everyone loves you," Lillian said. "But the gossip *now* is that you are too single-minded. You think of nothing but trade deals, smuggling, importation, exportation. You don't go to balls. You don't attend the opera. You don't visit gentlemen's clubs except to talk of Parliament."

"And to make jokes about baby elephants," his mother muttered.

Lillian continued on as if she had not been interrupted. "Next they'll be talking mental instability."

Next to her, her husband was nodding. "It could become dire."

Christian shrugged. "Well, that sounds surprisingly accurate for *ton* gossip. The long chain of whispers has managed to discover truth for once. This seems cause for celebration."

His mother set down her cup and saucer. "Christian. You are my only child. You are my life's work. I…" Her voice caught for a moment and she looked at Lillian and her husband as if for support. "I gave up *everything* to make sure that no rumors circulated of your condition. You know how gossip is. Go to a few parties. Dance with a few young ladies." She shrugged. "Marry one of them, and nobody will ever speak ill of you again."

Christian couldn't help himself. He burst into laughter. Well, at least he'd tried to be serious. "Go to a few parties. Dance a few dances. Commit yourself in a public, binding ceremony to another person for the rest of your life. One of these things is rather different in scope than the others, don't you think?"

"Christian," she said repressively.

"Since you've been so solicitous, here is some advice on soothing your sensibilities: Buy a few ballgowns. Walk in the park with a friend. Renounce your British citizenship and move to the Maldives."

She glared at him.

"Ah, see, no one likes the rapid escalation game, do they? I commend baby elephants to you as superior amusement in every way."

"Christian, I am trying to be serious."

"I know," he said. "I'm sorry. I tried, too. It lasted about a minute before I decided it wouldn't help one bit. I am who I am. I don't care if people think I'm off, or if they wonder if I'm ever going to get married. I don't mind if they strike me from whatever list they've put me on. I am never going to stop being the person that I am, and I don't see why I should apologize for it."

She leaned toward him. "We made sure that nobody knew of your night terrors. We never spoke of the list-making or the counting or any of the other oddities about you. People think you're witty and charming and the little peculiarities, well... Nobody has minded until now. We must make sure that this continues. We must make plans."

"Oh," said Christian. "I have an idea. I could speak on behalf of a bill in Parliament. I could write an editorial for the newspaper. Or—how about this for a difference in scope—I could tell everyone my father wanted to put me in a madhouse when I was a child."

"Christian!"

"Mmm." He took another bite of his sandwich. "I see you still don't like the game you invented."

His mother looked around, as if to make sure that none of the footmen were present. "It was not a madhouse," she finally said primly. "That makes people think of Bedlam. And you never went; I made sure of that."

"Yes," Christian said. "I recall."

"But it's those very facts that we must be vigilant about. It's embarrassing—no, *damaging*—for everyone to think you're obsessed with the details of the opium trade in the Orient. An interest is allowed; an obsession borders on the radical. Can you not just set it aside for the next decade or so? What is wrong with championing another cause? There are orphans here in England already. Orphans make an excellent cause."

"Mmm." Christian shook his head. "Given my track record with young elephants, I cannot think that trusting me with orphans would be a wise choice."

Lillian set her fingers to her temples. "Lord Ashford. Christian. We love you. We want you to be happy. Just come with me to tea a few times. I can have Lady Ennish invite you tomorrow. You can make your jokes, and people will laugh. Behave yourself. Fit in. That's all anyone wants to see—that you're still a part of *us.*"

That was precisely the problem. He was afraid that he wasn't any longer.

"I know," Christian said. "I understand. I'm sorry." He patted her hand. "I love you all, too, and I'm only telling jokes because I can't make this right. You see…" He'd stopped being one of *them*. He wasn't sure when it had happened, but it had. "I don't drink tea any longer."

"Pretend," Lillian begged. "You used to at least pretend before."

He *had* pretended. He'd pretended very well for years. He'd told himself when his friend's ship had sailed that Anthony would be back in seven years, having learned his lesson. Everything would come right again. Anthony would confess his error. Christian had pretended for years, even after he heard that Anthony had been…misplaced.

He'd pretended those reports were in error even while he sent his own men to investigate. His pretenses had all started to break down, month by month, as the men he had sent returned, armed with interviews and notes, all of which amounted to one thing: Anthony was no longer in this world.

There would be no apology. There would be no promises. There would never be a reconciliation. What Christian had done was irrevocable, and all the doubts he'd pretended out of existence had welled up in his dreams with the fury of phantasms that would no longer be suppressed.

"I'm truly sorry," he said. "I can't pretend. Not anymore."

It was three days after Judith had last seen Christian. Daisy had come over and was perched on a rickety chair. Theresa and Benedict sat on the sofa next to her.

"I want to talk to you about tomorrow."

Theresa raised a hand. "Pardon me, but we can't start. We have to wait for all the cats to arrive."

Judith grimaced at her sister. Squid sat proudly on the sofa next to Theresa, his paws stretched in front of him in the regal pose that had earned him his full name: Lord Squid, Baron of Kittensley. Caramel was curled on Benedict's lap. Her brother rubbed her ears idly. Parson sat on the side table.

"The cats are mostly here," Judith said. "Besides, I've seen little evidence that they attend to English in the first place."

"Not the way *you* speak it," Theresa muttered.

"So if Evelyn—"

"She's Lady Evil at the moment."

A more appropriate name for the cat could not have been given. Judith accepted the interruption without even blinking.

"As I was saying. Since I cannot communicate with Lady Evil, I'll leave it to you to do so when she graces us with her presence."

Theresa snorted. "*This* is why the cats never listen to you."

This was why doing the simplest thing in the Worth household took nine hours and a committee. Judith sighed. "Please hold your tongue, Theresa."

"I told you, it's literally *impossible* to hold one's tongue."

Judith ignored this. "I am going to have to leave town extremely early tomorrow morning on business," she continued. "I shall be gone until very late in the evening. Theresa, Benedict, you'll have to look after yourselves."

Her two siblings exchanged glances. Then Theresa burst into a delighted smile that made the hair on the back of Judith's neck stand up.

"Lovely," Theresa said. "Why all the fuss and ceremony? Don't worry about us. We'll see you when you return."

Judith persisted. "If there is an emergency, if you need someone, you will go find Daisy, who has kindly volunteered to help. She'll be at the flower shop until two in the afternoon, and then in her flat across the way. Understood?"

Theresa rolled her eyes. "Yes."

"A badly made sandwich is not an emergency. A desire to see the circus is not an emergency. It's not an emergency unless you are in peril of your *life.*"

"Or a cat's life," Theresa put in.

Ducks alive. There was a loophole to end all loopholes.

"Only Squid, Parson, and Caramel," Judith said. "No other cats."

Theresa's eyes rounded in horror. "Not Lady Evil?"

"Definitely not Lady Evil. I'd drown her myself."

"Oh." Theresa scrunched up her nose. "You're teasing me. Lady Evil is your favorite."

Technically, she was. Judith refused to admit it, not when she could tweak her sister instead.

"You're *mean.*" Theresa frowned at her.

"Like a queen," Judith agreed.

"Eating beans," Theresa finished.

"Where are you going?" Benedict asked.

No point dissembling there. "I am going to see our uncle William."

Theresa sat up. "Will you see Camilla?"

Benedict frowned. "For what purpose?"

Judith didn't look at Daisy. She had never told Daisy of her past before they met. If Daisy knew that her uncle was a viscount, that her father had been an earl, she'd think that Judith had been making fun of her with their game.

"I'm simply seeking out answers to some questions. That's all."

"Are you going to bring Camilla back?" Theresa asked.

"She's always welcome, but—"

"Where will she sleep? In our room? There isn't room for three in that bed, not if we want Lady Evil and Squid and Parson and Caramel to still be able to stretch out."

"You are getting ahead of yourself, Tee."

"But I don't *want* to put the cats out of the room."

"It's a social call," Judith said a little more loudly. "Nothing more. Nothing less. And your sister is more important than a bunch of cats."

Theresa inhaled in horror. "What!?"

"It's a social call. On a relative." *Who might be embezzling the trusts I so painstakingly earned for you,* Judith did not say aloud. "Please stop extrapolating from a single visit to the end of the world."

"But if the world *is* coming to an end, I would very much like to make sure that the cats are taken care of. The cats are my responsibility. You always say so. I'm just trying to be responsible. Is that so very wrong?"

There was nothing to do but completely ignore this. Judith gestured. "Daisy will look in on you once she's finished at the shop. Mind her when she talks to you. Do not use the kitchen stove yourself. Do not try to burn the house   down.   Do   not   get   into   a   knife fight—"

"I have *never* wanted to fight with knives." Theresa tossed her head scornfully.

Judith, of course, noticed that her sister did not disclaim interest in any of the other items on the list.

"And whatever you do, do not adopt any more cats," Judith finished. "Four is enough cats. Understand?"

Two had been enough cats. *One* had been enough cat.

"But what if—"

"There are no buts," Judith said, "just as there are no more cats. Or fires. Or any of the other things on the list. The only thing I want to hear right now is 'Yes, Judith.' If you can't say that, hold your tongue."

"Yes, Judith." Theresa rolled her eyes. "But I still hate that expression. 'Hold your tongue.' Have you ever *tried* to hold your tongue? I have." She stuck out her tongue. "Look." She tried to grip it with her fingers. "It'th too thlippewy. Like a fifth." She frowned. "A fifsth." She spat out her own fingers. "Like a fish, even. The tongue is an unholdable object. Why does anyone still say that?"

Judith narrowed her eyes. "That was not a simple 'Yes, Judith.'"

"Wait. You didn't make Benedict say 'Yes, Judith.' So he's allowed to get in a knife fight? It's not *fair*. If he gets to cut people, I want to, too!"

Judith sighed. "Benedict?"

"Yes, Judith," Benedict said. He had been watching her with a somber expression, without any of his usual liveliness in his eyes. His reply was almost perfunctory. "I'll do none of those things."

When it came to Benedict, Judith just hoped he would leave his room.

"Lovely." Judith stood. "Daisy is going to make sure that you all have something to eat in the evening. I'll be gone before you wake. Please, for me, try to behave a little. Go for a walk. A sedate walk. Along the river will be nice this time of year, don't you think?"

Benedict shrugged.

"Lovely," Judith repeated. "Then… Daisy, thank you for stopping by. I'll walk you to the door?"

It was an excuse to get her friend alone, and a none-too-transparent one.

"Judith," Daisy said, turning to her once they were out of eavesdropping distance, "are you in difficulties?"

Judith sighed. "Nothing I can't manage."

"Because if you're going away for a day, I can't help remember that there was a man who visited. He was too well-dressed, too…too…" She paused. "He really could have been a marquess. Not that I would know anything about them."

"No," Judith said. "All your experience is with dukes, as I recall."

Daisy sighed. "Dukes and scoundrels. All I am trying to say is that if you…that is, if he… If this is not precisely a matter of business, one that will take you to see this supposed long-lost uncle who has not extended a hand to help out in all the years I've known you—if it's something else, if you've decided to, um…"

"Um?"

"Sell your virtue," Daisy said after a mortified pause.

They rarely said a word to each other about their problems, but Judith knew that she worried about Daisy and how many turnips she purchased because she'd had some bad months in the beginning when she'd counted carrots, too. If Daisy was worried about Judith's virtue, it was probably because she'd had her own tussel with reality on that score. Judith wanted to protect Daisy from the worst that had happened to her; clearly, Daisy felt the same way. She could have hugged her.

There was a reason they so rarely talked of reality. Reality had far too much ugliness in it. In many ways, it would have been easier for Judith if she'd simply lost her virtue. That, one needn't speak of. Losing one's father, one's brother, was another level of impropriety entirely. If Daisy thought that street-walking was beyond words, Judith didn't want to know what she might think of her father selling his loyalty.

"I am calling on my uncle," Judith said. "And you're right, he has done an excellent job of ignoring our branch of the family these last years. I don't imagine that it will be a particularly pleasant call. Any time money is involved, it rarely is."

"And the man yesterday? Is he bothering you?"

"An old family friend." Judith shut her eyes. True, yes. True and so false. "From before we moved here. Our stations are no longer congruent. I believe we horrified him sufficiently."

"If you say so." Daisy looked her over. "But, please…" She trailed off.

Judith reached out and took Daisy's hand. "Of all the things you have to worry about, my virtue should not be on the list. I know how you feel about such things."

Daisy shifted uncomfortably.

"You're a good friend," Judith said. "An excellent friend. Thank you for looking in on the monkeys tomorrow. Are you sure I can't pay—"

Daisy cut her off with an embarrassed motion. "I wouldn't think of it. You've looked in on my mother too many times."

Judith nodded. "See you in a few days, then."

"Of course." But when Daisy left, she glanced over her shoulder. And Judith remembered everything she was holding back.

Chapter Nine

The Waterloo Bridge station fell away as the train made its way out of London. Across the seat from Christian, Judith looked very—well, not *proper*. Proper was absolutely not the right word.

She was wearing a demure brown traveling gown. At least he *thought* it was brown; colors were not his forte.

There was nothing improper about her, not from the top of her head, covered by a wide-brimmed, sober traveling bonnet, to her ankles, which were properly hidden from view by the dark folds of her skirt. A dark cloak hung on a hook and her fingertips were gloved in gray.

But this was the same gown she'd worn to the solicitor's office. The cuffs had long since lost their crisp, sharp edge; the fabric at the elbows had been maintained carefully, but it had worn just a little thin, showing years of use.

Not that Christian was exactly *good* at identifying clothing. If there was an opposite of a fashion expert, it was he. His female relations had long since learned that "What do you think of my new bonnet?" was likely to be met with a frown and a response of "How very…brown…and…hatlike it is."

Which was usually met with shrieks of horror, because invariably, brown bonnets were not "brown."

They were some other color that women could magically detect, something like "plum" or "burgundy" or "red."

Brown. They were basically all brown. There were only three colors, as far as Christian could tell; everything else had just been made up. So Christian knew that if *he* noticed Judith's gown, something was truly amiss, and it wasn't just the fine dusting of cat hair.

This was not a *proper* gown. A proper gown would have been fitted to her figure, allowing him to see every curve he knew she had. A proper gown would have shown the skin of her neck, the little bones of her wrist.

No, this was a *sensible* gown. Sensible ladies could be a great many things—respectable, dignified, astute, clever, and realistic. They weren't inherently improper; in fact, quite the reverse.

But they were never the sort of woman his mother would hold up as a lady to be admired for anything other than her fortitude in handling unfortunate circumstances.

Christian was the unfortunate circumstance at the moment. Judith sat across from him, not looking his way, very carefully reading a newspaper. Even in her sensible gown, even turned away from him, he could hardly make himself look away. She read very methodically, very deliberately. Reading every column in order, without stopping to think or skipping ahead or pausing to converse with him.

When she'd finished the final sheet of the paper, she frowned at it and started once again at the beginning.

Which was not very flattering, as the first sheet of *The Morning Post* was given to advertisements announcing charity balls and governesses for hire. That was where Christian ranked with her: somewhere below the notice of royal charter for incorporation of the London Company for Fire, Life, and Marine Assurances. Probably below mice, roaches, and other vermin.

This was what sensible ladies did when forced to spend several hours in the company of unfortunate circumstances like former family friends.

"What do you make of the transatlantic cable?" Christian asked.

Out the window, wheat fields gave way to grassy meadows. Waving fresh stalks, hip-high, lined the banks of a slow-moving river. Willow trees along an avenue gave way to an orchard, one of brilliant leaves and tiny, scarcely detectable fruits.

She looked up at him. "I beg your pardon. Which problem?"

"The transatlantic cable that it is being laid," Christian repeated. "It's mentioned on page two of the *Morning Post*, in some considerable detail."

She blinked. "Likely," she finally said, "you, as a member of the House of Lords, are more versed in the matters involved than I am." She looked back at her paper.

"I ask because you seemed to take an interest in the lengthy discussion regarding Foilhammerum Bay. You read the entire three columns about it, after all. Twice."

Judith sniffed. "I have no interest in Foilhammerum Bay. Or transatlantic cables. I am not certain it will do us much good to be able to send messages at such speeds. Such rapid communication will only give us the opportunity to embroil ourselves in affairs that would otherwise resolve themselves without our intervention."

She rustled the paper and brought it up again.

"We represent the British Empire," Christian said, watching her. "Embroiling ourselves in conflicts where we do not belong is our imperial business."

But she didn't glare at him. She didn't even recognize that what he'd said touched on the heart of her family's treachery. She simply glanced at him over the edge of the paper and raised one eyebrow. "Pushing yourself unwanted into someone's attention may be *your* particular specialty, but I cannot think it a national pastime."

"Why, thank you," Christian said. "I *am* particularly good at that. In this case, though, it seemed to me you might have opinions about what you were reading."

"Oh, might I, please?" She gave him a brilliant smile.

Even though he knew she was being sarcastic, that her expression was manufactured, that smile nearly knocked him backward against the seat with its force.

"Thank you so much, Lord Ashford. I didn't know it was allowed."

"You see?" Christian said, smiling in response. "That's better. Much better. We have an alliance to strengthen and if you don't talk with me, how can I do my part? Rapid communication. That is the key to your hatred and our mutual antipathy. Why, if we didn't tell each other how we felt, we might lapse into a mere tepid disregard. We can't have that."

She inclined her head. "I see your point. That would be dreadful."

"So yes, Lady Judith. I give you my full, outright permission to think, to create your own opinions." He gave her a little sitting bow. "If it's too difficult to come up with your own, of course, I remind you that I'm a man, and I'm more than happy to share mine."

She was trying not to smile in truth now.

"It's one of the things I admire most about English gentlemen," she said. "They are always willing to provide their opinions to ladies. One hardly even needs to solicit one any longer."

"Perfect." Christian nodded soberly. "I was worried that my brilliant good looks and easy manners would make me impossible to hate, thus ruining our fragile alliance. But this will be simple. Just tell me all the subjects you are an expert in, and I shall endeavor to explain them to you."

Her lips twitched.

"Clockwork. You do still like clockwork, yes?"

She tilted her head to look out the window. "I do."

"Well, I saw a clockwork horse the other day. Clever thing. It tossed its head back with a little…um, moving motion. That takes some complicated gears and thingummies."

"Probably a crank spindle," Judith murmured. "Fitted to—"

He frowned at her. "I'm pretty sure that *thingummy* is proper terminology," he said as stuffily as he could. "The clockwork-ologists *I* know all referred to it as a thingummy."

She laughed. "You are such a goose. You obviously remember Mr. Mortimer, don't you?"

Her father's man of business. He'd been dreadfully stuffy, always lecturing Judith as if she were his concern. Christian had helped her escape from the man a time or twenty, even before he'd thought of her as anything more than an underfoot pest. For a moment, they smiled at one another across the train, as if remembering the time that

Christian had replaced all the ink in the man's desk with acorns.

Then Judith pulled back as if stung.

"Oh, damn," Christian said. "That was a slip. I'm being remiss in my duties."

She picked up her newspaper.

"It's just a little slip," he said. "We can fix it. Do you know what will fix it? A list."

"A list?" She looked up. Her nose wrinkled.

"A list!" He nodded vigorously. "Lists fix everything. Watch: here's a list of reasons you hate me. One, that book you got in trouble for losing when you were eleven? That was me. I did it."

"What, the Gilbert? The one on heathen mythology?"

"Yes," he said. "I dropped it in the stream one afternoon. I didn't want to tell you because the cover said it was for young ladies."

"And you never told anyone? I was made to stay inside for five days for mislaying it, and you know how I hate staying inside."

"I know," Christian said sadly. "Look at my despicable character. Formed at a young age, and my bad habits were never unlearned."

"Oh, good." Judith leaned back. "Keep going. This is working."

"Two," Christian said. "That was a lie. Sorry. I didn't lose the book. I had nothing to do with it. I just told you that I had so you would hate me more. Look at me; I'm a hardened teller of falsehoods. You can't trust a thing I say."

She narrowed her eyes at him and folded her arms. Her fingers tapped dangerously against her sleeve. "Let me do the next one," she said. "Where were we? Ah, yes. Item C—you never can be serious, not even when you're making a list, which I know you hold sacred."

"What did you say?" Christian drew back.

"You're never serious."

"No, no. Before that. Item *C?*" He looked at her in horror. "This is a list. It started with numbers. It goes one, two, *three.*"

"Not this list," Judith said with a glint of a smile. "This list goes one, two, C."

Oh, God. She knew him too well. He put his hands over his ears. "No."

"Right," she continued. "On to Roman numeral IV."

Like this, glaring at him... She looked like a beautiful, victorious warrior queen, one who used badly-numbered lists instead of spears. In his case, the former was a more effective weapon.

"*Gah.*" He winced and rubbed his face. "Knives are stabbing my ears. I am being murdered. Someone fetch a constable and take this woman into custody."

"Roman numeral IV," Judith said, "you are given to excessive histrionics. Also, you are trying to have me falsely imprisoned. You have a tendency to do that with my family, don't you?"

"Please stop. Please use numbers."

"Very well. Eight—"

"No! You skipped six and seven!"

"Eight," Judith said meaningfully. "I hate you because you let my brother die."

He swallowed.

"Nine," she continued, "I hate you because you didn't care what would happen to me after."

"Judith…"

"Eleven," she went on, glowering at him.

"Ten?" he offered.

"*Eleven.* I hate you because you make me remember everything I could have had."

Christian shut his eyes. It was almost physically painful to leave the list as she had. One—the book. Two, the lie. Three—not *C,* it would never be *C*—he wasn't serious. He went through the rest of the list, putting everything in proper, numerical order in his mind.

When he finally opened his eyes, Judith was looking at him. She tapped her fingers impatiently.

"You have a task, Christian," she said. "You can't let me forget that I hate you. If I forget, you'll make me laugh. Then, when I do remember, it will hurt all over again. If I have to remember for the both of us, I'll make sure you won't like it. Are we understood?"

He knew precisely what she meant. For a moment there, they'd been laughing together. They hadn't been at odds. Losing that sense of camaraderie again reminded him of that empty hole in his life.

He didn't need any more reminders.

He gave her a nod. "Understood."

Chapter Ten

Christian's man had telegraphed ahead for an open carriage. The team was badly matched; the bay on the left pulled a little too hard, and the gray mare on the right kept trying to slow down—but the seats were clean and comfortable and he could handle mismatched cattle for eight miles. Persuading the team to pull in approximately the same direction at approximately the same time couldn't prove more difficult than trying to work with Judith.

She sat next to him on the single front-facing seat, looking ahead with a fixed expression that suggested she would allow him no latitude at all.

He waited until they'd left the houses behind, until the road was nothing but dust surrounded by fields.

He waited until the horses had reluctantly fallen into a productive trot and he could spare a hand from the reins.

Then he reached into his satchel. "I have a confession to make."

Her eyes darted to him.

"I did a thing," he told her. "A very bad thing. Something that absolutely violates our agreement. I bring the matter to your attention so that you might deal with it appropriately, but in my defense—no, no, there can be no defense."

"Christian, what are you talking about?"

He removed a package wrapped in waxed paper from his bag. "I brought you a sandwich."

She looked at the package suspiciously, then narrowed her eyes in his direction.

"I know," he said. "What was I thinking? It's a veritable peace offering."

Her head tilted slightly. "What sort of sandwich is it?"

"That's the worst part. I know you have Opinions on Sandwiches." She had once made him a list of her Opinions on Sandwiches, and they had been so opinionated that he couldn't imagine them without capitals. That list had been properly numbered, and he hadn't forgotten any of the items.

She was becoming more suspicious. "What have you done?"

He shook his head. "I'm terribly sorry. It's indefensible. I have no excuse. It's curry chicken salad and cucumber."

My favorite, she did not say, but her lips pressed together.

He gestured to his satchel. "Unless you prefer egg and ham?"

My other favorite, she also did not say.

"This is salvageable," he said. "I simply forgot our ceasefire of mutually agreed upon hostility when I was ordering today's luncheon. But I can fix this." He turned to look her in the eyes. "I can make this better. I'll eat them both in front of you, singing their praises. Nothing could be more inclined to push you into a rage."

For a moment, their eyes met. She didn't seem on the verge of raging. Her gaze dropped to the waxed paper in his hand, as if contemplating giving it up.

Her chin squared in determination and she snatched the packet from his hands. "No such sacrifice is needed. I'll eat it."

"But will that serve? Our agreement, after all, requires—"

"I'll eat it resentfully," she told him, and unwrapped the sandwich. She looked at it, then looked at him. Her lips pursed. Her eyes narrowed.

A woman ought not look beautiful because she was looking askance at a sandwich, but then, Judith had never done the things she ought to have done. And because he knew her, he knew precisely what the problem was. Judith loved food. All food—fruit, biscuits, sandwiches, chocolates. If one could eat it, Judith appreciated it. He'd known. She'd made him lists about food.

This was not just a sandwich of cucumber and curried chicken. It was composed of bread, precisely three-quarters of an inch thick, crusty and dark on the outside and soft and spongy on the interior. There were perfectly crisp cucumbers, sliced and laid so as to evenly cover said bread. And there was the curry chicken filling, not stingily dabbed in place, but with chunks of meat alternating with a tangy spicy sauce and a bit of pickled carrot. If Judith had been the editor of a lady's magazine entitled *Perfect Sandwiches According to Judith*, this would have been the featured sandwich of the year. Every year.

Possibly Christian had miscalculated. He'd wanted to see her smile; he hadn't thought beyond that.

"Oh, you *cad*," she said in horror.

"Yes, that's the problem with maintaining a solid front of ill will," Christian said. "The major difficulty we have is that once we get past the mutual hatred and the ruining-your-life thing, we're actually extremely good friends."

She glared at him.

"Good friends," he said hastily, "who are utterly repulsed by one another. Look at me and my nasty, suggestive sandwiches."

"Suggestive?" She shook her head. "No need to worry. It is a logical fallacy to conflate a man with his sandwich. I am perfectly capable of castigating you while devouring your food." She took a bite. "Oh, ducklings." She chewed. "Mmm."

"By all means," he said in a low voice. "Conflate me with my sandwich. That sandwich is me in effigy. *Eat* my sandwich. Eat it with your mouth."

Her eyes flickered open briefly into narrow, disapproving slits. "What are you doing now?"

He was…damn it, he was flirting with her. He hadn't intended to do it. Really.

"I'm being reprehensible," he said instead. "It's part of our agreement. You can't complain about reprehensibility; it's precisely what you bargained for."

Judith considered this as she swallowed her bite. "Very well. If I must eat you in effigy, then I am eating your sandwich with my teeth. Like this." She took an exaggerated bite, snapping her teeth together.

"There you are," Christian said. "Kill the sandwich. Kill it as if it were me. Rend it to pieces."

She took another vicious bite of chicken curry. "Your sandwich," she said after she swallowed, "tastes like victory."

"Kill it," he said. "Kill it dead."

She took another bite.

Just as she was chewing, he leaned toward her. "Who is England's greatest chicken-curry killer?"

She looked up at him, her eyes widening. He didn't give her time to react. He whispered, *"You are."*

It happened so swiftly. She laughed first. Then she choked, and *then* she spat out little bits of bread and chewed chicken.

"Christian." She put one hand over her face and fumbled in her pocket with the other. "I hate you."

"There you are." He handed her a handkerchief. "Never trust me. Let your guard down once, and next thing you know, you'll have curry chicken up your nose."

"I think," she said, "you may very well be the worst person in the world."

He bowed at the waist and took up the reins again. "At your service."

Judith had spent almost two years under her uncle's care. Odd, that she should have to use chicanery now to obtain entrance. But the butler took Christian's card and ushered her in as his guest.

"Lord Ashford," the butler said. "Lady Ashford."

Her entire soul twitched at that designation, but she did not correct his mistake.

This place seemed so odd and yet so familiar. She'd skipped through these halls when she was seventeen and her father had gone abroad as part of the ambassadorial attaché. She'd never really noticed that the entry table was marble and mahogany. She'd paid no mind to the golden urn, higher than her head, that graced it, or the crystal chandelier that was lowered and lit every evening, so it might sparkle with the light of a hundred sweet-scented beeswax candles.

Back then, her uncle's house had seemed like just a normal, ordinary *house* to her. These sorts of riches had been expected. There had been no such thing as unpolished wood or banisters that creaked dangerously if you put any weight on them. She'd never thought about how much work she'd made for the servants when she tracked dirt in on the Turkish carpets.

This had been what her life looked like: clean, rich, bright, and unexamined.

She sat on the sofa next to Christian and inhaled. Lemon polish; apple blossoms. Everything here smelled perfectly fresh. This was what her uncle had offered, what Judith had turned down. It was what Camilla had, and Judith could only hope her sister was happy. That they might easily resolve her uncle's role in all of this.

She heard his footsteps coming down the hall. Her uncle entered the room all smiles.

The wisps of hair Judith remembered had faded to baldness, but he was still serious and polite.

Christian stood to greet him.

"Lord Ashford." Her uncle shook Christian's hand enthusiastically. "Always good to see you. You're very welcome to drop by any time you find yourself passing through Farnborough; no reason to wait for business to rear its head. And you said you'd have someone with you. This must be…"

Uncle William—no, she needed to think of him as *Viscount Hawley*—turned to Judith. He frowned.

"This is…" He must have placed her features then, a few seconds too late. He jumped back as if stung. "Oh, dear Lord. It's Judith."

Christian didn't miss a beat. "Yes. Oh-dear-Lord-it's-Judith. My favorite Judith, to tell the truth. Far better than good-heavens-Judith, or Judith-my-ar—"

Judith cleared her throat. "Lord Ashford," she said a little too loudly, "and I have visited for some informational purposes. We thought you might be of assistance."

Her uncle swallowed and looked back and forth between the two of them. He pulled a handkerchief from a pocket and dabbed at his head, perhaps realizing that he'd been ambushed.

She had pondered for hours, wondering how best to phrase her question.

I'm sorry to raise a crass matter of finances, Uncle, but I suspect you have embezzled the funds that I had rightfully earned, was not the way she wanted to start the conversation.

"We have come to request your assistance on a little matter," she finally said. "I wanted to talk with you about Lady Theresa's guardianship."

He shook his head vehemently. "You know I don't want anything to do with that girl. You keep her."

She tried not to blink.

"You can try to convince me she's reformed—but that girl is a…a…" He gave a little shudder. "Your pardon; she is your sister. But if you're trying to pawn her off on me? No."

It wasn't him. She doubted he could have feigned that little shiver, as if Theresa had sent a brigade of cats running over his grave. Judith tried another tack. "But if I were to seek out someone else as guardian, who might I consider? Surely you've talked to someone in the family…"

He shrugged. "I have no idea. Honestly, I do not. Nobody else would be willing."

"No?" Perhaps there was another way to get at the matter. She had thought about it and thought about it. Mr. Ennis had said he might answer Lady Camilla's questions in person. So…

"I also thought we might visit with my sister. Is Lady Camilla present?" Judith hadn't realized that her heart was aching until she asked the question.

It has been so many years. They'd argued when Camilla said she wanted to go to her uncle.

He's stuffy. He doesn't love us, Judith had said.

I won't starve, Camilla had shot back.

Fine. Have your wealth and your gowns. If you don't want to be loved, we don't want to love you. Those had been the last words she'd spoken to her sister. Afterward, Judith had written and written, taking back those words over and over. *I was wrong, Camilla. I lied. I love you. I will always love you.*

Camilla had never answered.

Her uncle's smile grew pained. "Uh. Well. As to that. Um." He scratched his head. "I'm sorry, m'dear. My hearing is not what it once was. Could you repeat yourself?"

"Yes, of course." She leaned closer and raised her voice. "I should love to see my sister, Lady Camilla."

Her throat was closing. Years of letters, all disappearing into the post with no reply. No word, no explanation, not even a "never speak to me again." She was nineteen now, surely on the verge of coming out.

"It has been an age," Judith said. "I would dearly love…" God, she would dearly love to know her sister might one day forgive her.

She hadn't known how much she wanted to see her sister until she said the words. Eight years was long enough that the coltish, long-legged adolescent in her memories would have transformed into a beautiful lady. Camilla would have had every opportunity growing up in Viscount Hawley's household. Why, maybe the scandal wouldn't dog her. Much.

"Ah." Her uncle took out a handkerchief and rubbed his head. "I had rather thought you asked that. Well. Hm. So."

The longing in Judith's chest shifted into full-blown anguish, a wanting that seemed all the more keen for its aching.

Her worst fears rose up. "Does she not want to see me? Surely a short visit would not be…so terrible for her?"

"Well, that's the thing." Her uncle gave her an uneasy smile. "She is, uh, not here. At the moment."

All of Judith's hopes deflated. Of course she would be gone. Judith had been out of society so long she'd forgotten what it was like. There would be house parties in the summer; eligible young ladies would be off visiting. Camilla might not have come out in London society, but under the circumstances it would be more sensible for her to take on polite society in small pieces as preparation. Judith should have realized it.

"Of course," Judith said. "Can you tell me when she will return?"

The handkerchief squished in her uncle's hands. "Ah. Um. You see, we are…not entirely expecting her to do so."

This information hit Judith like an arrow. "Is she ill? Is she *married?*"

"No, no," her uncle said. He did not meet her gaze. "Not that I know, at any rate. It was just…ah, you see, for the first weeks or so, she was a lovely, biddable child. But you know young ladies, eh? They do chatter and ask questions. And, um, sometimes cut up the peace, and I'm not the age I once was. Which is to say, do you remember my second cousin, James Rollins?"

"No." Judith was beginning to feel faintly horrified.

"Well," the viscount continued. "He lives in the Peak District. I can give you his direction if you like. He had two daughters who were around Camilla's age. We got to talking once, and, uh, we all agreed that your sister would be so much better off with them."

"Did you." Judith's voice sounded as if it were coming from very far away. She had come here thinking that her uncle might have taken over guardianship of her sisters, her brother. That he might have done so for so foolish a sum as the several hundred pounds she'd laid aside for them. She should have seen it from the moment she walked in the door. He had a marble table set with a golden urn in his front entry. He had a crystal chandelier that was worth more than all she'd managed to set aside in the eight years since her father had passed way.

His morals might allow him to abscond with her sisters' money, but to him, it would be like stooping to pick a penny off the ground—unworthy of his time and attention.

As for the guardianship of her sisters? She'd imagined everyone would want the task, treasuring it as she did.

Her uncle had abdicated it altogether.

"Well." Her uncle smiled. "Is that all you wished to discuss? I'll get the direction for Lady Camilla, if you wish."

"How long?" Judith heard herself ask.

He frowned. "I beg your pardon?"

"How long was it?" She looked at him. "How long did it take you to toss my sister out after promising her a home, a place to stay, clothing, a come-out… How long did it take you?"

His lips froze in a pained smile. "I did what was best for her," he finally said. "Camilla has been with the Rollins family for seven and a half years."

She had known the answer would be hurtful. She had thought he might have withstood at least a year. But it had taken him *six months*.

He couldn't even tolerate her sister for six months.

"And my letters?" Judith asked. "What happened with the letters I sent? Did you send them on? Did you consider writing to me and giving me her new direction?"

"Ah." Her uncle rubbed his forehead. "I felt she was better off…not remembering her old family. I instructed the servants to toss them out. Never tell me you're still writing."

Camilla's old family? That was how he saw her now—as something more dangerous to her sister's wellbeing than a complete stranger. Judith imagined herself calmly turning away from him and finding that golden urn in the entry. It would make the most satisfying crash when it dented his bald head.

But it wouldn't get her sister back.

"I have no other questions." If she looked at him any longer, she would lose her temper in truth. "Get me my sister's direction."

Chapter Eleven

T he sun, which had seemed so pleasant afterward, beat down oppressively. Christian sat next to Judith. Her hands were folded on her lap, her gaze trained on the fields ahead of them.

Someone who didn't know her might have thought her serene.

Christian knew better. She was upset. So upset that she'd folded all her emotions deep, hiding them under the quiet of her tilted mouth.

"Do you think he was the one to take the money?" he asked.

She shook her head. "I should have realized the idea was foolish the moment I saw his home. What point would there be in his stealing a few hundred pounds?"

"Not everyone is rational about their dishonesty," Christian pointed out.

"But he could not have snowed the solicitor. How could he claim to be Theresa's guardian when he isn't even housing Camilla any longer? And why wouldn't Mr. Ennis tell me about him? None of this makes sense." She folded her arms. "I hate to think that Mr. Ennis was lying to me."

Christian glanced down at her. From her perspective...

Well, from her perspective, this was downright chilling. Her father had betrayed the family; her brother had been transported for the same reason. Her uncle had refused to take Theresa in, forcing Judith to take on that burden herself, and then at the first possible instant, he'd put her other sister out, too.

No wonder she didn't want to think of Mr. Ennis as a liar. He was the only person in her life who *hadn't* betrayed her, Christian included in that number.

Her hands trembled. Christian did not reach out to take them; that would violate their agreement. But he wanted to.

Her eyes shivered shut. "Oh, Camilla."

"You don't think she'd be happier with other young ladies her age?"

Judith made a noise in her throat. "She and I talked about this. We argued, really. He told her she would never want for anything. She'd have clothing, a come-out—even if it was only a come-out in country society, where the scandal would be less fatal to her chances. He'd never had children; he promised to treat her as if she were his own daughter." Her voice shook. "Instead, he abandoned her to his second cousin, someone that Camilla didn't even know."

"Maybe," Christian said dubiously, "she is happy with them."

"Maybe." But Judith sounded as convinced as he felt. "But at least I have her direction now." Her tone firmed. Her jaw lifted. "And whatever might have gone awry, I am sure that I can fix it."

Those words had a well-worn sound to them, as if she'd trotted them out so many times that they provided only threadbare comfort. "Find where the money for the younger girls has gone," she said, holding up a finger. "Fix

Benedict's difficulties at Eton. Teach Theresa enough deportment that she might be able to marry with reasonable success. Find Camilla and assure myself that she is happy, that someone is looking after her future." She was nodding as she spoke, ticking off fingers. "It's not so much, these things. I can do them."

"And what of Judith?" Christian asked.

The hand she'd used to tick off tasks fell to flatten against her gown. "What of her?"

"What are you doing to secure her future happiness?"

She didn't speak, not for a long time. "I'm not unhappy now," she finally said. "There's no reason to worry about me."

Odd. She'd said there was money in trust for the two younger girls. Why was there nothing for her? She ought to have had money as well. She ought to have brought her own damned chicken curry sandwich. She ought to have had more than one good, sensible gown. She wasn't worried about herself, but she should have been. Someone needed to care about what happened to her, even if it was the man who had promised to make her hate him.

He pulled the horse to the side of the road. They were just outside town, with a field of turnips bordering one side of the dusty road and a bit of grass and a footpath on the other.

Her eyes opened. "What are you doing?"

"Nothing," he said. "Nothing at all."

"But—"

She didn't trust him, not one bit, and he could hardly blame her. She'd been struggling under a tremendous burden for the past eight years. It was a miracle she could still keep her head held high, an even greater miracle that she'd accomplished what she had.

"I have one task," he said, "and that is to make sure you hate me. Somewhere in all those years of managing and arguing and planning, it seems to me that Judith fell off your lists."

She looked down.

"The Judith I remembered," he said, "would never hesitate to explore. She'd enjoy the summer sunshine. She'd wander the footpath just to see what was at the other end. She wouldn't worry about anyone's guardianship or her brother's schooling. She wouldn't have to."

Judith glanced down the footpath.

"She would take a little time to herself every day, so she wouldn't forget."

"Forget what?" Judith said, her voice subdued. "That the world lied and told her that she was important?"

"No," Christian replied. "She wouldn't forget that somewhere, beneath the duties and the obligations, she still deserved joy."

Her hands clutched her skirt. "You're supposed to make me hate you."

He looked at her, waiting, until she lifted her face and looked him in the eye. Until she let him see all the anguish written in her expression. He couldn't hold her hand in comfort; holding her gaze would have to do.

"I trust you'll recall that if there is a dearth of happiness in your life, it's because I've taken it from you." He shrugged. "Now, I plan to sit here and read. So go and take care of Judith."

He took a book from his satchel and didn't look up. Not when she unlaced her bonnet strings. Not when she took off her gloves, one by one, and laid them on the seat.

If he watched her take off her gloves, he might start thinking of the buttons on her gown. The laces of her corset. The nape of her neck, where he might lean down and... No, the last thing Judith needed at the moment was a man who couldn't keep his eyes where they belonged.

He let her disembark from the carriage on her own, giving her this moment of solitude.

He didn't look up, but he imagined her as he'd known her years ago. She would go out into the summer sun. She'd lift her face until the sun's rays outlined the dimple on her cheek, the curve of her lips. She would inhale and turn and finally—finally—she would smile.

The footpath led to a stream, one that chirped merrily over graveled banks overhung by ferns and grasses. The sun was high overhead, and Christian had been right—she needed this. She needed to breathe clear air, to feel the cobwebs in her chest loosen and break up.

Eight years of London fog and London smoke had taken their toll. She'd not had many idyllic moments.

Christian had it right—it was hard to hate him because despite everything that had transpired, despite everything he had done, they *knew* one another. She could keep telling him to make her hate him, but being hateful simply wasn't in his character.

No matter how she wished for it, no matter what she told herself, she knew him too well. He would not stop bringing her her favorite sandwiches or making her laugh. He would always be the one to stop the carriage so she could have a moment for herself.

He would know when she needed it.

Standing next to the stream, with the sun tickling the back of her neck, it was hard to remember that she didn't like him. Judith reached for the righteousness of her anger, but it slipped away, burbling like the water in the stream.

She tried. It was his fault Camilla had been abandoned, after all. Wasn't it?

The words no longer rang true. It was Judith's fault, too; she'd told her sister not to come crying to her when their uncle was cold and unfeeling. It was her uncle's fault for not living up to his grandiose promises.

Next to those two huge wrongs, Christian's fault hardly even registered.

There, on the banks of the stream, she tilted her face to the sun and quietly, painfully let go. She trailed her fingers in the cold water, imagining the worst of her hate bleeding from her like dark ink. Her hand grew numb as she envisioned all her hurts slowly drifting away, the darkness dissipating into clear water.

It wasn't his fault Camilla thought she was unloved. It wasn't his fault her father had committed treason. He was just the easiest, nearest target.

She made her way back to the carriage after fifteen minutes. Christian didn't ask her how her time had gone. He didn't tease her. He simply put down his book.

"We need to negotiate a new treaty," Judith said.

"Yes?"

"There's a problem with the former one." She insisted on meeting his gaze head on. "You can't remind me that I hate you if I don't hate you."

His hands stilled in the act of gathering up the reins.

"I wish I could," she confessed. "It would make everything so easy if I did. I'm angry with you. I can never forgive you." She looked over into his eyes. "It's simple if it's all just hatred. But nothing is ever simple, least of all us."

His gaze dropped down from her eyes to her lips, and then very slowly, traveled back up. She felt the path it took like heat from the sun.

"You're right," she said. "We know each other too well to really hate one another."

"Come," he said in a low voice. "You can't be reasonable *now*. I don't want you to be reasonable. It gives me…ideas. And hope." His voice dropped even lower. "I will never forgive you if you give me hope."

"Don't hope." She looked away. "I never said I would forgive you. How could I?"

He exhaled. "What now? We've only managed to uncover more problems. You still haven't figured out what is happening, and I still don't have Anthony's journals. The money—"

She looked away. "At this point, the money is the least of my worries. I need to find my sister. I need to know that she is well. I think it's best that we see each other as little as possible. I'll look into Camilla's whereabouts; nothing else matters until I know she's safe. You…"

"I'll ask for some private legal advice," Christian said. "I'll see what circumstances might lead to this oddity that we've discovered, and find out if there's any way to force Mr. Ennis to disclose what he knows without creating a public scandal."

She snorted.

"A larger public scandal," Christian amended.

"It sounds like we have an agreement."

Christian fingered the reins. "As to our new armistice, might I make a suggestion?"

She looked over at him.

"We can try not to hurt each other," he said.

"You mean, I'll try not to call you a colossal idiot, and you in turn will—"

He reached out and touched her hand, interrupting her speech. In truth, she couldn't have formed a word. His hand on hers snuffed out all her rational thought, like fingers pinching out a candle—a sharp heat all at once, and only the imprint of light against her vision.

"Judith," he said, "I asked you to marry me once. You sent me one letter after eight years and I appeared on your doorstep within four hours. Yes, I want Anthony's journals. But let us not be foolish; we both know that is not all I think about. You know precisely how you can hurt me. Please. Don't."

Do, his eyes suggested. *Turn your hand over. Take mine. Let it all go, and hurt me.*

The thing about admitting to herself that he wasn't entirely at fault was discovering that she must have hurt him.

He'd wanted to marry her. He'd said he loved her, and likely he had. He had said he would never forget her, and he hadn't.

She couldn't apologize. Not now. Not with his hand on hers. Not with her heart still so raw.

She pulled her hand away. "I think last time we hurt each other enough for a lifetime. The less we talk, the better it will be."

He nodded. "Agreed. Hopefully, everything will go right from here on out." He picked up the reins and started the horses.

"Wrong," Judith reminded him. "Remember, we want everything to go wrong between us."

Chapter Twelve

The house was quiet when Judith finally returned home. It was only eight in the evening, and still light out at this point in the summer, but nobody greeted her at the front door.

She walked in. The entryway had been freshly swept. To her right, no detritus of meals had been left on the table.

Curious.

There *was* a single place set in front of her chair. A fork and a knife stood guard over an aging metal cover. She lifted it.

Dinner awaited her. Someone had made a creditable roast potato and some buttered carrots. These rested alongside slices of crusty bread and cheese. A little note was folded under the edge of the plate.

Judith lifted it with trepidation.

Welcome home, Judith, the note read. *We love you. We missed you today.*

Both Benedict and Theresa had signed it. How…sweet.

How suspicious.

She let the cover drop. It was sweet like tea with four lumps of sugar added. One only dumped sweeteners in to hide the fact that the beverage had been overbrewed.

The singular lack of carnage continued as she made her way through the house. No books were heaped on the stairs that she ascended. No piles of petticoats had been unceremoniously abandoned in the hall.

Her siblings were sucking up to her, and Judith was afraid. Very afraid.

As she came to the upstairs landing, she could finally hear their voices. They were in the bedroom that Judith and Theresa shared, speaking quietly with one another.

"No, no," Benedict was saying. "Stop. It tickles."

"Lie still," came Theresa's response. "You can't possibly move. You'll crush them."

Them. Oh, dear. Judith lifted her hand to shove open the door and announce her presence when Benedict laughed. Oh, God. He *laughed*. Judith's heart stood still. He was laughing again. She'd feared that whatever had happened to him at Eton had broken him in some irretrievable way. But if he could still laugh, everything was going to turn up right.

So instead of shoving the door open, she gave it a gentle push—enough for it to swing open a few inches.

Her brother and sister sat cross-legged on the bed, and they were surrounded by kittens. The word *surrounded* did not do justice to the multitude of kittens that thronged her bed. So many kittens. There were three on Benedict alone. He twitched his finger invitingly, and one calico kitten pounced. A second one—black, with a single white paw—curled, sleeping in the crook of his arm. A third tiny cat, all fluffy white fur and pink nose, was ascending his arm with the uneasy determination of an exceedingly clumsy mountain climber.

Those were not the only kittens. Two played in Theresa's skirts; another three rolled in a tussle at the end of the bed.

Oh, for the love of…kittens. She had said no more cats. They'd *agreed*.

This many uncountable kittens, however cute, would turn into approximately eighty trillion grown cats, given time, milk, and free rein to indulge their cat-lusts. If only they weren't so cute.

If only Benedict were not laughing.

At that moment, Theresa looked up and caught sight of Judith standing in the doorway. The amused smile froze on her face.

"Oh, look who is home. Judith!" Theresa gave a scarcely credible fake smile and attempted to unhook kitten claws from her hair. "How good to see you." These kitten claws, it turned out, didn't unhook; she ended up dragging a cat body across her face. "We were just…um…"

Benedict wasn't smiling any longer. He touched his finger to the little kitten sleeping in his arms and looked at Judith with a worried furrow marking his forehead. "I know you said no more cats, but… These are kittens. Kittens aren't cats, right?"

Judith swallowed. "Benedict, love. Kittens are still cats, and you both know it."

Two heads dropped in disappointment.

"You told us to walk by the river. We found them in a sack with rocks in the bottom, down by the Thames," Theresa said. "Someone had thrown them over the edge, but the sack caught on a hook and didn't fall all the way in. We couldn't just leave them."

Benedict, obviously misinterpreting Judith's look of consternation, interjected. "Don't worry. I was quite safe climbing down to get them. It wasn't in the *middle* of the bridge where the drop to the water could have been significant. Near the edge." He looked uneasy. "Pretty near, I'd say. Not quite at the center."

She shivered imagining what his *pretty near* actually looked like. It didn't matter. The drop was heart-stopping anywhere along those bridges.

"Can we keep them?" Theresa asked. "There's only eleven of them."

Only eleven kittens. She could have wept. The cat population in the Worth household—already approaching dangerously Malthusian levels—had nearly quadrupled with the retrieval of that sack.

But she'd promised her brother and sister that even if they didn't always have fine clothing and servants, they would always have love. She thought of Camilla, sent away because girls of her age talked too much. One of her sisters was *somewhere* in England—and maybe not loved at all.

She thought of Benedict laughing, looked at him running a finger down the soft fur of that little black kitten.

And she thought of Christian. He'd been everything to her once. At least, he'd been the promise of everything. For all that he'd wanted to marry her—for all that he cared still—when push came to shove, he'd not thought of her wellbeing at all.

She came over to the edge of the bed and picked up a little yellow cat who emitted a mew of protest.

"Benedict," she said, "Theresa. There was a rule. The rule was: No cats."

Theresa's lip trembled. Judith took off her bonnet and let the strings trail on the bed. It was instant mayhem: three kittens leapt at once, pouncing on this new and exciting prey.

"I'm proud of you," Judith said. "I wouldn't want siblings who thought that rules were more important than kittens. You did the right thing."

Their faces lifted, twin expressions of joy lighting them.

"Here are the new rules," Judith told them. "We can each keep *one* kitten. You have to find homes for all the others."

"Yes, Judith."

"You have to keep order. No teaching them to climb or whatever it is that you do. And it is your job to keep the females locked in a room when they go into heat."

Her two scapegrace siblings smiled and nodded. Of course they did; they'd say anything now. Judith knew who was going to be stuck actually enforcing these rules.

But Benedict was smiling again, and Judith didn't care.

"If you don't pay any mind," she reminded them, "you'll discover that inattention on that score is how sacks of kittens end up hanging from hooks on bridges or worse. Do not fail me."

"Yes." Theresa nodded vigorously. "Thank you. Oh, thank you, Judith."

"And so, until we can find them all homes…"

She looked at them, and then snapped her wrist so her bonnet strings trailed over her brother's lap. "It's kitten wars!"

Four little cats raced over him, claws out. They were still small enough that they would do no more than tickle. Kittens batted. They pawed. They pounced. Her brother shrieked, and she ran the bonnet strings across his legs.

Benedict dissolved into laughter as the cats regrouped, rolling around and pouncing once more. "Can't. Breathe." He choked. "Too many kittens."

"Just *eleven*, did you say?" Judith narrowed her eyes at her brother and sister. "Fear my wrath. *Feel the claws.*"

"No, no!" he shrieked. "No claws. No claws! I will retaliate!"

He didn't. He laughed and gathered the kittens in his arms.

"Do your worst," Judith said. "I'll be waiting."

Christian awoke at the toll of noon the next day.

Acceptable, if this had been mid-Season, and he'd been burning the midnight oil in a socially acceptable fashion. Embarrassing, since he'd gone to bed at eleven. His head ached with the subtle pressure that came from not enough sleep. His eyes felt as if they'd been dragged through gravel. He'd dreamed again last night, a wisp of memory that had largely vanished from his conscious mind. Something about empty rooms and unending corridors in the Tower of London.

By the time he made his way downstairs, he'd done his best to dull the ache of his head with willowbark tea.

He'd managed to lose the most persistent throb of his head, if not the sense of unease that accompanied it.

The voices that he heard in the parlor didn't make him feel more comfortable.

He inhaled and strode past the open door.

"Christian."

The voice was like a noose, catching him up. He turned.

"Where do you think you are going?"

His mother and his cousin sat together, looking suspiciously innocent. Like a pair of panthers that had been lying in wait at the watering hole for prey to wander past.

"Come." Lillian patted the sofa nearest her. "Join us. Tell us how you've been."

"I've an appointment."

"Oh, you mean the one you had Mr. Lawrence make at your solicitor's office?" His mother smiled. "No, you don't. I've moved it."

"Mother." He strode into the room. "I'm twenty-eight, for God's sake. I have responsibilities, duties, *business*. You can't move my appointments as if I were a child."

Her smile sharpened. "I would agree, dear, except—"

Lillian set a hand on his mother's arm, clearly a prearranged signal.

She sighed and subsided. "Christian. We are worried about you."

This was not going to be simple. He sank into a chair near her. "Am I shirking my responsibilities?"

"Yes," Lillian said. "You're not taking care of yourself. You must have lost a stone this last year. You only ever make jokes; you hardly laugh at anyone else's. You're so pale. You don't go riding any longer. You don't have any fun."

A snippet from last night's dream snapped back into his head—of turning a corner of one interminable hallway and seeing Anthony Worth in front of him. His friend had been dressed in the blue-and-something undress uniform of a beef-eater.

"That's not yours," Christian had said. "You shouldn't be wearing it."

Dream Anthony had simply shaken his head and frowned. "Who are you?" he'd asked. "I don't know you."

In his dream, just as in reality, Christian had called for help, screaming. Guards had come—this time, the real yeoman warders of the Tower of London, their faces shadowed in dark clouds. They'd laid hands on Anthony, and his friend had burst into shards like a vase shattered with a stone.

Christ. No wonder he could scarcely sleep. A year ago, the last of the investigators had returned. The man had talked to three of the convicts on Anthony's prison ship. All three of them had reported the same thing: Anthony had not disembarked at any point from that ship.

Up until that point, Christian had held onto hope. He'd held onto all his hope as hard as he could. He'd tried his best to believe that Anthony couldn't be dead.

"I think you should see my doctor," his mother said.

His mother meant well; she loved him. With his father gone, it was his job to protect her, even if the thing he protected her from was the truth.

He had been an odd child, given to making lists and counting objects. He'd thrown tantrums about colors, of all things—he hadn't been able to learn his colors like the other children. But it was the nightmares that had been the final straw. He had used to throw fits in the middle of the night—massive screaming, shouting fits that he could not be woken from, and that he did not remember the next day.

His father had worried that he was mad. In fact, he'd wanted to have Christian put away. His mother had protected him from that. She'd found a physician, and together, they'd helped him sleep through the night.

He could never let himself forget that: His mother had acted out of love. She had protected him. She had saved him.

If she ever found out what had resulted from her efforts, she'd never forgive herself. He couldn't protect her from what was happening to him now, but he could protect her from that discovery.

And so instead of telling her to never mention that physician to him again, he simply folded his arms. "There's nothing wrong with me that a physician can cure," he said gruffly. "And you know I hate the taste of his mixtures."

Lillian reached out and took his hand. "Christian. We're your family. We love you. If something's wrong with you, we want to help."

He looked at his hand in hers. There were worse things than being loved, far worse things than having a cousin and a mother who cared for him and worried over him.

"What is it, Christian?"

He could have made a joke, but even he couldn't figure out how to work England's greatest chicken killers into this moment.

"It's guilt," he said. "Good, ordinary British guilt. Nothing more."

The two women watched him intently. "Go on," his mother said.

"I worry," he said. "What I did with Anthony Worth—"

"Hush." His mother patted his hand. "Nonsense. Nothing to do with you."

He saved my life when you almost killed me, and I couldn't even return the favor.

"Nonetheless," Christian said. "Ever since I've realized that Anthony..." He could say the word. He could.

"Perished?" his mother provided.

"Perished." He swallowed. "Ever since I've been sure he did, I've felt haunted."

She looked down. "Now, Christian. I know you think yourself above my physician's treatments. I know you'll say you're not a child any longer, that you've outgrown such things. But consider. Just consider..."

"No," he said swiftly, before she could make the offer.

He *did* want. He *wasn't* above. He still wished, after all these years of not giving in. A tiny taste of oblivion; one night, when he might escape it all. He clenched his fists, digging his nails into his palms until the pain drove out that sick desire.

If there was anything more horrific than escaping Anthony's memory with a cup of laudanum, Christian didn't know it.

"It might help me sleep," he said instead. "It won't help me sleep well. Laudanum only intensifies my dreams."

She sighed. "If you insist. But you might give it a try, don't you think?"

He ignored this. "I have a better solution in mind. I'm speaking with Judith Worth. She's agreed to lend me her brother's journals. Once I've had a chance to go through them, I'll finally be able to set this all in the past where it belongs."

His mother frowned. "I had not thought the two of you were on such terms as to allow easy conversation."

"We aren't. Matters are improving. Mildly." They weren't friends, and yet they were…something. Maybe now, maybe now she knew he'd help, maybe now she would trust him with them early.

Because the sooner he had those journals, the sooner he could relieve his worries, and the less likely that his mother would finally offer him the one thing he didn't want to crave in a way he couldn't refuse.

"In fact," Christian said, "I'll send along a note with the request now. Maybe we can have this all settled by sundown."

Chapter Thirteen

Thank you for agreeing to see me," Christian said. They'd chosen a neutral venue for their rendezvous—a dock near Judith's home, not so cozy as her house nor so intimate as his.

A walk along the wharf would remind neither of them of their old walks in the orchard. For one thing, the air was perfumed by the gritty pollution belched from steamships' smokestacks. For another, Christian was not alone with Judith.

The wharf was crowded. A world's worth of sailors thronged the docks. Lascars from India. A crowd of mariners from Portugal talking together. A Scotsman at the edge called out a chant as bare-chested men hefted a weight in the air.

And Judith did not take his arm.

She walked beside him in a gray gown that might have been called "serviceable," emphasis on *service*, had his mother seen the thing.

"You said you had news from your solicitor." Judith looked over at him expectantly.

"It is the news of bafflement and protest," Christian said. "Nobody has any inkling over there. If I could give some further particulars—"

"No," Judith said. "No particulars."

"My solicitor can dispatch a man to comb through the relevant precedents, but searching for such odd cases will take time. Weeks, he says."

Judith's nose wrinkled. "*Weeks.*" She blew out a breath. "But… Wait. All my urgency was because I thought Camilla would be coming out soon, and I wanted it to be known that she wasn't completely penniless." She frowned. "Now that I don't know where she is, the urgency is…"

She trailed off, as if recognizing the stupidity of saying that matters were less urgent because her sister could not be found.

"There's no urgency on your end, perhaps." Christian swallowed. "On mine… I had a question."

She looked over at him, her eyes narrowing. Not suspicion; that was real fear he saw reflected there. The last time he'd put a question to her on a walk… Oh, God.

Back then, they must have spent hours every day walking demurely together. Demurely on her part, that was; he'd spent the entire summer consumed by lust, remembering her brother's warning, and telling himself the entire time that he had to wait. She had not yet come out; he could not claim her. She had not yet come out; he wasn't even supposed to flirt with her.

Friendly banter and long walks it had been. Followed, on his part, by lengthy dips in ice-cold rivers.

He had behaved himself. Oh, very well; he had *mostly* behaved himself. Somewhat behaved himself until his last night there. That last night had been warm and magical. The apples were still hard lumps above them, but they were beginning to look apple-shaped. Summer had been coming to a close.

They'd both been out on what had started ostensibly as separate strolls—he, because he didn't care for the cloying smell of cigar smoke in her father's library. He didn't know her excuse. At that point, they had intended to accidentally cross paths so many times that all excuses had blurred together into a sea of flatly unbelievable pretext.

He'd bowed to her most properly. He'd offered her his arm a little stiffly. He had asked whether she would mind if he intruded on her solitary walk, and she'd put her head to one side as if she had to think the matter over.

"I suppose not," she had said.

Sometimes, when he thought of her, the crook of his elbow still burned with the memory of her fingers on that night. With the imagined path he'd wanted her hand to trace down his arm.

But Anthony had warned him off. Judith deserved a Season. She deserved a choice. Don't do anything irrevocable; not anything mildly untoward.

And Christian had agreed. He'd *hated* that he had agreed that night. Hated it, because his thoughts had been consumed with all the lovely, lascivious irrevocable things he wanted to do to her.

"You'll dance with me at my come-out?" she had asked near the end of their walk.

"If you still wish me to do so," he'd said, trying valiantly to be honorable.

Back then, she had looked at him as if he hung the stars for her, as if he were the embodiment of every clichéd hero.

"How could I not?" she had asked.

"You say that now, but you'll be surrounded by men. Fellows will admire your beauty. Noble, serious men. Your card will be full, and you might regret having promised a spot to your elder brother's mildly amusing friend. I would hate to impose upon you under those circumstances, Lady Judith."

Her fingers had tensed on his arm. He turned to her.

Slowly, ever so slowly, they had started moving, up from his elbow to his bicep. He swallowed.

"Don't you dare Lady Judith me," she had said. "Not you. Not tonight. Not unless you want me to call you Lord Ashford in retaliation." Her fingers had flirted with his shoulder, the lapel of his jacket. "Don't be a goose."

His breath had sucked in. "You wouldn't dare. You wouldn't dare *not* call me Christian."

"I wouldn't count on my not daring it, were I you."

He'd taken her hand in his. Honestly, he'd meant to return it to his elbow after her fingers had wandered. But somehow, once his hand had clasped hers, he hadn't quite been able to let go.

"We mustn't do this," he'd said as their hands intertwined. "They'll get the wrong idea about us walking together in the moonlight. They'll think..." He trailed off as Judith took his other hand. His fingers convulsed around hers.

"They'll think what?" she said. "That we have an understanding instead of a friendship?"

"Judith." His voice cracked. "We *can't* have an understanding. Not until you're out."

"Is that so?" She'd looked at him. "Pardon me, but I think we do have an understanding."

"Judith."

"What are you telling yourself, I wonder?" She looked at him. "That you must let me have my Season? That you must watch me fall in love with another man? Why, when you could watch me fall in love with you instead? I know I'm not perfect. Are you afraid that I will drive you mad?"

"I'm afraid of the day you don't," he'd whispered. And then he'd pulled her close. Twigs had crunched underfoot—the sound of Christian breaking the promise he'd made her brother. He'd taken her face in his hands and kissed her.

It had been a slow, sweet kiss. Her lips brushed tenderly against his. His fingers splayed against her jaw, tilting her head up, and then he'd pulled her close—close enough that their bodies touched, close enough that he could feel her tremble. It was the kind of kiss that had brought his entire body to life, like waking up at the seashore to the sound of the ocean, the smell of salt, and the expectation of sun and sand.

Eventually, he'd managed to pull away. "I will dance with you at your come-out," he said. "If you want. I'll squire you to every event that we both should attend. I'll take you on walks through the park and on horseback rides and I'll buy you ices and I'll try not to be boring long enough that I can fool you. And next May, when you've had a chance to see a few other gentlemen, I'll ask if you prefer me still."

"And when I do?"

His breath sucked in. He'd leaned down and kissed her again. This kiss had been more: more sweetness, more tenderness. More passion, because he knew what she wanted, and she knew it as well. She'd opened her mouth to his. His hands had slipped down her back, down her spine, pulling her up into him.

Just a few months, he had told himself. A few months until he saw her again, and then the entirety of the Season to wait. Back then, it had seemed an impossibly long time.

"And then," he had said, "after all that, I will offer you the right to drive me mad legally, all the time, in perpetuity, for as long as we both shall live."

She had never had that Season. They had never had the chance. And when he'd asked that question…

Afterward, when he was feeling selfish and lonely and lustful late at night, he'd sometimes wished that he had broken his promise to greater effect. That he'd done something truly irrevocable that night. That he had coaxed her to his bed—it would hardly have taken any effort; she'd been as curious and delighted as he was—and presented their immediate marriage to her brother as a necessity.

If he had actually been married to Judith Worth, they'd never have asked him to assist in her father's trial.

God, he wished he had been selfish.

He didn't know why Anthony had *stopped* him. He must have known then what he'd done. Hadn't he wanted his sister protected?

Maybe he hadn't expected to be caught. Maybe he'd been protecting Christian from entangling himself with the family before he knew all the facts. *Maybe,* whispered that guilty portion of his conscience, *maybe he didn't…*

"Why do you want Anthony's journals?" Judith said, effectively interrupting his reverie.

It took him a moment to collect his thoughts: the journals. She was asking about the journals.

"I told you already."

She exhaled. "Spare me that claptrap about your friendship. If it had meant anything at all, you'd have asked years ago. You sent me a note making that request five months back. The truth, Christian."

He shut his eyes. "How well did you follow your father's trial?"

"I was *there* for Anthony's. All of it." Her words were tightly controlled. He looked down and detected fists at her side.

"Then you know that Anthony—that your father—had a plan. Britain needed China to legalize the opium trade. Your father had his own ideas. Diplomacy was failing on the question; war was inevitable. And your father did not think that—"

She held up a hand. "Skip my father, please. I have granted you that…there may have been some justice on that score. That doesn't mean I want to hear about his treachery in detail. Tell me what this has to do with Anthony."

"The fact that your brother was guilty of treason is—"

She looked away. "You can't really believe that. Deep in your heart, Christian, you knew him. You can't believe he would be so evil."

He had never believed Anthony evil; that was the trouble. "Do you think I'd have released the information if I didn't know it was true?" He wasn't going to shout at her on the docks about this. "I believe your brother committed treason—in fact, I believe your brother's sentence was unrelentingly kind, under the circumstances."

She glared up at him. "You spent *summers* in our house."

"Your father sent the Chinese information about the targets Britain planned to shell," Christian retorted. "Anthony knew of it and did nothing. What do you want from me? I spent summers in your house. I didn't realize that required me to be party to betraying my country. The evidence—"

"Damn the evidence." Judith's voice shook. "There's more to evidence than papers in a trial. You had the evidence of years of friendship. You had the evidence of his character."

Christian held her eyes as she spoke.

"You knew Anthony. That's what I can never forgive—that you put your stupid evidence in logs and missives and bank transactions above your friendship. You *knew* Anthony. He was the one who would always tell the truth when something went awry. When he ran in the house and broke the china vase, he confessed. When he got angry and threw me in the river that one time, he apologized and told my father. He accepted his punishment. He was the most annoyingly proper brother in the entire world. How can you look me in the eyes and tell me that you think he could have committed treason?"

"It's simple," Christian bit off. "Sweetheart, I knew him better than you did."

She gasped. "How dare you!"

"Not only do I think your brother was *capable* of committing treason," Christian said, "I know why he did it. You are perfectly right; your brother would never do anything he thought was wrong, and if he found himself in the wrong, he would do everything he could to correct it."

"Precisely!" she crowed. "So—"

"So what would your brother do if he thought that England was committing a grievous harm?" Christian said. "Really, Judith. What would he do?"

She swallowed. "He would… He would…" She shook her head. "No, he wouldn't. He would try something else. He would ask my father to…petition the House of Lords, or he would write a piece for a newspaper or he would…" Her hands made fists again. "He would do anything other than commit treason. He *would*."

That was what woke Christian in the middle of the night. Not the fear that Anthony was innocent; the suspicion that Christian—and all the rest of Britain with him—was guilty. If Anthony was right, if there was no solution but what he had taken on.

Everything Christian owned, everything he had, every sheet on his bed, every silk gown his mother owned? They were all stolen. There was nothing to do but either suffocate in that knowledge or…

He couldn't believe Anthony was right. He couldn't.

"That's why I need the journals," Christian said in a low voice. "Something happened to Anthony in his years in China. He saw something. He observed people doing things they shouldn't. He thought treason was the only solution." Christian looked away. "I have to believe there were other options. That justice is not impossible, even after all these years."

Judith's hands curled into fists at her side. "You want my brother's journals so you can prove Anthony not only a traitor, but a stupid, misguided, ineffective traitor at that?"

"No." It sounded worse when she put it that way.

"I've *read* his journals. There's nothing in them, nothing like that at all."

"No, there wouldn't be. Not that you'd notice. But—"

"It's not enough for you to take Anthony's family, his father, or his life. You have to destroy his memory as well?"

"It's not like that, Judith. I want to do something. I want to know that I didn't make a mistake. I can hardly sleep. I'm—"

"That's what you want from me?" She looked him over. "I promised you my brother's journals because I need your help. But I will *never* tell you that you made the right choice. Maybe, if you can't live with yourself, there's a reason for it."

"Judith." He reached out and took her hand. For a moment, he remembered that walk in the orchard. He remembered what trust looked like in her eyes.

It didn't look like this. She yanked her hand away. "Earn the damned journals," she hissed. "We're not friends. We may not hate each other. But when I think of what you did to my brother... Well, you shouldn't be able to sleep."

In the days that followed their meeting, Judith wanted nothing to do with Christian. She didn't want to think about him or his accusation that she didn't know Anthony. The notion was utterly ridiculous.

How could she not know her own brother?

The Monday after he'd leveled that piece of poppycock at her, as she was reconciling the account books, she only let herself dwell on his words for a few seconds. A few seconds while she tapped her pencil against the sums.

Christian thought he knew Anthony better than *she* did? Ha. She'd known him since he was three. He'd been telling on her—and on himself—since she could walk. Her brother had been kind, loving, honest, trustworthy... and possessed of the most rigidly annoying morality that she'd ever encountered in her life.

Christian didn't know a thing about him, and she would simply have to put his wild accusations out of her mind. They were nothing more than an attempt to justify the unjustifiable.

She had, after all, books to reconcile and a scant hundred and fifty pounds remaining to her name—not enough to see Benedict through his schooling, and certainly not enough to start him on the road to the rest of his life. Christian wasn't worth a shilling on her accounts.

She refused to think about Christian's claim on Tuesday, but she let herself imagine his face when she punched the bread dough down.

On Wednesday, she wasn't thinking of him when she received a letter in the mail. She refused to think of their trip to the country, refused to think of him stopping the carriage and letting her sit in the field. If she admitted that he understood her well enough to know she'd needed to enjoy herself, perhaps her brother, who he...

No. She wouldn't go down that road. She refused to do it.

She opened the letter instead. It was from the Rollins family in the Peak District.

Miss Worth, Mr. Rollins wrote. Not *Lady Judith;* that was already a slap in her face. *I believe you have been misled. Your sister did indeed stay with us, but on a temporary basis only. She left after two weeks, and that was quite a number of years ago.*

I hesitate to speak ill of anyone, but Camilla was in need of a stricter hand, someone who would teach her the truth about her new place in life.

"What new place in life?" Judith asked the letter aloud.

It didn't answer. Instead, it went on in a similarly offensive fashion.

For her own good, we sent her to my aunt Charlene in Redding, whose unbending nature would fashion your sister into a young woman who behaved as one of her station ought. Her direction is enclosed.

Judith crumpled the paper, her whole body aching. Two weeks? Camilla had not even had the security of two weeks with them? "Lies," she said. "Why is everyone lying about my siblings?"

She wrote a letter, trying not to feel bitter, to this Charlene.

The next day, though, brought good news in the post. *Somewhat* good news. It was from the man she worked with in Edinburgh, the one who sold her designs.

Lady Judith, the letter read. *The Wittfield factory in Bristol wishes to use your design of circus cats for a production of five hundred units; they offer a payment of twenty pounds.*

She looked over the offered terms; they weren't what she once might have received, but then, her designs no longer earned what they had. Clockwork figurines were no longer quite the rage. The novelty was wearing off. She'd need something different, something that would appeal to more people if she were ever to make as much as she had. Still, any income at all was better than nothing.

She sent back an acceptance.

Friday, the post brought an answer from Aunt Charlene—or, as she was called, Charlene Heilford.

Miss Worth,

I do recall your sister Camilla, and rather fondly, if with some exasperation. She stayed with me for two years. By the end, she was an excellent companion. So excellent, in fact, that I passed her on to my friend, Miss Abigail Troworth, in Bath. I have asked my secretary to enclose her direction below.

Passed her *on?* As if she were a package or a horse? And companion? Camilla was a young lady, not a *companion.* Judith tried not to scream. At least Camilla had stayed with the woman for two years.

At least.

At least she'd had time to grow fond of the woman before she was handed over.

Judith should have done more than send letters to her uncle all these years. She'd imagined that her sister had cut off all ties with the embarrassing side of her family. Judith hadn't realized her sister hadn't received those letters. Judith should have done more. She should have...

But she hadn't. Judith's friends, most of her family, had denounced her entirely and stopped answering her letters. She had assumed that Camilla had joined them.

By now, Judith practically had her letter of inquiry memorized.

Dear Miss Abigail Troworth, she wrote. *Your friend, Mrs. Charlene Heilford of Leeds, told me that we had a mutual acquaintance—my younger sister, Camilla Worth, who you so graciously hosted sometime starting in the years 1860 or 1861. I am hopeful that she may still be with you at this time. If she is, might you be so kind as to inform me of the fact, and to let her know that her elder sister is desirous of speaking with her? If not, I would be most obliged if you could pass on whatever you know of her current direction.*

She sealed this letter, stamped it, and—before she handed it over to the postmistress—kissed it for good luck.

This time, she'd get a real response.

This time, she would find her sister.

Chapter Fourteen

The dreams had worsened. Christian had woken at two that morning, bathed in cold sweat. Tossing for two hours hadn't helped. Counting beads hadn't helped. Even making a list of all the ways he might try to get the journals from Judith—somehow, anyhow—hadn't helped. Finally, he'd found a robe and wandered the halls of his home, searching for a plan in the darkened rooms.

"One." He said the number aloud as if it were a flag he could plant in shifting sands, one that would hold them in place. As if *this* list would fix everything when months of lists had accomplished nothing. The number one was a beginning, and beginnings begat endings. One: He couldn't count on receiving Anthony's journals. He'd pinned his hopes on that eventuality, but it might be months—or not at all—before he received them.

He was fairly certain that he couldn't manage many more months scarcely sleeping.

"Two." He stopped in front of a window looking out over a side street. The cobblestones were indistinct dark blobs in the evening. "I will have to come to terms with the fact that Anthony is dead, and I am at fault."

Oh, God. His heart beat faster, shallow and thready, just hearing those words spoken aloud. But that was the crux of the matter, was it not?

Even if his plan was successful, it wouldn't change anything. Anthony had saved Christian's life, and in return, Christian had ruined his.

"Three," he said.

"Christian?"

He jumped, mid-plan, to see his mother behind him. She was watching him with a worried expression. She'd worn that worried expression much over the past months.

"Mother," he breathed. "Why are you awake?"

She didn't answer. Instead, she shook her head. "This can't go on."

No, it couldn't. He had thought he would sleep eventually, when the exhaustion finally set in. Now, he was almost too exhausted to sleep.

"You have to let me help." She came to stand by him.

"Not the way you want." He put his arm around her. "Sometimes, you can't help in the way you would like. I'm begging you, Mother. I know you and Lillian mean well, but your physician's suggestions are not the solution. You have to stop asking me about them."

He was beginning to get desperate.

"But…" She bit her lip. "But you never used to mind, back then. If you would just recall…"

He recalled all too well, more than a decade later. That familiar taste on his tongue. The slow slide into a welcome stupor.

He grappled for an acceptable answer. "Laudanum doesn't stop dreams, Mama," he said. "It makes them more vivid. I don't dare." His hands shook. "Please. I haven't the energy to fight you, too. Please. I need you to stop."

She inhaled. "Christian."

"Think on it. I love you, but if you can't stop, I can't be around you. I'll take rooms elsewhere."

"*Christian.*"

He set his hand on her shoulder. "Neither of us wants that. Please let me solve this my way."

She sniffed. No, she *sniffled*. He'd made her cry. It was the last thing he'd wanted. He put his arm around her and pulled her close, letting her weep because there was nothing she could do.

Nothing *he* could do.

Three. There was nothing he could do. He couldn't change anything in the past. He couldn't bring Anthony back to life, not with plans, not with lists, not with journals. This was his future: his friend was gone. Death was forever.

Four. He had to find another way.

"I have to find another way," he said aloud.

He'd let guilt tangle him up for too long. He'd tried to cut directly through it all, to turn guilt into not guilt. He'd focused only on his own feelings.

But maybe there was another way. A better way. A way to take all that guilt and use it. He'd wanted Anthony's journals because he'd believed that with them, he could reform the past.

But the past was the past. If he got the chance to look those journals over, he'd take it, but even that wouldn't change what had transpired. Nothing could.

He could only change the future.

Five.

No, not five. "E," he said aloud. His skin twitched at the sound.

"Your pardon?" His mother stirred in his arms.

He had the sensation that he was seeing the universe stripped to gears and coils, everything laid out in order. Not from largest to smallest, but as Judith had set the pieces of the clock on the table so long before: in order of use.

"E," he said to his mother. "It's the ordinal that follows four this time."

She shook her head in confusion.

"I'm sorry," he said. "I'm a difficult son. I was difficult from the beginning, and I'm terrible now. I can't change the past. I can't make this past year easier for you to bear. But I can change the future. I can be better."

"You really are a good son, Christian," she said. "I've never worried about anything financially. You've never caused any horrific dust-ups in town. I'm very lucky to have you. It's why I wish so for your happiness."

"I'm lucky to have you, too," he said. "I'm glad you were here tonight, Mama. Just like this, you were enough. You helped."

Maybe that was all she had needed to know, because he could feel a subtle tension leave her frame.

Item E: Judith wanted to know what had become of the money. Well, if he wanted to get rid of the guilt he felt, he needed to stop thinking about *him*. It had been his dreams, his journals, his hopes that had been his main focus.

Item E: He had thought of himself quite enough these past years, thank you, and that selfishness had the tang of mind-clouding laudanum to him now. Cloying. Blinding.

He felt as if he were waking from an opium dream to the clarity of reality.

Christian needed to help Judith. Not to earn Anthony's journals. Not to bring her round to his cause. He needed to do it without expectation of any return.

He could only change the future, and there was one thing he was certain of: If he ever intended to look dream-Anthony in the eyes, he needed to do the things that Anthony wasn't here to do for her.

Chapter Fifteen

A few days later, with milk warming on the stove and kittens to feed, a knock sounded at Judith's door. She wasn't expecting any deliveries, and this wasn't Daisy's half-day at the flower shop. She had no idea who it was until suddenly…

It's Camilla, whispered the part of her brain that refused to be cautious. *It's Camilla. She received the letter. She's come. She's come.*

"Theresa," she said, handing over a spoon and wiping her hands on her apron. "Please stir the milk, and when it's warm, take it off the stove."

Doing things for the cats was one of the few tasks she was sure she could trust to her sister.

"Whoever it is," Theresa said, "ask them if they want a kitten! Or three."

If it was Camilla, Judith would let her keep all the kittens. No; she couldn't let herself build up that imaginary future. It would hurt too much when her hopes were dashed to pieces.

It was a good thing she hadn't done so. When she opened the door, it was not Camilla. It was Christian, standing on her stoop, holding a basket of strawberries. He stood somewhat awkwardly, shifting from foot to foot.

He *should* be awkward. He'd told her she didn't know her own brother. He was the anti-Camilla—the last person she wanted to see at the moment. Her hopes didn't just fall; they shattered.

For a second, Judith imagined slamming the door on his face. Then she imagined opening it again, just to slam it once more.

"Here," Christian said, holding out the basket. "These are for you. I'm sorry."

The berries inside were a little larger than thumb-sized and a brilliant red. It had been forever since she'd had a strawberry. She could smell them—that faint, sweet, tart smell that was so reminiscent of her childhood summers. They were so dear in London; she couldn't even remember what strawberries tasted like.

She only remembered that she had once loved them. She'd loved them even when they were a common treat, easily obtained from the hothouse on her father's estate.

He knew she loved strawberries.

For a second, Judith imagined taking the strawberries...and *then* slamming the door on his face.

Alas. If only she were a hair pettier. She would have much more fun, if less self-respect.

"I'm sorry," Christian repeated. "I've been thinking. I'm sure over the years you've heard enough abuse leveled at your family. You didn't need to hear it from me. You asked me to help. I should help."

He did not look particularly well.

He looked as if he'd not slept since last she saw him. His eyes were red and ringed by dark circles. He was clean-shaven, but so newly shorn that she could see small nicks where the razor had broken his skin.

"Please," he said. "You're right. Not about any of the other things I said—but I can't live with myself. Anthony's not here because of me. I owe you because of that."

"You owe me strawberries?"

"No." He swallowed. "Help."

It would be easier if he were not so innately fair. She'd spent eight years building him up in her mind as a villain. Someone who jumped to conclusions. Someone, perhaps, who had purposefully hurt her and her family. Someone who was unthinking, uncaring, unfeeling. It hurt to be reminded that he thought, he cared, and he felt.

On the one hand, she didn't understand how he could be the person who had destroyed her family.

On the other hand...strawberries.

Gluttony won over principles. She took the strawberries. "Thank you," she said. "Come in. Have a kitten."

"A what?"

"A kitten," she said, stepping to the side and allowing him to enter. "In fact, have two."

He frowned. "Is that a euphemism for...?" But he stopped in the entrance, cocking his head. Inside, the mewing from down the hall was immediately evident.

"Wait your turn." Theresa's voice floated down to them. "Stop clawing. Smidge, that's not nice. There. That's better."

"Oh." He gave her a confused smile. "I suppose it's not a euphemism for anything." When he smiled, all his weariness slid away, leaving him simply...sweet.

She didn't want him to be sweet.

"Under the circumstances, two kittens is actually a euphemism. Anything under ten is a euphemism. Welcome to the hopefully temporary cat menagerie!" Judith said brightly, shaking off her unease. "These things happen in the Worth household. Think nothing of it."

"Ah." Christian cleared his throat. "All in a day's work." He took off his hat and set it on the side table. "I've been thinking. I was hoping to be of service to you in another way."

Judith clapped her hands together. "Don't tell me. You want *three* kittens. Oh, today is a good day! The kitten emporium is open to all customers. We accept strawberries as barter."

"Actually." He looked upward. "I hadn't contemplated kittens at all. I was thinking about Benedict."

She shut her mouth. "Ah." Her brother was upstairs. He was doing better, at least on the outside. His bruises had faded; he would go out on walks in the afternoon. He would even smile and laugh, particularly if there were kittens involved.

But only when Judith was watching. When she wasn't, he would curl up and make himself small. He would look off into a corner of the room, as if seeing something she could not see. And she wasn't sure what the expression on his face denoted, but it made her want to find the boys who had done this to him, the ones who had stolen the joy from his life, and…and…

And there her imagination failed. She was an adult. It wasn't appropriate for her to beat small children to a pulp, no matter what they'd done to her brother. Not that she'd have the choice, of course, because Benedict wouldn't tell her who had done this to him. That left her with no tools for dealing with this mess except kittens, ginger-ginger biscuits, and attempting to coax false smiles from her brother.

"What of Benedict?" She looked over at him. "If you tell me he needs a man's influence, I will hit you with a...a..." She looked around the entry for a reasonable weapon. "With a chair," she finished. "Eton was nothing but men and boys, and look how well that went."

"No," Christian said. "Not a man's influence. Just the company of someone who had his own problems at Eton."

She looked over at him. She had never heard of any problems. Christian was funny. Everyone liked him.

And she could bake a tower of biscuits, and it wouldn't make a difference. Besides, she'd taken the strawberries. "Do you think you can help?"

"I don't know if I can," he said with a shrug. "But at least I can make sure someone is asking the right questions of him."

"Are there right questions?"

"No," he said, "but there are wrong answers. Boys can be very cruel to one another, and if you've never experienced it, you might not understand."

"Very well," she finally said, and led him upstairs.

Benedict was sitting on his bed, reading a book, with three cats—Squid, the adult, and two kittens—cuddled up to him. He looked up as Judith tapped on the door.

His bruise had vanished. His lip was healed. He didn't *look* like a boy who had been hurt so badly he refused to go back to school.

But he was.

"Benedict," she said, "do you recall Christian Trent, Lord Ashford?"

At the words *Lord Ashford*, her brother curled up on the bed, an arm going protectively around the two kittens. She wasn't even sure Benedict was aware he was doing it.

"He's the one from the other day," Benedict said in a low voice. "Is he…here to take a kitten?"

Christian shook his head. "What is the business with all the kittens?"

"Yes." Judith ignored Christian. "He *is* taking a kitten, but not Snippet or Smidgen, so stop worrying."

Benedict's eyes narrowed. "Scrap?"

"Scrap is my kitten. He can't have Scrap."

Christian blinked. "But what if I want Scrap?"

Of course he'd ask. "Then your wishes will be thwarted," Judith said primly. "You can't have my kitten, not for any strawberries. Might I suggest Fillet? She's sweet, kind, and excessively pouncy. She would be an excellent companion."

"What kind of monster names a cat *Fillet?*"

"When she's curled up," Benedict offered, "with her markings—she looks a little like a fillet of beef. With a stripe of fat along the side."

Judith cast Christian a scornful look. "Who names a cat 'Fillet'? Someone who has eleven kittens to name." She put her hands on her hips. "I will hear no criticism from anyone who has named a smaller number of kittens."

Christian just nodded thoughtfully. "An excellent point. I am not a professional kitten-namer. I am not even a hobbyist. I suppose I ought to leave the kitten-naming to the kitten-naming-specialists. This young man is one of them?"

A tiny smile touched Benedict's lips. A real smile, and Judith's heart twinged. Oh, Christian was good. She'd forgotten how good he could be at this. No—*forgotten* was a lie. She had purposefully purged all of his good qualities from her memory.

Christian sat in a chair, and Judith followed suit.

"Your sister," Christian said, "when she asked if you remembered me, was asking if you remembered me from eight years ago. I was a friend of your elder brother's. I visited your home over a great many holidays. Before you were born, and after."

Benedict sat straight up at that. "You knew Anthony?"

"I did," Christian said. "We went to Eton together."

Benedict's shoulders slumped and he shot Judith an accusatory glance. "Oh," he said in an entirely different tone.

Christian ignored this. "We both know that there are a number of ways that boys mistreat each other there. I had nightmares when I was a child—ones that made me scream and kick out. Sometimes I would walk in my sleep, too, and I'd fight anyone who tried to stop me. And worst of all, I could never recall any of it in the morning."

Judith blinked at him in surprise. She'd never heard of any of this—but then again, boys of that age were unlikely to confide in their friend's younger sister. There was a ring of truth to his voice.

"Boys at Eton are like a flock of chickens," Christian continued. "You know what chickens are like."

Benedict shook his head. "We've never kept chickens."

"Ah, well." Christian shrugged. "Then I'll tell you what chickens are like. They're stupid, cruel, prone to fighting. If they think one chicken is weak, the others will peck it. If one draws blood, the rest move in and if nobody intervenes, next thing you know—dead chicken."

Benedict nodded pensively.

"I was weak," Christian said. "And what was worse, I thought it was my fault. I thought there was something about me that demanded henpecking, the same thing that made me thrash about at night. So I thought I would tell you three things that your brother told me then, three things that changed my life. Since he's not here, I'll tell you in his stead."

Benedict leaned forward.

"Number one," Christian said. "It—whatever those boys did to you—is not your fault. You didn't do anything wrong. You aren't to blame, whatever they or anyone else told you."

Benedict inhaled. Judith felt a sore spot in her chest. When Christian spoke, he unconsciously leaned back against the chair and looked at Benedict. For a second, she had caught a hint of Anthony in his voice, in the cadence of his words. She could almost see her elder brother, sitting in that chair, saying those things.

"Number two." Christian didn't seem aware that they were both watching him. "You're better than them. Anyone can be a chicken pecking in the yard. But the top chicken never lasts. It is always dethroned. Some day, there will be a younger chicken, a stronger chicken. The only way to win is to not be a chicken. You're not a chicken, are you?"

"No."

"There you are. You're better than them."

Benedict considered this. "What is number three?"

"Number three." Christian folded his arms and smiled. "Ah, that's the fun one. It's this: They will pay, and you will make them do it. Since you were the one they wronged, you will determine what you think is adequate recompense. But we—your sister, of course, and me, if you wish it—will help you execute your vengeance. Whatever it is you think you need to feel better."

Benedict took this in. He closed his book and stroked a kitten's head. "I don't *want* vengeance. If I do to them what they did to me, I'll be no better than they are." He very carefully did not look at Judith.

"That's the other thing." Christian looked over at him. "For me, it was the usual—some ritual beatings, a great many snide remarks, the occasional dunking of my smallclothes in the communal chamber pot. I gather that you experienced all that?"

Benedict nodded.

"They likely stole your food, too—anything sent from home, and the choice bits from your meals."

Another nod.

"See? I told you they were nothing but chickens."

Benedict smiled.

"I suppose they jumped you more than they did me. Daily? Twice daily?"

"At least."

Oh, she hurt just thinking of what it must have been like for Benedict.

"And made it out to be your fault, so that if anyone interfered, you were punished more than they, I suppose."

Judith felt her fists clench.

Benedict shut his eyes. "Yes."

"Anything worse?" Christian asked casually.

What could be worse?

Benedict didn't look up from his kitten. "No." His voice broke. "Nothing worse. It wasn't even as bad as it could have been, and I still can't go back."

"There." Christian shook his head. "You're allowed to hate the way you were treated even if it could have been worse."

What could be worse than what had happened? She stared at him in confusion for a moment—and then came to a realization, one that choked her voice from her. She hadn't even thought to ask, didn't know what she would have done in any event. Thank God. She wanted to vomit.

But Christian nodded, as if this were all entirely normal. "Remember: You're not to blame. You're not a chicken, Benedict. What do you want to do?"

Benedict considered. "What did *you* do? What was your vengeance?"

Christian shrugged. "Well, they would always steal the sweets my mother sent me from home. So I asked her to send me an enormous hamper. The worst offenders gathered in my quarters one Saturday, gorging themselves on cake and cordial, to which I had added a generous libation of spirits." He looked upward and smiled. "They fell asleep. Your brother and I removed the door to their room from its hinges. We nailed a sheet of wood in its place, and then covered the wood with a thin coat of plaster. We had just enough time to apply a matching coat of paint.

"They left my room late that afternoon, staggeringly drunk, only to discover that they had nowhere to go. No room. No door. Nothing. There was only an empty hallway where they'd once lived."

Benedict grinned. "That's brilliant."

"It was utterly glorious. They were sent down for knocking holes in the wall."

Benedict considered this. "I still don't want to go back. I'd have to go back to do that."

"You don't have to go back to get even," Christian countered.

"But how?"

"Well, that's the trick. *You'll* have to figure it out. It has to be your idea, see. Because they stole something from you. They stole from you the belief that you could make a difference in your life. You have to take it back. I know you can do that."

Benedict stroked his kitten's head once again. "Hmm."

"They're chickens," Christian said, "but…" He leaned down to him. "Who is the greatest chicken-killer in English literature?"

Judith choked in her seat.

Benedict, though, looked up, his eyes wide. "Who?"

If he said Hamlet's uncle…

"You will be," Christian said. "I promise you."

If anything, Benedict looked more perturbed. "But—"

"Metaphorical chickens," Christian said. "Figurative killing."

"Oh. I suppose that isn't a problem."

"Think on it."

They left Benedict looking thoughtful rather than wary. It was a marked improvement.

Judith, too, was immersed in thought. She frowned as they descended the staircase.

She shook her head and gestured upstairs. "That was very kind, what you just told my brother. I'm not sure it will work—he's refused to listen to all talk of his returning—but—"

"You'll have to put that out of your mind," Christian said. "If he goes back, it needs to be on his own terms. If he only returns because you're forcing him, he'll feel powerless. That's no way to take on bullies."

"I don't want to force him to go back," Judith said. "I just want…"

"You want to set up his life so that he makes precisely the choices you think he should?"

Well. Put like that. It made her feel uneasy.

She pressed on. "Whatever you said just now, it was very kind. Doubly kind to attribute all those sentiments to Anthony, when we both know he wouldn't have made that last point."

Christian turned and looked at her. His eyebrows crinkled, and he shook his head. "Drat. Now I must contradict you again. Not only *would* Anthony say such things, he *did* say them. To me."

"Oh, I believe he said that bit about being better than the other boys and such like. But revenge? Plastering over a door? We both know Anthony…" She trailed off.

He gave her a pained smile, and all the weariness in his face returned, dropping on his shoulders like a burden he'd carried a hundred leagues. "You really don't know Anthony, do you?" He sighed. "Judith, your brother was a rigid *moralist*. He was *not* a rigid follower of rules. Don't confuse the two. When the authorities looked the other way—when the schoolyard was ruled by those who favored swagger and intimidation over fair play, and bullies were given free rein? Revenge under such circumstances, according to Anthony, was *justice*, not a violation."

His voice was low. His eyes were dark. And for one moment, she felt as if she were looking straight though the veneer of humor that he painted on everything, straight into the heart of him. He was looking at her steadfastly, as if willing her to believe. As if he needed her to understand that her brother could violate rules, laws…everything.

If she could believe that, she could understand what Christian had done. And if she could comprehend that…

"Plastering over the door was my idea," Christian said to her. "But yes, your brother helped. He approved. And he never told. It was justice."

She couldn't comprehend it. She didn't want to believe him.

But when he said *it was justice,* he had that same ring in his voice. The one that she'd heard earlier. The one that had so reminded her of her brother.

He'd come, bearing strawberries and an apology. He'd spoken to Benedict and brought a light to his eyes that had been missing ever since he returned home. It didn't change anything.

He believed her brother was a traitor. He knew Judith well enough to comprehend her likes and dislikes, and he'd only spent summers with her. He'd reached Benedict in a way that even Judith hadn't, and he hadn't seen him in eight years. If he could do all of that, how could he *not* have known Anthony?

He had to be wrong. He had to be.

She swallowed. "I understand what you're trying to say. Anthony wasn't as good as I believed."

"No." He shook his head. His voice dropped. "I'm trying to say that he was better. Not so cribbed in by rules. He never feared consequences on his own behalf. I think Anthony was a traitor to his country. I have never believed he was a bad person—just a misguided one. *You* may have never heard him say that revenge is the only response to injustice, but he used to tell *me* that all the time."

"And what has that to do with treachery?"

"You know that already," Christian said evenly. "The only reason you won't consider the possibility is that you don't want to admit the truth."

"The truth about my brother?"

"No." Christian set his hand on hers. "The truth about us."

She looked up into his eyes. Some part of her—oh, very well, some *large* part of her—still missed him. Not just her heart, but her body. Her skin. Her thighs. They all seemed to tingle with his proximity. For a moment, the world seemed to tilt toward him. Her shoulder brushed his lightly. Wool whispered against muslin.

She would hate kissing him as much as she yearned for it. She straightened, moving away from him. "There is no *us.*"

"There is. If your brother was a traitor, he didn't just betray England by selling her military secrets. He betrayed you, by risking your entire future. He betrayed your sisters and your brother, by leaving them without support if he were ever found out. And he betrayed *me,* putting me in the unenviable position of having to keep quiet to save him."

Judith swallowed.

"I understand. You won't accept any evidence I can give you of what happened. You don't want to admit that your brother is a traitor, because if you do, you'll have to admit the truth about us."

She didn't ask *what truth*. She didn't want to hear it.

She already knew.

"If your brother was a traitor," Christian said, "then I am not your enemy. I am not the cause of all the harm you've ever experienced. I'm not the villain. Instead, I am the only person in the world who loved Anthony as much as you did. I'm the only person who can understand how much you hurt."

Her eyes stung.

"If your brother was a traitor," he said, "you would have to admit that we have a great deal in common. That there is nobody else on earth who can understand you as I do. And you know, Judith…"

He reached out. She ought to move away. She ought to slap his hand. But she couldn't. His fingertips grazed her cheek and her eyes fluttered shut. He knew her too well, if he knew this, too.

He knew that there were nights when matters had seemed impossible, when she'd laid in bed examining the ceiling, wishing her brother had spoken in his defense. Why had he not said anything? Why hadn't he explained?

Sometimes, she'd hated her brother, too. She'd wanted to grab him and shake him and demand to know why he'd done what he had.

She wasn't proud of those moments. They'd left her feeling even more bereft of hope, even lonelier, than the times she'd despaired.

"If my brother were a traitor," she said thickly, "then I *would* hate him for what he did to me. I could never forgive him. I would be filled with bitterness. How could I trust anyone at all?"

"You could trust me," he said in a low voice.

"If my brother were a traitor…" She could scarcely get the words out. "I couldn't trust myself."

For a second, she let him touch her. For a second, she could feel a world of possibilities opening up to her. His fingers grazed down her cheek. She opened her eyes to see him looking down at her. He was close, so close that she might have kissed him.

"My brother was not a traitor," she said. "And I don't trust you."

But he didn't lean down to her. He didn't kiss her. He left the possibility of the kiss floating in the air, waiting for her response.

He let his hand fall to his side. "It's all right," he said. "You don't have to trust me."

Chapter Sixteen

eside Judith, Daisy swung her basket on the way home.

There was very little in her friend's basket. Some carrots and potatoes, and little else. Daisy had bargained for those vociferously, walking away from the butcher when he'd refused to sell her soup bones for the price she'd offered.

But she smiled as if nothing were wrong. "It's been an age since the queen came to tea," Daisy said. "But lo, she sent over her messenger just this morning. She'll be by shortly."

It was difficult for Judith to fall back into their little game. She'd spent the last few days being forcibly reminded that their game had once been a near-reality for her.

"What a compliment," Judith made herself offer cheerily. "She hasn't called on me since the Prince Consort passed away."

"You have all the luck." Daisy looked upward and sighed miserably. "Now you see my difficulty. I am naturally of such a cheerful disposition that dampening my usual vivacity in deference to her mourning will prove difficult."

"Have you considered adding brandy to her tea?"

Daisy giggled. They paused at the street corner, ready to part ways.

"Think on it," Judith said. "Brandy and queens. They go hand in hand. But as I'm sure you're busy, I'll take my—"

"Wait." Daisy bit her lip. "I have a small favor to ask of you."

"After you looked in on the terrible ones a few days back? I should think that a large favor would be in order. How can I help?"

Daisy looked at her, as if considering the matter. Finally, she shook her head. "There's nothing you can do."

"Surely there's something. Even if it's only to offer support."

Daisy considered this. Finally, she fumbled in her pocket. "That is precisely what I need," she said slowly. "A little support. That's all. The queen's visit has left me feeling a little out of sorts, and it might help if someone would…know."

She held out a folded sheet of paper.

Judith took it, and Daisy's cheeks flamed red.

For a second, she thought that maybe this was a letter from Crash, Daisy's…sweetheart? Friend? Enemy? She wasn't sure which. He'd taken an interest in Daisy once, and Judith wasn't sure at all why the thing hadn't come off. But Daisy's expression wasn't the flush of embarrassment. It was pure shame.

Judith unfolded the letter.

This is your final notice. I have been entirely too understanding, but your rents are two weeks in arrears. If you do not have the payment for me by tomorrow afternoon, I'll have the constables put you on the street.

Daisy looked at her defiantly.

Judith felt a lump in her throat.

Here she'd been, mentally bemoaning her own problems—hundreds of pounds missing, Christian causing trouble. Daisy's father was dead, her mother was ill, and she was going to be homeless tomorrow.

"Daisy," Judith said slowly. "I… We… That is, I could… If hosting the queen would be a strain on your household," she managed to say, "I have some room over my way. We could make space."

"We don't need help." Daisy's hands tightened on her basket. "We only need—that is to say… Nothing. We don't need anything."

Judith swallowed the lump in her throat. She thought of the wilted carrots her friend had purchased and the soup bones she had not.

Daisy nodded. "Well, then." She took the paper back. "I suppose I should make sure the silver gets a proper shining for her arrival, then."

Judith set her hand over her friend's fingers. "Daisy. I can help. Isn't there one thing I can provide?"

Daisy swallowed, appearing to think this over. "Do you have a room where I might be private for a moment? Before I return home?"

Judith nodded, and the two of them walked down the street.

When Judith had first moved here, everything had seemed so impossible. So crowded, so messy, so *noisy.* Now, when she'd visited Christian's household, Mayfair seemed unconscionably bright, everyone so spread out.

This place had become home.

It wouldn't be home without Daisy.

She opened the door to her rickety row house and led her friend up two flights of stairs to her attic. "There," she said. "We're private."

Daisy nodded, sat on the chair in front of Judith's clockwork arrangement, and burst into tears. She didn't say anything, didn't ask for anything. She just wept.

Judith could hardly blame her. She'd have wept, too.

"Daisy." Judith handed her a handkerchief and put her arm around her friend. "Let me help."

Her friend sniffled. "It wouldn't serve. We have a flat with two rooms—far too much space for us. We should have moved houses a year ago. When my father…" Her voice caught. "It's simply that I grew *up* in those rooms."

All of the emotions Judith had refused to feel these past weeks—the aching, gnawing hurt of seeing Christian again, the sharper piercing despair at discovering that Camilla had been handed about like an unwanted parcel, the knowledge that her childhood home was lost to her… It all seemed suddenly overwhelming. She could suppress her own tears. She couldn't hold back the ones she had for Daisy's loss, too.

"I know." Her eyes stung and she wiped at them. "I know. It's too much."

Daisy buried her head in Judith's shoulder.

It was too much. Anthony. When it came down to it, there *was* a part of Judith that hated him. She always would. She hated him for staying silent on the witness stand, hated him for not defending himself, hated him for not shouting that he wasn't a traitor, for not explaining anything. She *hated* him.

She hated him most because deep down, she feared that Christian was right. He'd betrayed his country. He'd betrayed her. He'd left her like this, to make do for their entire family under this terrible burden.

He was dead, and she didn't want to hate him. She *loved* him.

But she hated him, too.

Minutes passed. A good weep was like a spring storm: all hard rain lashing the windows until the sun came out. Daisy gave a little hiccough and sat up straight. She wiped at her eyes, inhaled, and then managed a tremulous smile.

"Stupid emotions." She shook her head. "There. Thank you. I needed that."

Judith folded her own handkerchief back into her pocket. "I have five pounds for you."

"No, you don't." Daisy shook her head. "No. It won't serve. We need to move anyway. If you loan me money, I don't know when I'll pay it back."

"It's not a loan." Judith opened her drawer and counted out coins. "I won't sleep at night if I'm worried over you. I can't solve any of my problems. Let me solve one of yours."

Daisy exhaled. "I can't. Judith…"

Judith set the coins in her friend's hand and closed her fingers on the money. "You can."

Daisy let out a shuddering sigh. But she didn't say no.

Sometimes, Judith regretted that she had never told Daisy the full truth. That her friend believed that she'd been born minor gentry, and her family had suffered a minor reversal. Sometimes, she wished she had told her everything.

Now was not the time to make a grand declaration. Her friend would feel hurt that she hadn't been trusted, betrayed even. She didn't need *more* emotions on top of everything.

Judith gave a little nod. "Do let me know where we should meet."

"Of course." Daisy gave her a tremulous smile and lifted her nose in the air in exaggerated pride. "Who else will I be able to complain to about the queen's terrible manners?"

The letter arrived two days later. It had been so long since Judith had written that she'd almost forgotten to hope. But this time, the envelope that had come was thick, not thin, and all the hope she had tried not to feel rose up in her.

She'd finally found her sister. This must be a letter from her. Everything would be well. She wasn't going to lose another sibling. She would discover that Camilla had been living a life of luxury with an aging woman, who would have loved her so well she had left her all her worldly goods.

She'd been traveling the globe, perhaps, and…and…

And there she went again. She was rather too apt to make a once-upon-a-time story of the world. Still, her fingers shook as she opened the letter.

The envelope, it turned out, was thick because it contained her own letter folded inside it.

An additional piece of creamy paper was on the very official letterhead of Darvin, Darvin, and Darvin, Solicitors at Law in Bath.

Miss Worth, the letter read. *Miss Abigail Troworth passed away five years ago. We have no records of your sister. She was not left a bequest. Upon inquiry to Miss Troworth's executor, her sister, Mrs. Harbough, we are informed that a Camilla or possibly a Camille did accompany Mrs. Troworth at some point in her later years, but she believed the girl was sent away after Miss Troworth's passing. Mrs. Harbough does not know where, or if, she obtained a further position.*

Yours truly,

Irwin Darvin

Judith wasn't sure when the paper crumpled in her hands. It made an excellent ball, one that she almost lobbed into the fire before realizing that she might need the solicitor's direction at some later time.

Once-upon-a-time thinking indeed. She might as well have imagined that the queen *would* visit. After all this time she was still telling herself lies. Everything would turn out right if only Judith worked hard enough. If she never quit. If her brother went to Eton, if she kept smiling, if she never gave up.

If she did all those things…then what? The wicked witch would bring her sister home, as if hard work were a magic wand that she could wave over the world?

No. There were no once-upon-a-times. There was only reality. Her father had killed himself. Her brother had refused to defend himself and disappeared without a trace. She would never know how he died, or what cause he perished for; all she would ever have was aching emptiness.

Her sister, who she had believed to be safe and well cared for, was missing, God knew where. She had to be alive; even now, even with bitterness filling her thoughts, Judith couldn't contemplate Camilla's death.

She couldn't bear the loss of another sibling.

But she couldn't even take care of her own little brother. If she had ten thousand pounds, she'd go in search of her sister. But she didn't have even a thousand pounds, and so…

Right at that moment, a great crash came from downstairs—the shriek of wood splintering, the sound of dishes crashing.

Judith shoved the letter in her skirt pocket and dashed down the stairs. As she descended the steps, she could see the carnage. The hutch in the parlor that housed all their dishes—plates, bowls, crockery—had fallen over. A mess of broken wood and shards of china met her.

As did her sister.

"It's all right," Theresa said, waving her hands. "It's all right! Don't worry!"

"Theresa." Judith could hardly speak. "What—how—"

"It's not as bad as it looks," Theresa said swiftly. "The cats are unharmed."

"What happened?" Judith's heart was racing.

"Well," Theresa said, "I was teaching Whiskers to climb, and—"

All of Judith's helplessness, all her bitterness, all the anger she'd stored came rushing to the surface. Her face heated. She could feel her hands balling into fists, almost of their own accord.

"Teaching her to climb." Her words sounded arctic. "What did I tell you? What were the rules?"

"But you said!" Theresa's chin wobbled. "You *said* that kittens were more important than rules."

"Oh, for the love of ducklings. I didn't mean you could ignore every rule with impunity, you nitwit."

Theresa's nose scrunched up. "I'm not a nitwit."

"Right now you are. Only a nitwit would tell me that kittens were more important than rules when she had just endangered her kittens' lives by teaching them to do the *exact* thing I'd told her not to."

"You're shouting." Theresa's arms folded around herself. "Ladies don't shout."

"Do you think that just because you paid no money for those cats, they were free? And what of crockery?" She picked up a shard of plate. "What of this, Theresa?"

"I don't know! I didn't think! I just—"

"You never think," Judith said. "You just break things. You break things *on purpose.*"

"No, I don't," Theresa said. And then, because she was honest, she continued. "Yes, I do. Sometimes. But I didn't, not this time. This was on *accident.*" She inhaled. "You're still shouting. Anthony would never talk to me like that."

Anthony wouldn't. Camilla wouldn't. All of Judith's anger had reached the boiling point.

"Anthony," Judith heard herself say, "is not here."

"No, but *he* promised he would always take care of me. *You* aren't taking care of me. You're screaming at me. You *never* listen. You *always* favor Benedict."

Judith made herself set the piece of plate down carefully. For all that she told herself she didn't begrudge the past years—for every smile that she'd managed to plaster on her face, thinking of the safety and security that she was winning for her sisters—a part of her, a part that she hated, a part that would not go away—that terrible part of her was always present, whispering that she would have been better off without her family. Without them, she'd have all the money she had earned for herself. Without them, she'd have been able to hire a full-time servant instead of scarcely getting by with a half-day charwoman twice a week. Without Theresa, she'd have been with Camilla in the first place, and none of this— *none* of it—would ever have happened.

She would never want to be without her brother and sister. She *hurt* because she didn't know where Camilla was. But some small, hateful part of her soul wished that she didn't have to carry that burden.

Judith hated that deep down, she was hateful.

"Anthony," Theresa was saying, "never talked down to me or told me that I was a nitwit. Anthony never corrected me. And when Anthony gets back—"

That hateful part of herself snapped. "Anthony," Judith said, "is dead."

Theresa stood in place. Her eyes widened. "Don't say that."

"He's dead," Judith said. "He disappeared in the middle of a storm eight years ago. He has not attempted to make contact, not with me, not with you, not with anyone at all in England. Anthony is a traitor. He could have argued his innocence, and if he had, he would have been here with you. Get this fact into your nitwitted skull: Anthony abandoned us. He doesn't care for us. He is *not alive*. He is dead."

Theresa's eyes grew even wider, if that were possible. She turned her head away and swiped at forming tears. "Don't say that! Don't say that, Judith."

"Anthony has not put food on your table," Judith continued. "Anthony has not provided for your future. Anthony has not scraped and scavenged and worked himself to the bone to save you. Anthony didn't spend months searching through secondhand stores to find decent teacups. I am sick and tired of hearing about Anthony doing this and Anthony doing that when all Anthony did was betray his country, his family, and then perish under circumstances that left a cloud over the title. Anthony was a terrible brother."

"No, he wasn't!" Theresa was screaming now. "You're saying that because you don't want to be criticized for your mistakes. You don't want me to realize the truth. Too late. I already know. You *are* the wicked half-sister. Anthony told me that he would be there when I most needed him, and he would *not* lie to me. You're a hateful person."

Judith knew she was hateful. She knew because every time she thought of Anthony, she could no longer simply mourn him. She hated him, too. Love was a knife, and try as you might to hold it properly, it would always twist in your grasp, cutting your fingers.

"Yes," she said spitefully. "Now you know the truth. Your eldest brother is dead. Your eldest sister is hateful. But do look on the bright side, Theresa—you are only a brat."

Theresa's nose quivered. She swallowed and looked away. "I am... I am..." Theresa was a great many things, but she was not a liar. She couldn't finish the sentence.

That was the thing about hateful truths. They hurt because they were *true*. Theresa knew that she was a brat. The part that hurt her? That Judith knew it, too.

"I hate you," Theresa said instead in a low voice. "I hate you. I hate you. I *hate* you. And when Anthony finally does come home…" Her eyes filled with tears. But she couldn't finish that sentence, either. Because deep down—deep, somewhere, behind the brattiness, and the difficulty, and the acting up—deep down, Theresa was not actually stupid.

And not being stupid, she knew the truth about her brother.

Anthony was not coming home. He was not ever coming home.

"I hate you," Theresa said, crying. "It's all your fault."

"It isn't all my fault," Judith said. "It's just all on my shoulders. Try it, sometime, and see how well you do."

"I hate you," Theresa repeated, stomping up the stairs. "I hate you, I *hate* you—you, you—" She floundered, trying to find a venomous enough word. "You *mallard*," she finally hurled at her.

The door to their joint room rattled as Theresa slammed it. One final piece of crockery fell to the floor from its perch on a broken shelf and shattered.

Anthony was dead. Judith was alone and surrounded by broken crockery, and *mallard* didn't seem a strong enough epithet to describe the wreckage.

She picked up a shattered plate and moved a door that had been wrested from its hinges. There, spilled over the floor where once they'd been hidden behind the doors of the bottom shelf, were three bound volumes. They'd once been blank; her elder brother had filled them with his cramped, scarcely readable writing while he was in China.

She stared at Anthony's journals for a very long time.

Then she gathered them up. "Duck it," she muttered. "Duck it all to shell."

Chapter Seventeen

ne of her umbrella spines snapped halfway to Christian's home, sending little lashings of summer rain into Judith's face every time the wind shifted.

An hour's walk should have been enough to calm her, to allow her to change her mind. But the image of the front parlor, a mess of wood and shattered plates, would not leave her.

Her mismatched teacups might not have been much, but they'd been *something*. For Judith, they'd been proof that after being thrust so precipitously from polite society, her family might still aspire to rise to the heights where they'd once effortlessly soared.

Myths. Lies. Nightmares.

Judith was done pretending.

By the time Judith rapped on Christian's door, the rain had stopped and the sun was on the verge of setting. Little gray scudding clouds were pinking up just over the edge of the Mayfair roofs. She was going to have to walk home in the dark—a prospect she didn't particularly care to think about at the moment.

The door opened a bare thirty seconds after her knock.

Every detail in the interior of Christian's house seemed too bright, too luxurious. Oil lamps were turned up full bore, so that a golden radiance spilled onto the front step. Cream paper graced the walls, with some ornate pattern traced on it in gold. Marble floors, polished wood furniture. Even on the front steps, she could detect some delicious scent wafting from the kitchen.

It hit her like a strike to the solar plexus. She forgot so easily how different that other life was, the one she'd once lived. It was a life where fabrics never itched and shoe leather never cracked, where a shattered plate was whisked away without any need to think about how it was to be replaced.

Here she stood in her gray shawl with the pilling yarn, holding her broken umbrella. She clutched a canvas satchel that had seen better days.

The butler blinked at her.

She had nothing but her manners. Judith swept her umbrella down, closing it. Her chin went up.

She handed the broken, dripping utensil to the man. "Do tell Lord Ashford that Lady Judith Worth is here."

The queen could not have said it better. The queen would not have hesitated to step inside the warm, dry room and so Judith did not, either.

"Of course," the butler said a little stiffly. "I shall inquire if my lord is at home, but I expect he is not."

This was servant-speak for *you'll be tossed out.*

"Jeffries."

Judith looked up the main stair. Marble steps were clothed in red and gold carpet, and Christian stood at the top like some conquering god set to descend his temple steps.

"I'm at home," Christian said. "I'm always at home to Lady Judith. Understood?"

"Yes, sir." The man glanced mulishly at Judith's skirts. She wasn't dripping; she'd checked. She'd cleaned too many floors in her brother and sister's wake to do so.

"Have Mary send in something warm to drink," Christian said. "And scones. Lady Judith?"

He gestured, and she ascended the stairs to meet him.

She would not be overawed. She would *not* be overawed. This was what she'd been born to. This was what she would have had, had Christian not...

Or maybe, had her brother not...

It didn't matter. Now, she might have been lady of smashed crockery and broken furniture, but she wasn't going to duck her head to him. She'd spent the past eight years working for something impossible, trying to fit pieces together in ways they would not go.

Maybe it was a fairy story to believe that things could still turn out for her family, but at least it was *her* fairy story. She might not choose the ink or the paper, but she could write the words. Christian and his marble and his carpet and his butler all put together could not stop her and her smashed teacups. Her fists clenched as she made her way to him.

"Judith." He looked utterly bemused. "Whatever brings you here? And what are you...?"

She hefted her canvas satchel. "Keep your tea," she said. "Keep your scones. Destroy what little remains of Anthony's reputation. I don't care any longer." She thrust her burden at him.

He staggered under the sudden weight. "What the devil, Judith?"

"Go ahead, then. They're Anthony's journals." Her chin was in the air, and she didn't think the queen could have said it more proudly if she *did* secretly visit Daisy. "It doesn't matter any longer. Take them."

He set the package on a side table. "What is going on?"

She turned to him. "Go ahead. Explain it to me if you please. Use small words if you must, so I'll be sure to understand. Tell me how you're so certain. How you *know* that my brother was a traitor. Tell me how it makes sense for *Anthony* to have betrayed everything he held dear. Tell me, Christian. Everything else is broken. Tell me *now.*"

She poked his chest as she spoke, and he looked down at her finger. Her hand was beginning to shake, and that wouldn't do.

"Well," he finally said. "I'm surely not going to shout the whole thing at you in the hall. Come." He opened a door to a spacious office lined with shelves. A desk and a few chairs sat near a fire.

"Come in," he said. "Have a seat. Have a scone."

"I don't want a scone." It was a lie.

She didn't want any of his quiet reassurances. She wanted justice. She wanted anger. She wanted to make his life turn topsy-turvy, as hers had done.

She also wouldn't have minded a scone. It was hard holding onto her hard-won anger when there was food available. Especially when she noticed a little brown kitten curled on a pillow before the fire.

She sat instead. The fire crackled pleasantly, and when Christian sat next to her on the sofa—a good three feet away—she refused to look at him.

"I'll make it simple," he said, "I believe that Anthony gave military secrets to the Chinese because he did not want Britain to win the war over opium."

Her hands were finally warming up in front of the fire, and that made them feel itchy. She rubbed them surreptitiously against her skirt. "That's the most ridiculous thing I've ever heard."

Christian simply inclined his head. "Do you know why Britain and China were at war?"

"I was seventeen," Judith said. "I remember something about trade dealings and tea." She frowned. "Something about the Chinese seizing a British ship."

"Close enough." The door opened and a servant brought in a tray. She set it on the side table near them, and Judith tried not to wonder what was on the plate beneath the cloth napkin. Of course Christian's teacups matched. She hadn't really expected anything else, but she still glowered at him as he poured pale liquid into a pink-edged china cup, and then set a little biscuit on a plate.

"Here." He set these unceremoniously to her left. "You didn't ask for it, so you needn't feel obliged to me when I give it to you."

She looked at him from beneath her lashes. She had never in her life *not* eaten food that was put in front of her, and he must have known that she was hardly going to start by spurning a sugary little biscuit. Especially not when little flecks of real vanilla were visible from this vantage point. When was the last time she'd had anything flavored with vanilla?

She wasn't fooling anyone. She picked it up and ate it in one bite.

Christian spoke again as she lifted her cup. "It was really about one thing from the British perspective: tea."

She looked down at the saucer in her hand. "Tea?"

"Tea. Tea comes from China."

"I know. It's why it is so very dear."

"And yet we cannot do without it," Christian said with a lopsided smile. "China has tea; Britain demands tea. Unfortunately, we have nothing that China wants in return. If life were fair, we'd simply send a vast quantity of money to China every year. They would grow wealthy. And we would not."

Judith looked at the cup in her hand once again. "Britain waged war for better tea prices? That seems…"

It seemed like a tremendous waste, even if only one life was lost over the matter. Even if the only life had been her brother's. And there had been many more lives lost than the one. Many more.

He noticed her frowning suspiciously at her cup. "It's a tisane," he told her. "Mint and chamomile. It's not tea."

She took a sip.

"It wasn't just about tea prices." Christian set another biscuit on her plate. "In truth, England found a much more effective way to balance the trade deficit than to lower tea prices. We found a product that the Chinese demanded."

"That's…good?"

His nose wrinkled in distaste. "Not when that product is opium. It's addictive. It ruins men, utterly ruins them. Men addicted to the drug can think of nothing but how and when they'll find their next smoke. Even men who manage to drag themselves away from the opium dens still feel its call years later. They'll catch a hint of a scent on a breeze, and next thing they know, they've abandoned all caution. One doesn't *stop* being an opium addict, not ever. One can only stop taking the drug. I'm simplifying decades of history, but the Chinese government outlawed the trade of opium. Britain couldn't afford that. Two wars later, and…" Christian shrugged.

Judith fell silent. "You think Britain was in the wrong."

"On balance? There's no question. But you didn't ask about my beliefs."

Judith felt a little *thump* to the side of her chair and looked over. Fillet had abandoned the fire to greet her. She was looking at Judith, blue eyes steady in her little brown, whiskered cat face. Judith reached over and stroked her between the ears.

Finally Judith spoke. "You think *Anthony* believed Britain was wrong. That he believed it so strongly he betrayed his own country."

"Yes."

"Why would he care?"

Christian looked away. His voice dropped. "He had a particular hatred of opium."

"I never knew it."

Fillet stepped daintily onto Judith's lap, kneading at her leg and letting off a low purr. Her feet crackled noisily as she did so; she was stepping on the letter in Judith's pocket.

Judith slid it out surreptitiously and moved it under her leg so it wouldn't make any noise.

"No. You wouldn't. He'd never tell another's secrets. But—you see—" Christian stopped again and inhaled. Then he looked over to her.

She had seen Christian unhappy. She'd seen him laughing. She'd seen him the way she always saw him—as if he had five jokes at the ready, and he wasn't afraid to use them.

Right now, it looked as if his jokes had all been stripped away. Every care he had, every worry, seemed to reflect in his eyes.

"You see," he said in a low voice, "his best friend was an opium addict."

Judith's hand stilled on the cat. "That's ridiculous. *You* were his…"

Christian stood. "Ah," he said. "I misspoke. I should have said his best friend *is* an opium addict. One doesn't stop being an opium addict, not even if it has been…" He swallowed and looked up. "Fourteen years and eight months, since one last had a dose."

Of all the things that Judith had expected to hear when she came, this had not been on the list.

"I had night terrors as a child," Christian said simply. "I've always had odd dreams; I'd scream out in the middle of the night, and kick at anyone who tried to calm me down. On top of my other oddities, it made my father believe that I belonged in an institution. My mother saved me from that fate by giving me a small dose of laudanum every night when I was young. The dreams didn't stop; the screaming did." He shrugged and gave her a smile that was not quite a smile. "By the time I started at Eton, the dose was no longer small."

She found her fingers trailing down Fillet's spine, searching out the rumble of her purr. Judith's heart was squeezing inside her.

"Anthony found out because one night, I took too much. I stopped breathing." Christian's voice became more ragged. "Anthony made me stand. Anthony slapped my face. Anthony walked me around the room until I coughed and took a breath again. He saved my life. And he told me I had to stop taking laudanum."

She could scarcely breathe.

"It took months. Every time I went home, my mother... Did you never wonder why I spent every holiday with your family? Every summer? Every spare moment?"

She shook her head. "It...just always was. I didn't even question it."

"I couldn't go home," Christian said. "My mother would set out my medicine, and...I couldn't say no, not those first years. It's as I said. Anthony saw what opium did. He sat with me when I was a gibbering mess. He kept my laudanum in his trunk and measured out smaller and smaller doses. He heard me beg and cry. He saw me at my absolute worst, and he would sit with me and help me make lists and sort things until the worst subsided."

Judith couldn't breathe.

"I hate opium the way one might hate an old lover—one has to hate it, because one doesn't dare return. Anthony hated it the way you hate me—as the thing that nearly destroyed a friend."

"Oh." Judith's chest felt heavy. She wanted to take his hand, to comfort him.

She wanted to comfort herself.

"So, yes," Christian said. "I believe that Anthony hated the opium trade enough to turn traitor to stop it. How could he not?"

"Oh," Judith repeated. Something inside her was breaking. Her anger. Her certainty. Her righteous fury.

"What I told you is true: I owe your family everything. Just not, perhaps, the way you imagine it."

She inhaled. She'd known. Deep down, maybe, she'd always known. She'd been angry at Christian, so angry in part because she had known. Anthony hadn't defended himself because he'd done it.

Everything was too much. "Of course." She picked Fillet off her lap and stood. "Of course." Her world had just altered in the blink of an eye and she wasn't certain what would take its place. She should say something to him. Offer him an apology. Something. Anything.

"Thank   you   for   explaining.   I'm   sorry for…everything." She didn't know what else to give him, so she handed him the cat.

"Judith?" He stood. "Judith, are you well?"

"Perfectly so."

"No." His hand touched her elbow. "No, you're not. I should have known. It's a great deal for anyone to take in. And you weren't well when you came in."

The words came out in a rush. "I have no idea where Camilla is," Judith heard herself saying. "Nobody has any idea. The cats broke everything. Benedict…"

He set the cat on his desk and put his arms around her. She should tell him to let go. She absolutely should not twine her hands in his lapels, nor breathe in his scent. She shouldn't let him hold her.

But, oh, how she wanted to be held. Even if it was by him.

Maybe *especially* if it was by him.

You don't want to admit I could be right. If you did, you would understand that I was the one person on Earth who shared your pain.

"How could he?" She choked on the words. "How *could* he? How could he simply do what he believed to be right without thinking of the consequences? Without asking what it would mean for Camilla and Theresa and Benedict?"

"And you." Christian whispered the words in her ear. "And you, Judith. How dare he leave you to fend for everyone? How dare he place that weight on your shoulders?" His hand crept around her waist.

"And you," she heard herself say. "He let you discover…everything. He made you feel responsiblefor what happened to him." Her voice shook. "He let me blame you, and I still don't know how I can ever forgive you."

"Sweetheart, I don't know how I can forgive myself."

She looked up at him.

Her life was a shambles. Everything had fallen to pieces. She had no idea where to turn next. But looking up into his eyes…

He was looking back at her, his dark eyes solemn. God, he'd asked her to marry him once. She'd said no; of course she had said no.

"Maybe we can figure that out," she said. "Maybe we can figure it out together."

He exhaled. He smelled of chamomile, of warm sugar.

He'd kissed her once long ago. That flutter in her belly said that whatever wounds her heart had sustained since then, she could let him do it again. Maybe if he did, maybe it would be as if all those years hadn't happened. As if there were no pain, no anger, no fury between them. As if this were only that perfect summer evening in the apple orchard.

But there were no trees here. There was no moon. And kisses couldn't wash away the pain she felt.

She looked down and the moment passed.

"Let me take you home," he said.

"I can make my own way."

"I know. Let me take you anyway."

Chapter Eighteen

Christian's carriage was well sprung and, despite the sound of wheels rattling against the uneven street, the ride was smooth. After so many years of having her teeth rattled from her jaw by indifferently sprung hacks, Judith had forgotten that a carriage might be like this, that she might pull the curtains, shut her eyes, and forget that the world was composed of rough streets and rowdy crowds.

Of course, one could not ignore one's companion. Christian sat across from her. He didn't speak. He didn't let his legs brush against her skirt, although he could have claimed the space was small enough to require it. He gave her all the room she needed.

She would never have enough.

Judith had known that matters didn't appear ideal for her brother's case. But she'd always made excuses. Too many excuses. Someone had planted the evidence; someone had misunderstood. Letters had been misattributed. She'd imagined any number of shadowy unnamed actors, because she'd not wanted to admit the truth. Something *must* have happened, because it was easier to believe that the universe and Christian had conspired to orchestrate her family's downfall than to comprehend that her brother might betray his family, his country, his every principle.

She might as well have convinced herself of the truth of those bedtime stories she had manufactured of Anthony, off fighting pirates and swimming to some unknown shore. Once-upon-a-time thinking, yet again.

The world in which he had betrayed her because of his principles was, for the first time, a colder, believable alternative. It was a lonelier place than the world she'd inhabited this morning.

She would adjust. She *had* to adjust. She always had so far.

She pulled her arms around herself and tried to imagine the truth.

Her brother was a traitor. He was not going to be vindicated posthumously. She was not going to have help. She glanced over at Christian and tried not to think.

Her thoughts were a muddle now. She hated Christian as much as she hated her brother—which was to say, she ached just to look at him. Her hand clenched over her skirt, reaching for the letter about her sister.

That was when she remembered that she'd left it in Christian's office, on his seat. She'd taken it out because Fillet had stepped all over it, drawing attention to her.

She'd almost forgotten her sister. That letter from the solicitor, blithely consigning Camilla to oblivion somewhere in this godforsaken country, was still at his house.

Maybe Christian's servants would throw it out.

She hardly had time to untangle her own feelings. She didn't have time for Camilla.

She could rush off to the last place her sister had been. She could ask a thousand questions, see what she could find. But if she did, she'd leave Benedict and

Theresa alone, unprotected. Who knew what might happen to them?

The closer the carriage drew to her home, the more everything hurt.

She couldn't concentrate on Camilla yet. Judith felt like a cat in a flood, trying to decide which of her kittens to save, knowing that whichever she chose, one of them would drown.

The carriage shifted right ever so slightly as it went around a turn.

Judith looked up to see Christian watching her.

You don't want to admit I'm right, he had told her. *If you did, you would know that I am the only person who can understand your pain.*

He had been right. She wasn't ready to admit that.

"Why have you never married?" she asked instead.

She could not see his face in the dark, and it was just as well. She didn't want to know whether he was looking at her with interest or with pity. Night lay between them like a velvet curtain. The darkness muted the emotions that she might otherwise have detected, hiding them in shadows.

"I thought about it," he finally said. "But here's the thing about having been in love that first time: I always knew, every time after, that what I was faced with was a pale imitation. I never found someone else I could trust with my soul. After the first time, nothing else was acceptable."

The pain was impossibly sharp. Trust him with her soul? Yes, that's what she'd done.

Like her brother, when Christian had to choose between her and his principles, he'd chosen his principles.

He didn't say anything else, and she didn't trust herself to speak. The carriage came to her street. The conveyance was too wide to bring down the narrow cobblestone road, and so the footman dismounted and held the horses.

"I'll see you to your door," Christian said.

"There's no need. I'm known hereabouts. I'll be perfectly safe."

"Nonetheless," he said, by which she understood that he intended to be stuffy.

"What of you?" he asked as they walked down the road in the dark. "You could have made a match. Not a brilliant one, I suppose. Not after that scandal. But you're an earl's daughter. You might have chosen someone who would have provided everything you wished."

He had asked her. After her father's funeral. He had found her and made her look at him. He'd told her he wanted to marry her, and damn what had happened with her family.

She'd been outraged.

She didn't answer. Not as they passed the dark-windowed house where her friend Daisy likely no longer lived on the second floor. Not as they skirted a group of men in the middle of the street, huddled under the single street lamp.

"Aw, Miss Worth," one of them called. "Come join us."

Christian took a step forward, but Judith set a hand on his arm. Once, she'd been scared of these men. Now she knew them. It was Fred Lotting, Mr. Padge, and the fellow that everyone just called Crash.

"Padge, you know I never gamble," Judith said. "Especially not on…what are you betting on tonight?"

Mr. Padge indicated the street, where rough circles were demarcated in chalk.

"We're betting on which of these, ah, crickets, will be the first to escape the third circle," answered Crash.

She looked over at him. "It's not that dark. Those are roaches, and I don't even want to know what you've attached to them to slow them so."

"It's—"

Judith set her hands over her ears, and the men laughed.

Crash took a step closer. "And who's your sweetheart?"

"Mr. Trent," Judith said repressively, "is a family friend."

"Aw, well, give her a nice, long friendly kiss good night for us, then," Fred put in.

Judith felt her cheeks flame. "Kiss your cockroaches," she snapped back.

They laughed once more, and she wished them good night and continued down the street.

Once, Judith had slipped on Theresa's discarded petticoat—who leaves petticoats on the *stairs?*—and had fallen, thump thump thump, down the steep steps of their house.

She'd had a wicked black and blue bruise on her hip for three weeks. She'd complained that everything hurt.

"Not everything," Theresa had told her. "What about your left middle finger?"

Her left middle finger had not hurt. And somehow, that one discovery had been a gateway to all the things that hadn't hurt. Not *everything* hurt.

"If I had married," Judith said, "I'd have thought men like that were rough and coarse and boorish all my life."

Christian tilted his head to look at her. "And aren't they?"

She shrugged. "I suppose. But Fred Lotting fixed my roof when it nearly collapsed after the snowstorm four years ago."

He frowned.

"Before you ask what he wanted in return, he did it because his wife said he should, and he adores the ground she walks upon. He doesn't even try to hide it. I've had men address me in an unwanted, unmannerly fashion before. It happens in Mayfair as much as it happens here. More, even."

"I see." He stopped in front of her house.

Not everything hurt. To discover that now, when so much had broken, seemed almost freeing.

"If I'd married," she said softly, "I would never know what I was capable of doing. It turns out that when you take away my kid gloves and my morning dresses, I can do quite a bit. This may sound ridiculous, but I'm proud of myself."

She climbed the steps.

She had intended to send him on his way, but when she opened the door, the entry had a view on her parlor. The events of that afternoon had seemed so distant that she'd almost put them out of her mind. But splintered wood and broken crockery were still spilled across the floor. She'd forgotten.

"Well," she said with as much faked brightness as she could manage. "Thank you very much. Good night."

"Really, Judith?" He shook his head in disgust and walked in. "It's almost as if I'm a complete stranger to you. You can't even move this much wood all on your own."

"Of course I can," she shot after his back. "No kid gloves. No morning dresses, if you recall?"

"Of course you can," he mimicked. "Just not easily. You do the crockery. I'll manage the wood."

Half the good plates were salvageable—just cracked and not actually shattered. There were two bowls, too, and almost all the wooden eatingware had survived. Her good tea service, though, had been on the top shelf. It had the farthest to fall.

And…

Christian set the last piece of her splintered hutch outdoors as she contemplated the one item that had been truly irreplaceable.

Her clockwork shepherdess with its dancing sheep. The china shepherdess was smashed beyond all possibility of repair. The base was in shards, and the inner clockwork was mangled, gears bent, springs broken.

He came to stand by her.

She remembered the day he'd given it to her. When she'd realized that he'd noticed her, really noticed her, and her imagination had built castles around the two of them. She hadn't been *wrong;* it was just that those castles existed in some other world, and she was living here.

Two of the sheep were unscathed. She gently pulled one off its little post.

"I can replace it," he said in a low voice, and she knew he was talking about more than the shepherdess.

"You can't."

"No, I can. I remember precisely where I got it. A visit, a little money, and…"

Judith felt suddenly tired. "You got it from Arthur Levitt," she said. "Four streets over, on Carlson Street. You can't replace it." She slid the sheep into her skirt pocket. "That first year, I sold everything I could. Gowns. Jewelry. Any property that hadn't been forfeited, I sold. I tried to sell the shepherdess back to Mr. Levitt six months after you asked me to marry you."

He inhaled.

"He wouldn't buy it," Judith said. "But he was very interested in the fact that I'd managed to make the sheep go backward. And when I showed him what I'd done, and how I'd managed it, he said he'd never seen the like. He offered to introduce me to a man he knew in Edinburgh, who arranged for the purchase of clockwork designs. It turns out that between my experience taking your shepherdess apart and that book you got me…" She shrugged. "Over the course of seven years, I made just over a thousand pounds."

He looked at her.

Not everything hurt.

"Mr. Levitt died six months ago. There really would have been nothing without his help," Judith said. "Instead, I made enough to send Benedict to school. Enough to set aside some money for my sisters. Some four hundred pounds apiece, sent anonymously because the only thing that would hurt their chances of some kind of decent marriage more than a lack of money would be having a sister who made that money in trade."

He hadn't looked away from her.

"There was a great deal of luck involved," Judith said. "But it's as I said. If I had married, there is much I would not have learned of myself. This has been hard and painful and horrible." She swallowed. "But I've learned that I'm stronger than hard, better than pain, and that with enough luck, horrible can go away."

"Judith."

She held out the second sheep to him. "Here," she said. "There's a reason I didn't tell you the full truth about the source of my sisters' money from the start."

"You thought I'd tell people the money was made in trade?"

She shook her head. "No. It's this: if you hadn't believed, long ago, that I deserved to take apart clockwork, I wouldn't be here. I didn't want to admit that I had any reason to be thankful to you. But... It doesn't hurt now. Thank you."

His hand closed. Not just around the sheep; around her fingers, clamping around them. He pulled her closer.

"This is a really, really, terrible idea," he said.

Her heart was pounding. "I know all about terrible." Her voice was a whisper. "Enough luck, enough time, and terrible..."

For a moment, it was if they stood in that apple orchard. As if all the years of hurt had washed away.

"Yes?" he asked. "What happens with enough time?"

She exhaled and looked up at him. "Even terrible turns to magic."

For a moment, he could not quite believe that he held her, that she was looking up at him with those wide, guileless eyes once more. It felt as if the empty years between them had vanished, as if they might start not with the new, but with the very, very old. The substance of what they'd been to each other had fallen into disrepair, but the foundation had been good. Hadn't it?

She rose up to him as he leaned down, her breath sighing. Their lips touched, and all the years disappeared in a moment of pure sweetness. It felt as blinding as the sun flashing across the clear water. Her lips were soft; her hand was warm in his. His other arm curled around her and she came to him, pressing against him, opening up to him.

Like that light glancing across the water, though, it did not take long to change. A minute, no more, until that first heady thrill of holding her, kissing her, gave way. Until he remembered her looking up at him and telling him she hated him.

Those eight years could not vanish, not with the first kiss, nor with the second. He remembered every one. Every night that first year, looking out his window and wondering how she did. Every night he'd imagined her coming to him. Every empty soirée he'd attended, every perfectly lovely young lady who would never do because she was not Judith. His hand slipped up her spine; her mouth opened to his.

Sweet gave way to bittersweet.

He couldn't erase those eight years for her, either. She'd put a good face on things—Judith always put a good face on things. But she had only conquered horrible because horrible first sought her out.

They couldn't kiss and forget. There was too much to remember on either side.

He took the sheep from her hand and set it on the table. Then he took her face in his hands and kissed her again.

"Judith," he said, "I wish I could take the shadows from your memory."

She looked up at him and shook her head. Her jaw shifted in the palm of his hand. God, he'd missed her so much. But the Judith he missed—the Judith of innocence and sunlight and orchards, the Judith to whom he'd handed half his soul, no longer existed.

This was the Judith of clockwork and rickety houses.

"You were right," Judith said. "We are more alike than I thought."

"How so?"

"I had thought to myself," she said, "that when you had to choose between me and your principles, you chose your principles." She reached up and touched his cheek. "I have just realized that I did the exact same thing to you. You asked me to choose you above my wounded heart, my pain, my pride, my love for my family. I didn't choose you either."

He let out a breath. "It's not comparable, Judith. The things you've lived with…"

"Maybe not. But I don't need to compare who has lost more to know I've hurt you. And if I hurt you a fraction as much as you…"

She stopped and shut her eyes.

Kissing her hurt. He did it again, letting himself feel every ounce of that pain. This, this is what they might have had. He might have had this tenderness without the accompanying shards of glass piercing his heart. He might have had this sweetness without regret or pain. He might have been able to kiss her without casting shadows.

He'd rather kiss her with shadows than not kiss her at all.

"This isn't going to work," Judith whispered as he kissed her again. "Too many things have broken between us. You can't trust someone with your soul twice."

"Maybe," Christian said. "But I'll help you pick up the pieces anyway."

She exhaled and leaned against him. The house creaked around them. She was here in his arms for now, at least.

"Thank you," she said. "Don't forget your sheep."

He smiled. "What do you mean by that, Fred?" he asked in a Cockney accent. "I never forget my sheep. How else are we to make Christmas jumpers for all the cygnets on the pond?"

There was a pause, and he could feel her shaking her head against his shoulder. But when she spoke, her voice was amused. "Christmas jumpers. Not Christmas jumpers again, Bill. Can't we just purchase sweets from the store like normal swans? You always buy the yarn; I always end up doing the knitting. My wings are getting tired."

No doubt they were. She'd faced down terrible, but from what he'd cleaned up today, and what she'd told him about Camilla, terrible kept coming back.

"Take a rest," Christian said. "This time, I've got it all in han—in wing." And he did. He knew precisely what he had to do.

She snorted at him. "I left a letter in your office," she said. "On accident. If you could send it back to me?"

"Of course." He reverted to his non-swan voice. "I'll be out of town for a little time on some business. If you need me, send a note to Jeffries and he'll cable me. I'll be back as soon as I can."

"And if I don't need you?"

"Send a note to Jeffries anyway," he said. "And he'll send it on to me, wherever I am."

"This isn't going to work," Judith said.

"I know. But…" Words failed him, and so instead of speaking, he pulled her close and kissed her again—one last time, one last kiss, drowning in the feel of her until he could scarcely breathe.

He let go only when it hurt too much to continue.

Chapter Nineteen

udith's head spun as she ascended the stairs. It felt as if today had been a year compressed by some housekeeper's trick to fit in the space of twenty-four hours. She'd lost one sister, found Christian, kissed him, and lost him yet again. She didn't know which direction was which, or what she should be doing.

She did know which direction she needed to address next: upstairs.

The bedrooms appeared dark as she ascended the creaking stairs. She checked on Benedict first. He was asleep, as best as she could tell, slumbering on his side under the covers. She opened the door to the room she shared with Theresa with more trepidation.

It looked like a cyclone had struck the room in her absence. Clothing had been yanked from the wardrobe and was strewn about the room, dangling over chairs and cavorting in piles on the floor. The blankets were piled high on the bed. Her sister clutched the edge of the pillow she held over her head. She might have been asleep...but as Judith was pondering the matter, Theresa turned, burrowing deeper into the bedclothes.

"Theresa," Judith said softly. "Tee."

Her sister didn't respond.

Judith sat next to her. "Tee, sweetheart. I'm sorry I shouted at you. I lost my temper. I shouldn't have done."

A sniffle met her.

"I love you, though," Judith said. "I will always love you, no matter how many cabinets you break, how many cats you bring home. I can't promise never to be angry with you, but I will still love you."

Her sister sniffed again, and then rearranged herself under the covers to curl against Judith's leg. Judith set her hand on the lump that was presumably Theresa's shoulder.

"I want so many things for you," Judith said. "I want you to be able to marry as well as you can."

Theresa didn't respond.

Not everything hurt, but one thing did. Judith looked at the anger, the bitterness that she'd carried for so long. She hadn't wanted to acknowledge any of it. But now…

"You were right, too," Judith said. "I am harder on you than on Benedict. In part, it's because you're…you. But also…" Her chest hurt thinking of it. "Our uncle offered to take in everyone but you. It wasn't your fault, sweetheart. You were six. But I think I've been unfair to you because of that. I've held it against you. Just a little, but it's always been there. I'm sorry. I'm going to do my best to let go."

Curious, how that admission lightened her heart. That ugliness that she'd tried to avoid… She remembered sitting by the stream after visiting her uncle, opening her hand in cold water. She felt as if it were all swirling away now.

"I'm sorry," she said again. "I love you. I wish you never had to worry about anything ever again."

A hand hooked over the edge of the blanket, and Theresa's face peered out.

"Judith," Theresa said, "I don't want to be a lady. You have to be a lady to not worry."

"Why don't you want to be a lady?"

Her sister looked away. "Because they have to sit still and smile."

Judith exhaled.

"Judith, do ladies make clockwork?"

"No." They didn't kiss men they weren't married to, either.

"So." Theresa pondered this. "Why do *I* have to be a lady if you don't?"

"Because I didn't have a choice," Judith said. "I did what I had to, for us to survive. I did what was best for you and Benedict. The truth is, I doubt I could ever go back, even if I wanted to do so."

"Oh."

"If my little clockwork habit came out, I'd be a terrible scandal. I haven't a choice."

"Oh." Theresa sounded a little too contemplative.

"I want you to have a choice," Judith said. "Because you might have a chance at so much more, if I keep out of the way and don't draw any scrutiny."

"A choice means I can choose not to be a lady," Theresa said.

"Yes. When you're of age."

Theresa inhaled. "I'm sorry, Judith," she finally said. "You're right. Is it…going to be dreadfully expensive to replace everything?"

"Dreadfully," Judith said. "But don't worry. You're going to help."

Theresa sat up. "How?"

"We're not buying bread for two months," Judith said. "You'll be making it instead."

Theresa fell bonelessly back against the covers, her pale hair spilling against the pillow. "Nooooo. I hate making bread."

Judith looked up at the ceiling. "We all do, Tee. But if you make bread, I'll have more time for my clockwork, and the money must come from somewhere."

"Wait." Theresa looked at her slyly. "Do ladies have to make bread?"

"Yes," Judith said decisively. "When ladies make a big smashing mess, they make bread."

"Damn."

"Theresa?"

"I know," Theresa said. "Ladies don't swear."

"Well. I'm glad you're aware, at least."

Theresa shrugged. "I'll stop, if I decide to be a lady."

"It doesn't work like that," Judith said. "I started swearing on waterfowl when I was eleven, and now I can't manage the real thing. Not even when I really, really need it."

"Well, then," Theresa said hopefully. "I definitely won't copy you. I'll swear on pig meat instead. What kind of fool wants to spend the rest of their life saying, 'Duck you all!' when you can say 'Ham it!' instead?"

"Goose." Judith mussed her sister's hair. "You shouldn't be able to make that joke. By the way, what happened with your clothing?"

Theresa frowned, and then looked around the room, as if seeing her stockings strewn over chairs for the first time.

"Oh, that," she said matter-of-factly. "I was going to run away from home because you didn't want me, but I had no way to put all the cats on leads. And then I got tired trying to gather them up, because they will *not* stay in one place, and there wasn't enough milk, and then I realized that I couldn't carry enough potatoes for more than a single meal if I wanted to bring extra stockings. Which I did, because extra stockings are an absolute necessity. I accidentally fell asleep until I heard you come home. Then there was nothing to do but hide."

Judith exhaled slowly. "Don't run away," she said, kissing the top of her sister's head. "And if you do, please have a plan for the future beyond potatoes."

"I would have brought salt."

"Oh, well." Judith shrugged. "That's good then. Salt makes everything better. Now scoot over. You have to leave some room for me."

Theresa moved over—nominally—as Judith dressed for bed.

But when Judith blew out her candle and climbed in bed, there was one last question.

"Judith," Theresa said, "When you were gone, Benedict said Anthony wasn't really...didn't really...that he wasn't..."

"Dead?" Judith asked.

"Yes." Her sister's voice was small.

No. Not another year of this. Judith rolled on her side and attempted to pat her sister's shoulder.

"Ow!"

"Sorry."

"Don't worry. It's dark. I shan't need my eye until morning."

Judith settled for a comforting noise rather than risk blinding her sister permanently. "Did Benedict say why he thought Anthony was alive?"

"Because he couldn't be dead. He just couldn't be."

Judith inhaled. "Theresa. If you're *not* going to be a lady, if you want to keep that as a choice, you're going to have to be able to look reality face on. You can't let what you *want* to believe influence you. Only ladies are allowed to believe comforting falsehoods. So tell me truly: do you think 'he couldn't be dead' is a good enough reason to explain away eight years of silence?"

Theresa inhaled. "No," she said in a small voice. "No, I don't." There was a longer pause. "Do I still have to make bread? I have just come to the conclusion that my elder brother has perished. I'm inconsolable."

Judith let out a long, tortured breath. "Really, Tee? You couldn't wait ten seconds before trying to mercilessly exploit Anthony's death to get out of punishment?"

"Well, if you're going to say it like *that,* of *course* I'll look like a grasping hag. But...ugh. Bread. One ought to be allowed to grasp haglike when bread is on the line."

Finding one nineteen-year-old woman should not have posed so great a difficulty.

For the third time that week, Christian told himself that he should have sent a man. That tramping about the streets of Bath on his own was a foolish waste of his efforts. But every time his rational mind offered this up—usually accompanied by a little footnote indicating that it was not too late to avoid the crowds, the invitations, and the incessant complaints over the waters, by the simple act of delegation—he imagined finding Lady Camilla. Perhaps she'd be attached to another elderly lady here in Bath. He knew her. He knew what she looked like. Nobody in his employ did.

It wasn't rational, but he could hardly bring himself to delegate this task, however annoying it was. And today he was reminded of precisely how annoying it could be. He was ensconced in the grand pump room, of all places. In the time of George's regency, the salon had been the height of grandeur. It had not changed since, and its age was beginning to show. A statue of some man who had died a century past, and whose greatest claim to fame had apparently been his fashion sense, stood in an alcove. Water came out of a serpent-headed pump that looked to be almost as old as the Roman empire.

Given the work recently done by John Snow and Louis Pasteur, Christian suspected that a central repository of aging water was more likely to be a hotbed of disease than health. But then, nobody had asked him.

"My granddaughter," the elderly woman next to him was saying, "Louise—after our dear Prince Consort's mother—but of course he passed away. What was I saying? My dear Louise would be a charming lady for you to meet. I had been thinking of sending for her; perhaps you might be interested in the introduction? Will you still be here?"

"Perhaps," Christian said, keeping his tone as politely noncommittal as he could manage. "Although I am here on business, and I may be called away just as swiftly."

Mrs. Wallace tapped a finger against her glass. "A shame," she said. "You know, it occurs to me that you could use someone competent to help you manage your schedule. My granddaughter—"

He couldn't help himself. He laughed. "Madam, I think you could sell a carriage to a sea tortoise."

Her eyes glinted. "Yes. Well. She *is* my seventeenth granddaughter, if you can believe such a thing, and I've popped all the others off. Three of them twice over. I can't wait until she's married and done with. When you've grandchildren to be married, you can scarcely take advantage of your dotage. No saying whatever you think; no shaking your fist and decrying all the things that are changing in the world. As soon as she's properly tied up, I'll be free to be the dragon I've always dreamed I could be." She sighed wistfully. "Ah. To tell everyone what the world was like in my day! To bemoan every last mother-loving alteration as if it were the end of days. Trains! Postage stamps! Stockings from machines! Harrumph! Until then, I must pretend I won't be the horrid relation by marriage you won't be able to escape. It's all smiles and 'Would you like to meet my granddaughter? She's a sweet girl.'"

"As an outside observer," Christian said. "I honestly wish you every success."

"She really is a sweet girl," Mrs. Wallace persisted. "Nothing like me. And never mind all the girls in the family—there's almost as many boys, too. We just produce and produce and produce. Like rabbits, but smarter and in smaller batches." She considered this. "And less gamey, I would imagine, although I have not yet put this to the test."

"Ah, well." Christian shrugged. "If she's not like you, I have no interest whatsoever."

"Flatterer." Her eyes narrowed. "You must want something from me. Maybe we can trade. My granddaughter for...?"

"I'm here, in fact, to inquire about the past. You were friends with Miss Abigail Troworth, were you not?"

"I was. I still miss her."

"She had a companion. A young girl. She would have been around fifteen at the time."

"No." Mrs. Wallace shook her head. "She absolutely didn't."

"Perhaps she would not have brought her about everywhere. But I am positive that Lady Camilla Worth was her companion."

"Angela Burbury was her companion, and she was fifty years of age." Mrs. Wallace frowned. "But... Camilla? *Lady* Camilla?"

"Yes."

Her frown deepened. "Tall thing? Skinny? Freckled? Dark hair, brown eyes?"

"Yes," Christian said. "So you *do* know her."

"She had a lady's maid named Camilla," Mrs. Wallace returned. "Something of a maid-of-all-work, actually. But not a lady. Surely not a lady, for all she could ape proper speech."

Christian didn't say anything.

"Camilla Worth. Oh, dear. That was the family name of the Earl of Linney, was it not? That...unfortunate one who..."

She looked over at him and her lips pressed together.

"Her father was a traitor," Christian said. "That doesn't mean she should be passed around and used as a maid."

"No, no." The woman shook her head. "I am quite in agreement. I hate to think that is what happened—but." Her frown grew. "She said something once. I am afraid—no, I am certain." Her fingers tapped on the table in front of her in agitation. "This is why I hate the present. One is always learning dreadful things that rather destroy one's appreciation of the past. When I was twenty, and I learned how sugar was made, I was most angry. I had not realized that sweets were so barbaric, and after that, I could never again appreciate a good biscuit." She looked upward and shook her fist at the painted ceiling. "Damn you, knowledge! Ruining everything good, once again. Learning things is most inconvenient."

It was likely less convenient, Christian suspected, to be the girl pressed into service. Or the slave who died producing white sugar.

"Do you happen to know where Lady Camilla went?"

"Ah." Mrs. Wallace set her fingers to her temples. "I believe she went to Edwina Hastings, who lived here temporarily for her husband's health. But then he died, thank God, and she went back to her mother's people in Sussex. I believe that Ca—Lady Camilla, that is, went with the household. She was said to be good with children."

Of course she had been.

Of course Judith had been in tears over what had happened to her sister. He could hardly blame her.

"Have you Mrs. Hasting's direction?" he asked.

She had.

Chapter Twenty

hen Christian sat down to write to Judith on the train to Sussex, he had at first intended to let her know everything he had discovered.

Somehow, however, his starts all became false starts.

Dear Judith,

Good news! Your sister is possibly not dead, although I won't be certain until—

No. That was not the way to write this letter. He crumpled the paper, tossed it to the side, and started once more.

Dear Judith,

It appears that Miss Troworth in Bath did not quite claim Camilla as a companion. Instead, she used her as something of an unpaid servant. But on the plus side, the family who hired her thereafter may have intended to give her wages, so—

Not that either. A second ball of paper joined the first on the floor of the train carriage.

Dear Judith,

I've been reading your brother's journals. You'll be delighted to know that I was indeed overly optimistic in imagining what I might make of these names. Your brother was neither stupid nor ineffective. While I can discover everyone who violated England's treaty with China, the more names I add to the list, the more I realize that I was foolish to imagine something could be done to held these men accountable. The small traders, perhaps, but some of these men are at the highest levels of government. I cannot imagine them being held to account.

What this means, I cannot say. In other news, your sister is still missing, so sorry, and...

No. He couldn't say any of that, either.

Dear Judith,

I have discovered where your sister was four years ago, and with any luck, she might still be in service—

Dear Judith,

I've slept properly for the first time in months. It turns out, I was wrong. I didn't need your brother's journals. I needed a better plan. I—

Dear Judith,

Have you noticed that I have an unfortunate propensity to make the worst possible joke at the worst possible instant?

Well. I've been researching Camilla's whereabouts, and I have absolutely nothing to say, so... Who was Shakespeare's greatest chicken-killer?

No. Even I can't continue after that. I give this letter up in disgust.

He settled on this:

Dear Judith,

My business is taking me longer than I had expected. I know you had a great many matters still pending when last we...

Talked? Kissed?

...saw one another. Please let me know if I can be of service.

Yours truly,

Christian Trent

Marquess of Ashford

Her reply made its way to him not in Sussex, but in Gloucester, where Mrs. Edwina Hastings had gone after remarrying.

Dear Christian,

Everything is as well as can be expected. It has only been five days, and I am entirely competent to manage my affairs for that length of time. We have shelter; we have bread. The latter is terrible, but I do what I must in the name of pedagogical soundness.

Thank you for your inquiry.

Judith Worth

Mistress of half the upper-floor bedroom

Dear Judith,

I see we're making a snail's progress: Climb two feet up the wall, slide down one while we're resting. I certainly didn't mean to imply any incompetence on your part. But as a personal matter, I've found that issues are easier dealt with when discussed with friends, instead of borne individually.

Try it; you might like it.

Christian

Master of all I see

(Particularly when my eyes are shut)

Dear Bill,

If you must know, I had been missing your advice—however ridiculous it is—with regards to my younger brother. He has suggested numerous occupations he might take on in lieu of returning to that group of youngsters who proclaimed him an ugly duckling.

To wit: He wants to join the Navy.

Or possibly, to just own a boat and/ or ship of some sort. (They are apparently not the same thing.)

Or maybe, he prefers to simply run away. He and his sister have had lengthy conversations on this exact point, which I find increasingly disturbing. Young swans these days haven't any sense whatsoever.

Any advice to give?

Yours,

Fred

Left pond, amongst the algae

My dearest Fred,

Young swans never have any sense, unfortunately. But luckily, they rarely have follow-through, either. Let him dream whatever he wishes for a few days, then demand that he figure out everything that must be done to achieve his dreams.

Chances are, the paperwork will catch him up.

Yours truly,

Bill

Dear Christian,

You were right. I assigned Benedict reading on trade routes, and he is currently complaining that everything is too difficult. It turns out, Newton is correct: Objects at rest tend to remain at rest, and twelve-year-old-boys are even more resistant to motion than regular matter.

Huzzah!

I have been so centered on my own worries that I have forgotten to inquire about your business. How goes it?

Judith

Dear Judith,

Well, I spent all yesterday walking to a town just north of Warwick. The stream had flooded, and while I could get past on the makeshift raft they'd rigged, the horses I'd hired from the station could not. It turns out that the man I'd needed to see was in Trowbridge, though, but the time wasn't wasted.

There were a great many ducks present, there to cavort in the flooded stream, and I passed the hours pleasantly thinking of you.

I was going to work in a joke about how I missed your mallard-dictions, but written down, it doesn't have quite the same flare. Maledictions. Mallard-dictions. It doesn't even look right. Some jokes just don't work in print, which is why I have nonetheless tried to render it here so you can laugh at my cleverness. Or abuse my stupidity.

Whichever brings you more joy.

In any event, I have high hopes for this fellow outside of Trowbridge. It can't be long now, and then I'll be back. Perhaps we might talk then.

Yours,
Christian

Judith knew she should not let herself dream.

Yet as she walked down the Mayfair street, she could feel herself wanting to do so. It was as if someone had attached a hot air balloon to her spirits and lifted them a hundred feet in the air despite her better impulses.

After weeks of friendly conversation—weeks of trying not to remembering his kiss, and failing utterly—Christian had sent a note around late last night.

Back in town. Need to see you. Can you come by in the afternoon? I'll send the carriage.

She'd told the boy there was no reason to send anything. But those words—*need to see you*—had somehow burrowed under her skin. They'd given her steps an extra spring. They'd felt like a cool breeze in the midst of a sweltering heat. It was all an indication of just how far she'd let her standards fall, that she *smiled* at the thought of Christian *needing* to see her the day he returned to London.

Don't, whispered her rational mind. *Don't believe. This is foolish.*

But the sun was shining and the skies were blue, and as foolish as it would be to construct a daydream about a future with Christian, rejecting her current happiness would be rather like throwing away perfectly good bread because children were starving in St. Giles.

Why not enjoy what she had while she could?

God. Bread. She was happy enough that even the thought of perfectly good bread—warm and fragrant, smelling of yeast and slathered with butter, instead of a hard, scarcely chewable lump that vaguely resembled coal in taste and texture—could not destroy her mood.

She smiled as she rapped on the door to Christian's home. She grinned as she ascended the steps to his office behind the butler. And when he stood for her as the door opened...

She'd forgotten what it was like to smile because someone else was smiling, to feel that they were linked, that his delight was her joy.

She'd missed him. His hair was in messy, dark curls, but he looked…rested, perhaps, was the right word for it. More at peace than she'd seen him.

She couldn't help but smile, and he apparently could not help but smile back. She might have basked in his smile for hours.

She was in desperate straits and she couldn't bring herself to care.

"Lord Ashford." She nodded at him.

"Lady Judith." His eyes rested on her. He'd looked at her precisely like that when he'd seen her on the street after eight years. But he'd not smiled, not like this.

He gestured to the seat in front of his desk. "Do you want anything to eat?"

"Real bread," she said immediately.

He blinked. "Not scones? Not biscuits?"

She shut her eyes and shook her head. "Real bread. Warm bread. Soft, but with a good, crisp crust. The kind where you can just sink your teeth into it and…and eat it."

A silence fell on the room, and she opened one eye to see Christian watching her.

"You're passionate about bread, all of a sudden."

"Theresa has been making punishment bread."

"Ah." He touched on his cravat, loosening it a little as if uncomfortable.

"The least said on the subject," Judith said primly, "the better. I am not going to give in and let her off her punishment. But I will eat your bread."

"I would never deny you the opportunity to eat my bread," he said in a rough voice.

"With butter?" Judith offered innocently. "Because I do love a good hot loaf, particularly when it has been lovingly caressed with a touch of butter, freshly churned."

He made an inarticulate noise.

"Sometimes," Judith confided, "I like to spread a layer of butter on my bread and then lick it—"

"Oh my God," Christian said, clapping a hand to his forehead. "You're doing it on *purpose.*"

She laughed. "Talking about how I'd like to lick your butter? Why, yes. I am. I always used to talk of food with you. Do you find it strange that I should do so now?"

"But…" He looked upward. "You were…back then. You were young. Innocent." He swallowed. "You used to eat strawberries…"

"Do nineteen-year-olds not eat?" She batted her eyes at him innocently.

He shut his eyes. "There was one time over breakfast when you were enjoying it. You were really enjoying it. I was uncomfortable. You asked me if something was wrong with the seat on my chair. You offered to come over and make me comfortable."

"I remember."

"I…just…" He looked over at her. "Were you doing it on purpose then, too?"

"For God's sake, Christian." She smiled. "I was nineteen, not stupid. Half my friends were already married. I tried to get you to kiss me for half the summer."

He made a choking noise.

"And you were so adorable," she continued, "trying so hard not to say anything. I thought you *knew.*"

"If you had any notion how much discomfort you caused me…"

"Then I wouldn't have changed a thing," Judith said.

His eyes met hers. "I wouldn't have wanted you to do so."

He rang a bell. When the servant appeared, he asked for bread and butter and lemonade.

"So," he said, as they waited for the servant to return. "I didn't ask you here to talk about food."

"No?"

"I asked you to talk about what I've done these last two weeks."

Judith looked up at him.

"I went to Bath to find your sister," he said. "I knew if I asked about I could find word of her."

She could feel her skin getting cold. "But you wrote me from Sussex. And Warwick. And…"

He nodded solemnly. "And all the other places I didn't tell you about."

"And she's not with you." Judith swallowed. "Dare I hope that…" But she couldn't complete her sentence. She was afraid to hope.

He shook his head. "But it's not as dire as it sounds. I found out where she was not two months ago. I believe that wherever she is, she is safe."

Her heart began to pound. Not swiftly, nor vehemently, but like a clock ticking just a little more loudly. Her throat felt dry. "Where was she?"

"Just outside Trowbridge. She was staying with the local miller. By all accounts, yes, she was acting as an unpaid servant."

Judith felt her hand clench into a fist.

"A rector who was traveling through found her, recognized her, and took pity on her. He took her in."

"Who was it?"

Christian made a face. "There things become murky once again. His last name started with a P. But don't look at me like that. The Church of England keeps records. There aren't that many rectors who could answer to that description, and traveling through that area? That limits it quite a bit. I came back to London because we can find her more easily from here. It's simply a matter of time and proper advertising."

"No." She wasn't sure if it was a denial or an agreement.

"Judith." He leaned forward. "We've almost found her. I've talked to people who saw her two months ago. She was well; they said she was happy. All we need to do is find this P-something fellow. We can advertise; I didn't want to do that without your permission. But we can find your sister. I assure you, you mustn't give up hope now."

"I haven't." Judith looked up at him. She was hoping more than she should. "I can maintain hope," she said quietly.

"Good. Because I'm not finished. I told you my solicitor had promised to do research on that one pesky question regarding your Mr. Ennis. The research is completed."

"Oh?"

"The answer is: nothing. They found nothing. Not one precedent that would lead to this behavior on your solicitor's part. No explanation."

"That sounds utterly awful. Why are you smiling?"

"Because that is the answer," Christian said. "I know you feel some degree of loyalty to your Mr. Ennis, but with that research in hand, you can go to him and threaten him with exposure. *Agh* is not some novel legal theory on his part. It was an admission of guilt."

Judith exhaled. She hadn't wanted to believe it. She still didn't.

"I don't believe you'll even have to bring suit against him," Christian said. "Your problem is solved."

The problem was solved. Solved, by discovering another person Judith could no longer trust?

Mallards.

But life was what it was. She'd lost Mr. Ennis. But perhaps she'd gained…

Christian was still smiling at her. She looked at him—really looked at him. "Christian. I thought you were away on *business.*"

"And so I was."

She turned to him. "I thought you were away on your own business. Something that was important."

His eyes met hers. Her heart was pounding a rhythm in her chest. "And so," he said slowly, "I was."

The door to the office opened and a maid in a brown uniform entered. "Here you are, my lord." She set a tray on the table.

It was bread. It had been sliced by the kitchen into thick, uniform slices. Warm. Steaming. How she'd had the luck to arrive when a freshly baked loaf was ready, Judith would never know.

"Thank you," Christian said, as Judith hoped her stomach did not gurgle too offensively. "That will be all."

Oh, to live in a world where one might order bread, real bread, and have it arrive in ten minutes.

You could live in that world.

Judith didn't want to think of it yet.

Christian slid the tray toward her end of the table. "Don't just stare. Have some."

She wanted so many things. Her sister back with her. An answer to her questions. Bread. The last was right here. There was no resisting any longer. Judith took a slice. It was hot in her hands, lovely and perfectly warming.

"Ohhhh." She shut her eyes and inhaled yeast. There was no point attempting to be articulate about good bread.

"Don't let me stop you," he said.

She picked up a knife. "Ha. As if you could." She dipped the utensil in the butter, so perfectly soft and spreadable. "I would stab you," she added by way of explanation.

"That knife is rather blunt."

She set it down and lifted the bread to her mouth. Her mouth watered; her teeth yearned to sink into it.

"Luckily," Judith said, "I have a great deal of experience with knives in need of sharpening. Hack away at anything long enough, and it will get the job done."

She took a bite. Oh, God. *Bread.* The difference between dry, indigestible leatherlike biscuit and real, soft, salivation-worthy bread was air, nothing but air trapped in perfect little pockets.

Air was *delicious.*

Salt tickled her tongue. The bread was warm and yeasty, the crust tearing in her teeth. She let out a moan.

"Oh," Christian said. "Just stab me now and be done with it."

She smirked at him. "Do you want me to go over there and make you comfortable?"

"Oh, for God's sake," he muttered. "Do you think I'll say no to that a second time? Yes. *Yes.*"

She did not set her bread down; she was not so selfless. Instead, she stood, kicked off her slippers, and made her way around the desk. He sat in place, watching her. Judith took another bite of bread. The crust had been baked to a perfect caramel, with just that hint of crisp sweetness.

Christian reached for a slice.

She set her hand on top of his. "No," she told him. "You gave it to me. It's my bread now."

"Is it?" he murmured. "What a shame."

"You know how it works when you want to eat someone else's bread," she told him. "You *ask*."

He looked at her lips and exhaled slowly. "May I have a taste, please?"

Judith held out her slice, bringing it to his mouth. His eyes met hers as he leaned forward and took a bite.

"It's good."

"*Good* is heresy," Judith said. "It's excellent."

"Not quite." He looked over at her. "You should know that I won't believe anything is truly excellent until I'm sure you've had your share."

"My share." Her voice sounded extremely quiet in the room.

"I've always been keen on giving it to you," he said. His eyes met hers. They were laughing, but this was no joke.

This was how Eve had been tempted. Not with an apple, although Judith never said no to a good apple. Not with anything so mundane. She'd been tempted with the promise of heat and salt and all the things she'd never known.

"Come here," he said, "and I'll show you."

She sank onto his lap. His arm came around her—and he took the bread. "Here." He held it out to her and she took a bite.

"God, yes," he whispered. "Have the rest."

She did, and when she finished, she licked butter off his fingers. His hand tightened around her waist. His eyes met hers and he leaned in, so that she could rest her forehead against him. "Might I have a taste, Judith?"

His breath whispered against her lips.

"Yes," she said quietly. "Please."

He let out a long sigh and then shifted up, melding their mouths together. He tasted of bread and lemonade, of hope and want and innocence all at once, of all the things she'd once believed and never allowed herself to feel.

He kissed her and she wanted. His hands slid to her shoulders. "Might I touch?"

She set her fingers on top of his, encouraging his hand to slide under the neckline of her gown. "Wherever you wish."

And then his mouth was back on hers. He pulled her close and as he kissed her, he undid the front buttons of her gown. His lips slid from her mouth to her chin. Her throat. He tasted her collarbone. And then his hands loosened her front-facing corset laces, sliding the heavy fabric away, before finding the hard nub of her nipple through the shift.

Pleasure rippled through her. "Oh, God," Judith whispered. "Don't stop. There. More."

Obligingly, he set his mouth to that sensitive spot—tasting, first with lips, then with the tip of his tongue. The sweet feel of his touch built inside her. She wanted more, needed more. Her hands went to his shoulders. She shifted to straddle him, pressing her hips against his. She could feel the length of him, hard and long, could feel his hips press up against her. It was necessary to feel him more—harder—against her.

"Judith," he murmured. "Oh, for God's sake. Judith."

"Don't stop."

"Let me help you more, sweetheart."

His hand slipped under her skirt, up her legs, caressing her as he went. His touch whispered against her petticoats, sliding them aside until he found the wetness between her thighs. He stroked her there, softly at first, and then a little less softly.

Touch was an act of trust. To let herself open for him. To let him bring her to this point. To allow herself to accept this, to accept him, to call out his name as her body clenched around his fingers, harder, tighter.

Touch was an act of trust, and somehow, she'd come to trust him. She let go and let her pleasure take her.

When she opened her eyes, he was watching her with a small smile on his face.

"Do you want more?" he asked.

More. More would mean more *him*. It would mean even more vulnerability, when trust was so new between them.

She ducked her head. "I'm not sure I could manage more at the moment."

He kissed her.

"What of you, Christian?"

He gave her a pained smile. "I've had my share for now."

She pulled back and ran her fingers down the front of his trousers. "Have you? I'm not actually naïve, Christian."

He exhaled. "Oh, damn it."

"Damn what?" She brushed the palm of her hand against the hard rod of his cock through his trousers.

"This isn't a quid pro quo. I don't want you doing anything simply because you feel grateful—"

She cut him off with a kiss. "I want to know."

"What it's like?"

"No." She ran her hand down the front of his trousers again. "I want to know if after all of this, we might trust each other again. If there's any hope at all..."

His hand found hers and pressed them to his buttons. "Then find out," he said on a low growl. "Please."

She released one button and then a second. A third. The fourth and final one, and then she could peel away his trousers and slide her hand against his skin.

He let out a gasp as she did. "God. Judith."

Trust. Running her forefinger down his hard member did not seem an act of trust, not until his hand found her knee. Until she heard his breath catch and felt him stiffen even further under her touch. He was hard and yet so vulnerable, all at once. His hand clenched against her waist.

This was trust: to give her pleasure over to another, and to believe that they would both gain in the process. She ran her finger down his length.

"Oh, God." His hand found hers. "Hold me. Like this."

This was trust: to tighten her grip around his hot shaft, to learn from the noises he made, the thrust of his hips. To exult in the feel of him, steel-hard and wanting. To know that she had brought him to this point.

His hand covered hers as she stroked the length of him. He let out a little moan, and then another.

"What do you want me to do?" she asked.

"Here." His fingers indicated. "Like this. Like—oh, God, yes."

He was hot to the touch, and as she slid her hand down his member, he became hotter still. His cock jumped, and she felt a swirl of pride, accomplishment, and the burning heat of exultation that she had done this to him. He grabbed a serviette from the tray at the last minute, spilling into it.

For a long moment, they looked into each other's eyes.

Then he put his arm around her and rested his head against her.

It had all happened swiftly—too swiftly, perhaps. There was still so much unspoken between them. But he'd been right. He was the one person who had understood the way that she'd been hurt, and she couldn't dredge up the slightest inkling of regret.

"Some time ago," Christian said, leaning forward to brush a finger against her cheek, "I asked you to not let me hope."

She exhaled.

"I was wrong. Let me hope. Please, let me hope." His hand caught hers.

After everything, it turned out that Judith still hadn't lost the ability to chase castles in the sky. If she could believe she could fall in love with Christian again, she could believe anything.

Hope seemed new and fragile—so fragile that she feared any further discussion.

Still, she kissed him again. "Hope," she whispered. "I'm learning how to do it myself."

Chapter Twenty-One

The house smelled of bread when Judith returned. Real bread. Yeasty bread. Mouth-watering bread, the kind she'd just had at Christian's house. The sort she'd never eat again without thinking of him and his mouth and his fingers and his promises.

What that delicious smell was doing in Judith's house, she had no idea.

Clearly something had gone terribly…right? She was unused to the possibility.

Judith walked through the parlor into the kitchen.

Theresa and Benedict stood in front of a loaf. A perfect, round loaf of bread. The only reason Judith knew it wasn't store-bought was the color—a light chocolate instead of golden-brown.

It seemed out of place in a house that had until now been the site of so much baking infamy.

"Theresa." She stepped into the room. "This looks lovely. What did you do?"

Theresa jumped and turned to her. "Judith. So, um. Yesterday. I may have added too much water to one of my loaves. I *meant* to clean it up, but, uh."

This was not what Judith had expected to hear. She blinked. "I didn't see bowls in need of washing."

Theresa waved this off. "Of course you didn't. I hid them from you until I could clean up. I'm not a complete imbecile, you know."

"Well, that's a...um." Delight? Pleasure? Stabbing headache? Judith wasn't sure how to finish the sentence.

Theresa bulled on with her explanation. "So. Then, early this morning, I saw it and panicked. It was this big mass of stringy yeast, cobwebby and, uh. Extremely disgusting." She looked at her sister. "So I punched it down and promised I would clean it out later."

"I...see."

"No point wasting your time on pointless explanations! I forgot about it again. The dough got really huge, and I never did knead it at all, and there was too much water and my bread is always terrible, so how could this really be any worse? So I decided to save time, and I just tossed it in the oven. And..." Theresa spread her hands. "This happened. It's got to taste terrible, but it looks like real bread. *Actual* bread."

"It really does." Benedict prodded it. "I am suspicious."

"Oh, I am, too. It's a miracle. It's as if my laziness and my impatience procreated and gave birth to a loaf of perfect bread."

Benedict shook his head. "I'm not sure that's a likely explanation."

"True." Theresa frowned. "Let us not consider the mechanics of how that procreation might occur. It sounds utterly disgusting."

"No." Benedict grimaced. "Virgin birth."

"Virgin birth," Theresa agreed. "Now, shall we try our miracle?"

Judith got a knife. The crust was a little dark, but the bread beneath let out a gust of steam as she sliced. It was the color of pale wheat inside, fluffy with the kind of air pockets one found only in the finest breads.

"Things should not go this well," Theresa said. "The course of good bread never did run smoothly. Or whatever it was that Shakespeare said. I'm sure he said something about bread."

"I'm sure he did." Judith nodded. He'd said something about chickens, after all.

"On second thought." Theresa frowned. "Now that I think of it, 'evil elves bewitched my bread' seems a more likely explanation. You all stand back—I'm going to eat this evil elf bread. If it turns me into a donkey, please don't sell me for less than fifty pounds."

She took the heel of the loaf and bit into it. A curious expression passed over her face as she chewed. She swallowed. Her eyes bulged, and then rolled upward. She twitched a few times, let out a choking noise, and collapsed to the floor in a boneless heap.

Judith's heart stopped. "Oh my God. Theresa." She fell to the floor beside her, fumbling to loosen her corset, raising her hand to her lips to see if her sister was still breathing—

Her sister's eyes popped open. "Needs salt," she said.

Judith stared into her sister's eyes for a moment, her heart racing in misplaced panic. Theresa had faked her death. Judith should have *known* she was faking it.

Judith grabbed a towel off the table. "Wait." She set one hand on her sister's head as her sister tried to sit up. "Wait. Lie back. I think something's wrong. Really wrong."

"What?" Theresa frowned.

"There's something on your tongue. Let me see it."

Slowly, Theresa stuck out her tongue.

"Further," Judith said. "It's right—" She kept her expression sincerely afraid, and Theresa's eyebrows rose in mirrored trepidation. Judith flexed her fingers beneath the towel and leaned forward. "It's here."

Before Theresa could react, Judith reached out and grabbed her sister's tongue through the towel. Theresa tried to pull away, but the cloth held her tongue firmly in place.

"Hey! What aw you do-egg?" Theresa exclaimed through the towel.

"Holding your tongue," Judith said. "You said it literally couldn't be done. It can. Never doubt me."

Her sister flapped her arms. "That'th got fair!"

"Nothing's fair," Judith said cheerfully, relinquishing the cloth.

Theresa sat up. "That was *brilliant*. I didn't know you could hold tongues like that. Here, let me try."

Behind them, Benedict just shook his head. "You two are missing all the bread. It's wonderful. Not enough salt, but…" His face suddenly went blank. "Oh. *Yes.*"

"Everything is better with salt," Theresa said with a nod.

Benedict stood up. "Everything is better with salt."

"Everything is better with salt," Judith agreed. "Why are we all saying that everything is better with salt?"

"Because." Benedict smiled, a bright wide smile. "Don't you understand? Everything is better with salt."

"Yes," Judith said. "We all know. But—"

"Everything is better with salt!" He pumped a fist in the air. "Theresa, Judith—we've figured it out. Don't you see? Everything is better with salt. And do you know how to make something even better than adding salt?"

Judith frowned. "No?"

Benedict cackled. "More salt!"

aisy!" Never had Judith been so happy as to see her friend waiting for her on the way to the market as she was the next morning. "I wasn't sure you would be here."

It had been a while since Daisy met her, and Judith had begun to worry. Her friend raised an eyebrow and held out a gloved hand. "The queen's visit was inconvenient, taxing, and *incredibly* boring—talking of matters of state does become *so* tedious. But while I feared I would perish of yawning, there was little danger."

"Are you settled in, then?"

"My mother and I are sharing a room, yes," Daisy sniffed. "It's closer to the seaside. The fresh air will do her good."

The docks, Daisy meant, which were hardly a source of fresh air. Still, Judith was relieved to hear her friend was well. Or at least not out on the streets.

She must not have hid these thoughts, because Daisy took her hand. "We're as well as can be," she said in a lower voice. "We've less space, but it's a blessing. With what you gave us, we'll have a nice, comfortable purse to hold on to, in case of difficulties. I won't have you worrying over me, Judith."

"Why not? I care."

"I know." Daisy squeezed her hand. "But worrying and pining never changed anything. Make me laugh instead."

"Theresa made bread," Judith said.

"Goodness." Daisy lapsed back into the game. "She is quite the accomplished young lady, is she not?"

"Well, up until yesterday," Judith said, "I had thought she was practicing the trade of brick-making." She went on to tell the whole story—embellishing, of course, the kittens into exotic cats, the crockery into priceless vases, and the punishment bread into... Well, the punishment bread needed no embellishment. It was embellished enough on its own. Daisy laughed the whole way to the market.

"And now I need to purchase ginger, ginger, flour, salt, and more ginger," Judith said.

"And gold leaf?"

"And concentrated citrate of magnesia," Judith said. "Really. Please don't ask about it."

Things must not have been altogether dire for her friend, because she purchased a ham hock in addition to her potatoes and parsley.

"So," Daisy said slyly on the way home. "Tell me about your marquess."

"My...what?" She hadn't told Daisy about Christian. Had she?

Oh. She had.

"Your *marquess*," Daisy said, exaggerating the word, as if to remind her that this was part of the game.

"Oh, Daisy." Judith shook her head. "I don't want to talk of him."

"No? Because Crash said he'd accompanied you home the other night."

"Since when are you speaking with Crash?"

Daisy flushed. "Since never. Just enough to be polite. You know Crash. One cannot put him off."

"Really? What did he do?"

"One cannot put me off, either." Daisy said with a faint smile. "Tell me. Come, come, come. I could use a little vicarious romance."

"Daisy."

"Or a little vicarious business, if that's all it is."

"He's—" But the lie died on her tongue.

She couldn't keep lying to Daisy—or at least, she couldn't keep telling her the truth in the guise of a lie.

But maybe... Maybe not everything needed to hurt. She looked over at her friend.

"I have a confession."

Daisy smiled. "Oh, I *love* confessions!"

"No. A real confession." Judith swung her basket heavily. "He... He really is a marquess." The words came out all in a rush. "His name is Christian Trent. He's the fifth Marquess of Ashford. He was my elder brother's best friend, and he wanted to marry me before we came here."

"There," Daisy said. "It will be all right. You'll see."

"Don't. Don't you comfort me." She looked over at Daisy. "You don't understand. I'm not making any of this up. My father was the Earl of Linney. He committed suicide after he'd been convicted of treason."

Daisy blinked at her.

"I didn't tell you. When we first met, it wasn't the time. It was too new to speak about. And then we started our game, and it's all felt like a lie ever since. You trusted me the other night with your secrets, and I haven't trusted you with mine. I'm sorry. So sorry. I should have explained—"

"Well, of course I know all that," Daisy said. "I'm not stupid. And people do gossip."

Judith came to a halt. "Oh. Well. I suppose that makes...sense."

Daisy looked upward. "While we're making confessions, I had intimate relations with Crash. Almost a year ago. I'm embarrassed. I never...that is...I never thought I was the sort to..."

Judith cleared her throat. "I, ah. I actually had guessed that. Based on the degree of awkwardness that descended between the two of you."

Daisy shrugged. "You see? Nothing to disclose."

Maybe nothing. Judith flushed. "Well, ah. If we're talking about intimate relations, Christian really is a marquess. He did want to marry me. And the other day... But no. I'm not going to complain to you about that. It would be utterly ridiculous."

Daisy shook her head. "You know, Judith, you have the strangest ideas about who is allowed to complain to whom. You watch my mother; I watch your brothers and sisters. I complain to you about losing my childhood home. Who else should you complain to about your problems?"

Judith spread her arms. "Anyone else?"

Daisy sniffed. "Don't be a goose. You're allowed to talk with your friends. That's what we're here for."

It was like tossing a loaf of odd, cobwebby bread into the oven and having evil elves turn it into something magical.

Judith smiled. "I love you, you know."

Daisy sniffed. "I know. But I am keeping score. If you marry him, you must have me over for tea. With gilt porcelain. And little tea cakes."

Judith laughed. "I can do better. We'll have curry chicken sandwiches with cucumber from a hot house in December."

"Yes. And when you meet the queen, I really don't care what the truth is." Daisy leaned in. "Whatever it is, *promise* me you'll tell me she breaks wind."

Not everything hurt. Judith laughed and bumped her shoulder against her friend's.

"She does," Judith promised. "She does. It's foul. There's a reason they use so many candles at Buckingham Palace, and it's *not* just for the light."

Chapter Twenty-Two

I t took the Worth siblings two full days to put Benedict's plan in action. Benedict scouted the lay of the land, as he called it, choosing every position carefully from the cover of the bushes.

It took twelve hours to prepare the ginger-ginger biscuits. Ginger-ginger biscuits were another one of Judith's creations. Regular ginger biscuits were made with powdered ginger. These were made with powdered ginger, essence of ginger, and candied ginger, for extra ginger flavor. They were bitingly spicy and were typically rolled in sugar. This batch had been produced in an atypical fashion.

This time, Benedict oversaw the preparation. The biscuits were baked, cooled, and then a single one was broken in thirds. Judith choked on her bit.

"These," Benedict said with a coughing nod, "are what we need. I truly believed that everything is better with salt until now, but..."

"These don't have too much salt," Theresa pointed out. "But maybe there is too little biscuit? I could not have made them any worse, and my skills at baking are unsurpassedly dismal."

Benedict had added to this a lovely, delightfully tasty lemonade.

"I want to try it," Theresa said as Judith decanted it into a soda-bottle she'd obtained for the purpose.

"No, you don't," Judith said. "You really don't."

They packed these delicious-seeming goods into a basket and took a walk—a four-mile walk—to a park. This one was just large enough for a cricket pitch. As it happened, three boys were playing.

"Will you be all right?" Judith whispered.

Benedict rolled his eyes. "Of course. I'm an old hat at this. And this time, I'm in charge." He took the basket and sauntered off. As he approached the pitch, the boys saw him.

"Hey! It's Worthless!" shouted one. Their cricket game was forgotten and children converged on her brother. Judith winced under cover of the nearby bushes.

"Worthless, what are you doing here?"

"Just passing through," her brother said.

"Passing through! It says it's passing through." The boy who had taken the lead had dark hair tucked under a cap.

"I'm meeting a friend," Benedict said, "I've brought something for him—oh, come on, let go." This last was directed to the boy who grabbed him by the elbow. "I'm not hurting you."

"You bother everything simply by existing," the leader said.

Another boy lifted up the lid of the basket. "Well," he said in a different tone of voice. "It never learns. We have us biscuits and a bit of—why, is this *lemonade*, Worthless?"

Benedict played his role perfectly. He balled his fists. "You can't have it, you weasel-heads!"

"Weasel-heads? Listen to it try to insult us like a man."

"I can have it," the boy said, "because I want it. I want it, and you don't wish for me to have it."

Benedict punched him in the stomach, and Judith almost cheered. The boy crumpled, falling to the ground. Benedict kicked at him, but it was too late. The other two boys grabbed hold of him. A backhand across the face; a wrench of the elbow, and then, another fist to the stomach when the dark-haired boy gained his feet again.

Benedict spat in his face. "You'll wish *you* were a weasel."

"Oh, go on." The other boy smiled. "We'll take your basket for your troubles, and if we see you again, you'll have twice as bad coming. Get off with you."

Benedict staggered back as they pushed him away.

"Go on." The boy made a shooing motion. "Get *off.*"

Benedict turned and ran. Not too far—he ducked behind a building, and then crept back to where he could join Theresa and Judith behind their bush.

"Are you all right?" Judith whispered, brushing at his face. "You're bleeding."

Benedict swiped Judith's concerns away. "If I miss this because you were weeping over a little blood—oh, God. He put the whole thing in his mouth at once."

The boy had.

Theresa peered through her fingers. "Everything's better with salt."

She had helped Benedict add the salt gleefully. All of it, a full cup, in place of the sugar. The boys spat and coughed.

"Almost everything," Benedict said. "And now they're going for the lemonade. They're passing it around."

"What exactly did you add to it?" Theresa said. "They're still drinking it. Does it not taste poorly?"

"Oh, it's not so bad," Benedict said. "But if those are the biscuits of death, that is the lemonade of incontinence. Give it some time."

They sat back on their heels and waited.

"Anyone want a ginger-ginger biscuit of deliciousness?" Judith opened the basket of treats she'd brought along and passed them out.

As they watched, she tried not to wince at the color gathering below Benedict's eye. They'd hit him again. But at least this time he was smiling. He grinned when the boys rushed off, yelping, leaving their cricket gear unattended.

He stood, walked back to the pitch, and left a note. She'd watched him write it last night, and so she knew what it said.

Dear Dean, Ralston, and Viridian—

I know what I'm worth.

Do you?

You Know Who

Benedict dry-washed his hands as he returned. "There we are," he said. "Revenge isn't sweet. It's salty. It's like they always say: Revenge is the only response to injustice. Come. Let's go home."

Judith stared at her little brother. Like *they* say? Which *they* said that? She had heard those words before.

From Christian, who had been quoting… Anthony. And there should be nothing odd about Benedict quoting Anthony, but he had been four years old when Anthony was transported. Benedict didn't remember his brother; what he knew about him, he knew because Judith had told him stories.

It could have been anything. Those words could have come from anywhere. For all she knew, it could have been an old Eton saying.

She pressed a hand to her mouth, but suspicion, great and terrible and painfully hopeful all at once, filled her. It *couldn't* be. It absolutely could not be.

She'd thought everything had been going well. *Too* well.

If she was right, everything had just become better. Better and impossibly worse.

She had a sudden memory of Mr. Ennis sitting behind his desk, resting his forehead against his hand, and saying, "Agh."

"Agh," Judith said.

"Agh?" Benedict looked at her, frowning.

Judith took hold of his wrist before he could dart away. "Wait," she said. "We're not going home. Not yet."

here *are* we going?" Benedict asked as Judith dragged him down the street.

"Are we there yet?" asked Theresa behind them.

"We're going on a walk." Judith bit out the words.

In truth, it was something closer to a forced march. She gripped her brother's hand, and she wasn't letting go. She would have yanked him by the ear, except that would have made him suspicious.

More suspicious.

More suspicious, perhaps, than Theresa. She followed behind them, carrying the basket of things they'd planned for their victory picnic afterward.

"Why are we going on a walk?" she asked. "Where are we going? Why now? Is Benedict in trouble?" The last was said with an almost hopeful gleam in her eyes.

If Judith's suspicions were true, Benedict was in *so much* trouble. "We're going on a walk," Judith said, "because our legs need stretching. So do our minds."

It couldn't be true. It would hurt too much if it were. And yet... Finally, everything fit, all of it, from the confusing answers that Mr. Ennis had given her to the way he'd fobbed her off with such apologetic helplessness. It all finally made sense, if having her world turned upside down for the second time in her life could be said to make sense. If she was right, she was going to collapse in a heap and cry.

Or commit murder.

Murder seemed a good option at the moment.

Possibly she could combine the two, and at her inevitable trial, she'd be able to use her tears as evidence of her mental unsoundness. She would have to ask Mr. Ennis, once she was done murdering everyone.

"I love you, Benedict," Judith made herself say as a reminder as they marched down the pavement. No, she was not *actually* going to kill him.

"Wait." Benedict suddenly stopped as Judith turned a corner. "Why are we going to see our *solicitor?*"

And there was her confirmation. She didn't let go of his wrist. "I don't know, Benedict," she said. "You've never been here with me. How did *you* know this was our solicitor's office?"

He gulped. "Ah. Um. I've seen the direction. On correspondence and such that he sent to you?"

"Smart boy." She gave him a grin, not relinquishing his hand. "Good try. Except you're a terrible liar."

"I could help him with that," Theresa said earnestly. "You see, you have to——"

At the forbidding look on Judith's face, she shut her mouth. "Or...perhaps not." She shook her head. "Benedict, you are going to have to make *so much* punishment bread."

Judith turned around. "Theresa, if you can't hold your tongue, I will..."

Theresa clapped her hand over her mouth.

"Good." Judith swept into the office.

The front room clerk, a distracted-looking fellow in spectacles, stood at her arrival. "Lady Judith." He frowned at her brother. "And young Mr. Worth. How good to see you both."

Judith raised an eyebrow at her little brother. "Never been here before?"

Benedict sighed.

"It turns out," Judith said, "I have a rather urgent question for Mr. Ennis. Has he a moment?"

The man actually looked to Benedict for permission first.

Her brother shrugged. "The jig is up," he said mournfully.

"The *jig?*" She was trying not to be incensed. "You—you—"

The solicitor came into the room. "Why, Lady Judith. Young Master Benedict. And this must be Lady Theresa."

"Maybe," Theresa responded. "I'm considering the matter. I don't have to decide for years, though."

Mr. Ennis made a confused face at that and shook his head. "How may I be of service?"

"Benedict." She pulled him forward. "It's *Benedict*, isn't it?"

Mr. Ennis gave a hopeful smile. "Your brother? Why, yes. Your brother is Benedict. Absolutely."

He was a worse liar than even Benedict.

"That's not what I meant. You said the guardian had turned over decision-making to someone else. That someone else is *Benedict.*"

Mr. Ennis's face became very still. "In a hypothetical sense? Yes. I suppose it could be. He wouldn't be the guardian himself; he'd merely be acting in an advisory capacity. But Lady Judith, your brother is twelve. Who would ever do such a ridiculous thing?"

If Benedict hadn't looked so dreadfully unhappy, she might have believed Mr. Ennis. Except he *hadn't* actually denied that Benedict had been put in that position. He'd just said it was ridiculous. And it was.

"It is utterly ridiculous," Judith said. "Let's not discuss this for now. We have another issue that must be discussed. Anthony has been missing for eight years. It is time to move on. We should have him declared dead, once and for all, so that Benedict can take his rightful title. If Anthony is dead, Benedict is the Earl of Linney."

"Ah." The solicitor frowned again. "Um."

"Might I suggest..." Judith leaned in. "*Agh.*"

"You appear to be legally astute." He sighed. "Yes. 'Agh' is my official legal response."

She had thought so. God, she was furious. "Lady Theresa has a guardian," Judith said, "but it is not me. The appointment of said guardian did not go through Chancery, and yet you accepted it unequivocally. And you won't file whatever necessary forms you need to declare Anthony dead."

She felt sick, elated, confused, and angry, all at once. Oh, God, she was so *angry*.

"That algae-sucking son-of-a-rooster." Her fists clenched. "I hate him. I will never, ever forgive him."

"What?" Theresa asked behind her. "Who? Who's in trouble?"

She would never do to Theresa what he had done to her. Never. She'd never keep her little sister in the dark, lying to her for whatever reasons she'd imagined.

"Anthony," Judith said. "Anthony is alive."

Theresa rolled her eyes. "Of course he is. I always said so, didn't I?"

"No," Judith said. "He is *actually* alive. He is in literal communication with our duck-nibbled solicitor. He left me to worry about you two all these years with no aid, without a word in communication, and then—"

"For what it's worth," Mr. Ennis put in, "I don't believe he was able to communicate until a few years ago."

"And he put *Benedict* in charge?"

"Yes, well." The solicitor pinched his spectacles. "That was not my idea. But it is rather difficult to argue with a man who leaves no forwarding address, and who takes five or six months to respond to any inquiry, which must be placed in the London papers in code. Trust me,

Lady Judith, I wholeheartedly share your outrage over the situation. I've sent the earl a most harshly worded message." Mr. Ennis sighed. "He may receive it in another five months. Or not."

"If it takes that long," Judith said, "why did nothing regarding Lady Theresa's trust come to my address? Surely Anthony…" She trailed off and looked at Benedict. "Surely…"

Benedict shrank in on himself. "I received the notice my first month at Eton," he whispered. "You said you had a plan. I'd go to school. I'd make friends. I would introduce my sisters about, and with a little money, they would make decent matches."

"Yes?"

"I thought…" Benedict swallowed. "I thought, maybe, if I never told you there was money… Maybe you'd come up with a new plan, and I wouldn't have to go back."

"Oh, Benny." Judith put her arm around him. Sometimes she forgot. He had old eyes and an old smile. But that didn't make him old. He was still a little boy.

"I won't go back," he said passionately. "I still won't. I hated everything about it. The people. Learning. Sitting still and memorizing Latin when nobody even speaks it anymore. I would have hated it even if I wasn't being pummeled. I know everyone is depending on me. Even Anthony said so. But I can't do it."

"Sweetheart." She held him. "I'm sorry. I'm so sorry I put all that on your shoulders. It's too much. But you should have…"

Told her, she had been going to say. But he *had* told her. He'd said he wasn't going back over and over. She just hadn't believed him.

"You should have told me Anthony was alive," Judith said. "And that you knew about it."

"But he said…" He trailed off. "No, you're right. He's not here. You are. I should have told you." He looked up at her. "Are you angry?"

"Shaking with rage," Judith said. "But I still love you."

"Please tell me," Theresa said, "that he's getting punishment bread for this."

She looked at her brother. He looked up at her with big, brown eyes. The same eyes she'd looked into when he was a baby. The same eyes, old eyes, that he'd had when he was five and he'd said that they just needed to add salt and it would be a proper turnip sandwich.

She looked at Theresa. "He is going to be making so much bread."

Mr. Ennis crossed the room and opened a file. He removed a small, folded square and held it out to Judith. "Here," he said. "Your elder brother asked me to give you this, if ever you found out."

Judith took the note and shoved it in her pocket.

"Don't worry," Theresa was saying to Benedict. "I'll explain how to make Theresa's Kindly Elf Bread. It's not that bad."

"Benedict?" Judith shook her head at Theresa. "I wasn't talking about *Benedict*. I meant Anthony. If I ever see him again, he will make bread for the rest of his life. Which will be unnaturally short."

"It's not fair." Theresa stomped her foot. "Benedict *never* gets in trouble for anything!"

"Benedict can't make bread," Judith said. "*You're* still on bread for another month and a half. Benedict is going to be washing bedsheets."

"Sheets!" Benedict looked at her. He gave her his best puppy-dog eyes. "Washing? But..."

"Ha!" Theresa smiled. "Punishment laundering! It's the only thing worse than bread."

"And," Judith said, "he's going to spend the rest of his time figuring out what he'll be doing. Now that he's not going back to Eton, he'll need another plan."

Chapter Twenty-Three

The river was dark and gray, a slow-moving mass of clouded water. Judith held on to the railing and watched little oil patterns swirl by.

She had brought her brother and sister home and, after assigning bread and laundry, had left. She'd needed to think. But wandering around the city couldn't calm her soul.

Anthony was *alive*. She'd let herself dream of it for too long when they'd first found themselves set adrift. She'd imagined her brother found living too many times. She'd created a fantasy in which he was discovered on some palm-shrouded isle in the Indian Ocean, where he'd been washed ashore. He would have come home. They would have sorted out all the unpleasantness surrounding his conviction. His name would be cleared.

And he would have saved her.

But Anthony was alive and he was a traitor. He'd betrayed her not just once, eight years ago, when he'd acted without concern for her wellbeing, not twice, when he'd stayed away, but a third time when he'd put her twelve-year-old brother in charge.

He'd left all the weight on her shoulders and given her none of the ability to make choices. She hated him so much for that.

She ducked into a church, found a coin, and lit a candle. Light flared, pushing back darkness.

"Why?" she asked. "Why, Anthony? Why?"

The candle flickered with her breath.

She took the hard lump of folded paper from her pocket.

"I hate you," she said. And then, because she missed him, she kissed it. "I love you."

She unfolded the letter.

Dear Judith, he had written. *I am sorry. I am so desperately, damnably sorry for everything I have done. The truth is, I don't expect that I will survive very long here.*

"Where is here?" she demanded. The candle didn't answer.

I know. You want to kill me a second time. You're shouting at me now—why Benedict?

It's simple: Benedict was four when I left.

You were at my trial. You heard the evidence. You were old enough to understand. I was convicted because the evidence showed I knew what our father was doing, and I allowed it to happen. From experience, I can tell you that the less you know, the better.

Benedict was the safest choice. Someone in the family had to know I was alive, and he was the least likely to understand the political implications and be punished for it.

Oh, that he had a reasonable response. She still wanted to punch him in the kidneys.

I grapple with it every day. I know I've wronged you. I know I've wronged Camilla and Theresa and Benedict. But we've wronged a great many others a great deal worse. I know you. You've no doubt found a way to undo half the harm I caused. I could not have put my family in more capable hands. You hold things together.

I won't explain what I'm doing. I won't justify myself. That, too, would be dangerous. The less you know, the safer you are.

I can imagine what you must think of me, and I'm sure I deserve your worst insults. But I dream every night of standing before my Maker and hearing him ask, "Did you do all you could?"

I hope that when that time comes, my answer will be yes.

Don't look for me. Don't write to me. Don't acknowledge me. When I'm dead, I'll make certain you are all informed. When she's old enough to understand, tell Tee-spoon that I send her all my love, and that Pri is well.

God. He'd always encouraged Theresa too much as it was. Judith had almost forgotten about Theresa's imaginary sister. It was just like Anthony to remember after all these years. Judith wiped tears from her face. "She's not a baby any longer, Anthony."

But then, Anthony had never taken the easy way. When they could have escaped all punishment by claiming a cat broke the vase, he'd always chosen to do what he believed was right, no matter whom it hurt.

He'd given up wealth, respect, and comfort. And he didn't need to tell her why; Christian already had.

She didn't wish she had a different brother; she wanted this one. He would never again stand near enough to hold, to yell at. She held a hand over the candle, close enough that the heat of the flame tickled her palm.

It had been a painful thing to admit that her brother was a traitor. It was even more painful to let herself believe that he'd betrayed his country for a good reason. A necessary one, even. And it was most painful of all to understand that he'd chosen his principles yet again—and that she could choose to either hold her anger close…or let it go altogether.

Slowly, painfully, she let go of the last of her resentment. "I'm proud of you," she whispered. "I wouldn't want a brother who put rules ahead of human misery."

She had a missing sister, an absent brother hell-bent on his own death, a younger brother who needed a new life, and a sister who would never be normal, no matter how much bread Judith made her bake. There were no knights, no castles, no magic. But there was laughter and there was love, and while Judith still had breath in her body, she would make sure they had enough.

Her life was already its own once-upon-a-time. There was enough joy in the story, enough sorrow mixed in. It might not be the sort of tale that mothers told their children, but it was still a good one. Not everything hurt. It would all turn out.

Benedict had given Mr. Ennis permission to share information about her sisters' trusts; the money was intact. He was going to decide what to do instead of returning to Eton. And Judith had been working on an idea for a bit of clockwork—something simple for a change. She had everything she wanted.

Almost everything.

There was one last thing she had to think about. She stared into the flame. Christian had ruined her brother once, and he'd said he would do it again. The point had seemed rather moot.

It wasn't moot any longer. If she were married to Christian, he would find out about Anthony. He would do what he always did—he would ask questions. He'd ask why Benedict was not declared the earl. He would ask what she'd heard from her solicitor. He would figure it out, and once he knew that Anthony was alive?

Her brother didn't stand a chance. Whatever he was doing, he obviously didn't want Judith to know. Christian would be a thousand times worse. The only way to keep Christian from asking questions was…

Judith stood in front of the candle and watched it flicker. The only way to keep Christian from asking questions was to not be around for him to ask. She ached, thinking of it. She trusted Christian with her soul.

But she couldn't trust him with her brother.

She knew this feeling, this crushing, squeezing pain inside. She'd felt it before, when her father had passed away. When Anthony had boarded the ship at Plymouth. She'd thought then that Christian was breaking her heart. The truth was, she was breaking it herself.

Nothing was resolved. She had no answers. She didn't know if she was ever going to get answers, but she had to move forward. She inhaled and bit her lip. She'd survived everything else life had thrown at her. She would survive this.

"Very well," she said to the candle. "You do everything you have to do, Anthony. I'll be here, holding things together."

She could do it. She could do it all.

She just couldn't do it all and have a husband.

You said you wanted to show me something."

Christian had expected the attic of Judith's house to be like any other attic—filled with cobwebs, old clothing, and unwanted furniture. Instead, it was clean and bright, tables laid out before them. A sheet of brass sat before him, with little toothed gears stamped from it. Three kittens lay in the sunlight streaming in from the single dormer window, a puddle of black and brown fur.

"I have something for you," Judith said.

"Yes?"

She plucked a little blob of white off the table. He couldn't quite see what it was; just a flash of gray in the palm of her hand. He heard the telltale sound of a clockwork mechanism winding. Then she set a key on the table, leaned down, and placed whatever she was holding on the floor.

It was a mouse—a little clockwork mouse of canvas and cotton batting, with wire whiskers. It immediately zipped away in a curving pattern across the floor.

Three predatory heads lifted from a nap. Six eyes widened in feline delight. And then twelve paws thundered after the mouse.

"Yes," Judith told him. "I know there are already a plethora of clockwork mice to be purchased. But they're so cheaply made that one good pounce will break the mechanism. These mice have been battle-tested."

"I approve." It seemed instantly appealing.

She brushed kittens aside and picked up the mouse. "Here. Let me show you again."

She wound it once more and let it go. The kitten battalion raced after it a second time, doing its best to rend and destroy. He had to admit, it made for an amusing tableau.

"Benedict tells me that he intends to go into trade," Judith said. "Please don't wince."

"I'm not wincing. I thought you intended to hide that fact."

Judith shrugged. "We had a discussion, and we decided it together as a family. We've hidden too much. It's time to stop pretending that we are anything other than what we are. We've traitors in the family. It's either cower beneath a bush and hope that some man chooses to look down on one of my sisters all the rest of her life, or defy them all. Benedict thinks we can start to manufacture the mice, and Theresa has agreed to use the money I'd set aside for her as seed money."

He wondered if this was her way of subtly testing him. To see if he would run shrieking. If so, it wasn't going to work. "I'm good at defying people," he said. "I offer my expertise on that score."

Her eyes dropped. "I spent so long trying to get my family back on the conventional path. Eton, trusts, Seasons, marriages—all without asking if it was the right path. We don't want the destination. No matter what his birth may have been, Benedict will never be a gentleman lounging in a club smoking cigars. Theresa will never be a giggling debutante. She would get bored and set the ballrooms on fire. Literally."

He took a step toward her. "What of you?"

Her eyes dropped and she inhaled. She picked up the clockwork key. "I am never going to be a lady."

He reached out and took her hand. "No? Because the position of Lady Ashford is open, and I'll be damned if I give it to someone who makes clockwork mice that break after a single pounce. It's been waiting for you these past eight years."

She inhaled.

"All that time, there's been a hole in my life." He stroked her palm. "It was so oddly shaped that I never quite understood how to fill it. But I know now. The hole is the shape of your younger brother, who won't go to Eton. It's shaped like your sister, who I fully expect to lead an armed revolt through the city streets. It's shaped like approximately eighteen cats and any number of clockwork mice."

Her fingers clenched on his arm. Her eyes were so wide, looking up at him.

"It's shaped like you," he whispered. "Strong, never giving up. Accomplishing miracles." He reached out and ran his finger down her cheek. "I know you have every reason to dislike me, but I intend to balance those scales out, over and over, until you can't remember why you ever felt that way. Tell me, Judith. Have I any chance?"

And Judith had thought that saying good-bye to Christian would be simple.

Here. We're well. We've figured everything out. We should avoid one another, lest we do anything irrevocable.

He was looking at her so intently that she yearned for irrevocable. If his attention could have changed worlds, she'd be in his arms now. But her world had shifted since the last time she'd seen him.

She looked down, where their hands joined. Her fingers seemed small in comparison to his. But her hands had put together clockwork. They'd learned baking and sewing and a thousand tasks that she'd never thought herself the equal of. She'd *managed*. The person she'd become was larger than the girl who'd once dreamed of a once-upon-a-time with this man.

A vision slipped into her mind of her hands running up his chest. She could almost taste him, could almost feel his skin, stubbled with dark hairs, beneath her hands.

She'd traded these hands for the knowledge of how he would feel. And, no, she wouldn't want it back. But... Still, before it all ended, she wanted to know. She wanted to know what she was missing.

"Christian."

He looked at her. His eyes were dark and so deep that she could have tumbled into them, if only she would let herself fall.

She wanted to *know*. If she didn't discover it now, she never would.

And so Judith did what she had wanted to do from the moment she took his arm in the carriage and yelled at him about swans. No, if she was being honest, she'd wanted it deep in her gut from the moment she'd sat across from him at her humble tea table. From the moment when he'd found her alone and given her a clockwork shepherdess. The moment he'd smiled at her and told her it wasn't proper, and she'd looked into those dark, deep eyes and told him that she didn't care.

Ever since then, she'd wanted to fall.

So now she did.

She took her hand from his.

He inhaled, his fingers questing toward her.

Their eyes met.

"I'm sorry," she said.

"No." He took a step toward her.

She set her hand on his chest. "I'm sorry that you had so much to worry about. I'm sorry I wasn't there to share it with you."

He didn't move away, and she stepped so close she could feel the heat of his body.

"Don't apologize." His voice was low. "Just say you'll be with me from here on out."

She took hold of his other hand, bringing it to press against her heart. His fingers convulsed lightly against her chest.

"I'm sorry," she said, "that we were never what we could have been."

He shook his head.

"It's not an apology." She ran her thumb down his hand, down the coarse hairs that dotted its back, to his cuff. "I only wish things had been different."

"So do I." His voice was hoarse. He leaned down to her. "So do I. I've wished it every day."

"Maybe they can be, for now."

"Forever." His breath feathered against her lips. His hand turned against her chest, sliding around her waist, pulling her hard against him. She wasn't sure if he leaned down to her or if she leaned up to him. She only knew that it felt right, the two of them together again, like two brass gears that had been machined for each other, turning in perfect harmony.

It was right when their lips touched, right when their hands tangled, his just enough larger that he could hold her in place. Their tongues met like a heavenly conjunction, spilling light through her. It hurt, the knowledge of how right they were together. She could have had this, this sweetness, this perfection. In some other world, she could have had this every day.

"Judith." His lips moved against her. "God, Judith."

She opened up to him and to the future she would never have.

Years from now, he wouldn't brush her nose with his. He wouldn't cup her face in his hand with that sweet tenderness. She wouldn't feel her breath coming faster, wouldn't feel her heart leap as his fingers brushed the edge of her bodice.

She wouldn't feel the sweetness of his touch, wouldn't taste the inevitability of their separation on his lips. She wouldn't know the cycle of his breath.

In the years to come, she'd have only her memories. So she'd make those memories as robust as she could.

For now, she kissed him. She opened to him. He was like a radiant sun, spilling light in her life.

"You'll see, Judith," he murmured against her lips. "This is as it should be—you and I. We should never have given up on us."

She couldn't let him see her cry. He would stop kissing her, and she didn't want him to stop. She leaned her head down, untucking the ends of his cravat.

"Judith. What are you doing?"

"What I wish," she said. "Have you any objections?"

She let her hand slide down the linen of his shirt.

"None." His eyes fluttered shut. "Absolutely none."

"And this?" Her fingers reached the band of his trousers. Found the button holding it in place.

"Oh, God. Judith. I should say no."

She halted.

"I won't. I keep thinking of that night in the orchard. How much I would give to go back and do more, to never have to know these past years."

"But then I wouldn't know me," Judith said. "I would not know what I was capable of doing. I wouldn't trade me for anything."

"I wouldn't trade you, either. And I'll have to convince you to keep me around." He said this with a smile, as if it were a foregone conclusion that he had already won her over.

She undid a button. Her heart hurt. No; she wasn't doing this just because she wanted to know what she would be missing. She wanted him to change her mind; she *needed* him to change her mind. God, if anyone could change the world with a kiss, it would be Christian.

"How do you think to convince me?"

He lifted her onto the sofa in her attic. "Here's one idea."

His hands slid her legs open, and he nestled between her thighs and licked her. He touched her so perfectly, so sweetly, she could have cried.

She did. "Oh, God."

"Now you can see for yourself," he said indistinctly, his tongue working against her. "What you have missed. How terrible it is. How impossible to endure."

His hands pressed her thighs wider, opening her up. His fingers slid inside her. God, that felt so good, there, just right. His tongue continued, and then, there was a pressure, a growing pressure.

As if all she'd wanted from him was building up inside her.

"Oh," she repeated. "Oh, God."

He didn't let up. He simply continued at the same leisurely pace. Nibbling her sensitive skin. Brushing his lips against her intimately, tasting her response with his tongue, until she wasn't sure of anything—not him, not her own name—not a single thing except the inevitability of this moment. He brought her higher, until her breath stopped working. Until her muscles all tensed at once, and she burst into little sparks of pleasure.

This. *This.* This was what she hadn't known, the pressure of his body against hers, the way he seemed to coax every last ounce of pleasure from her. The way he lifted his head in triumph with her last gasp, that self-satisfied silly grin on his face. The gentle caress of his hand on her hip.

He was hard again, almost impossibly so. She could feel his cock through layers of fabric, a heavy, solid weight against her thigh. He slid up her body to kiss her, and when she did she could taste herself on his tongue.

Her fingers found the button of his trousers again, circling round one. Undoing the first, then another. His hands undid the laces of her gown. For a brief moment, it felt as if she were drowning in fabric as he pulled her gown over her head.

Then he freed her.

His jacket was next, then her corset. They stripped each other bare, until his skin was warm against hers. Until his body pressed against hers, and he took her lips hungrily.

She could feel his member pressing against her, sliding as he cupped her face in his hands once more and kissed her deeply.

"We'd better stop," he said softly. "We had better stop now, if we intend to leave anything for later."

There could be no later. Judith shut her eyes. "No. Don't stop. Please don't stop."

His hands gripped her waist. "Judith. God. I want you so badly."

She looked up into his eyes. "I want you, too. I have always wanted you."

He bent his head and took her nipple in his mouth. She found herself gasping; she'd not known she could feel *more* pleasure after what had transpired.

But she could. His hand traced her hips. Very slowly, he notched his penis to the cleft between her legs. And, oh, God. There was even more. A stretching. A fullness. A togetherness. She was on the verge of tears.

He cupped her face with his hand.

"Sweetheart, is that…acceptable?"

"Yes." She set her hands on his hips. "It's very acceptable. It's utterly lovely. I don't want to stop accepting it."

He grinned. "Well. Then."

Her hands slid up his ribs to his chest, and he exhaled. He filled her; his body pressed against hers. This was what the wedding ceremony called two becoming one. In a sense, they were one. His body joined with hers. His mouth found hers. His breath escaped him and she inhaled it, turning Christian into Judith.

And yet she couldn't give all of herself to him. If anything had ever kept them apart, it was that—that they could never quite give each other everything.

Even as she opened herself to him, even as he tasted her, kissing her mouth, her nipples, even as his hands gripped her hips and his breath came faster—even then, they were two separate people.

Separate needs.

Separate families.

"There," he said. "There. I almost have you."

And he did. He'd found that spot with his fingers, one that had her gasping and hoping, hoping, hoping that this wasn't the end. Her second orgasm blazed up, so hot that it might have burned everything away. He made a noise deep in his throat and thrust hard against her, again, and then again.

And then it was done. For long minutes, they didn't speak.

His chest heaved. A faint sheen of sweat covered his skin. She held him, not wanting to let go. Not yet.

But she couldn't stop time, even if she'd wanted to do so. He pulled away eventually, and there was nothing between them, nothing at all. Nothing except the farewells they had not yet said.

Chapter Twenty-Four

After the shooting pleasure, after the little aftershocks had faded, after he'd pulled out and found a cloth and cleaned her up, Christian started to realize that not all was as it should be.

Judith wasn't talking to him

He tried to take her in his arms, but there was something in her eyes when he did, something that was both sad and joyous all at once.

"I'm glad we did this," she said.

So was he. And yet.

"Glad is such a tepid word." He reached for her fingers. "I'm not *glad*, Judith." Her palm lay passively against his. She didn't precisely resist when he pulled her close. She just didn't...participate.

What had felt so perfectly right mere minutes before now seemed subtly wrong. He could smell her. He could feel her skin bare against his. He belonged here, like this, with her.

So why did it not feel as if she belonged here with him?

Her eyes were open, staring at the ceiling.

"I'm a little overwhelmed," he said again.

"As am I." Her voice was low, and once again, it felt as if there were an unspoken *and yet* whispered after her words.

He waited, hoping he was imagining it.

She inhaled. "I don't know how I can walk away from this."

He'd not been imagining that she was pulling away. "Don't." His hands closed around her. "Don't. Stay forever, Judith."

Her fingers flexed, her hands dug into his arm. Her grip wasn't hard enough to hurt, but it held him in place.

"I'm sorry," she said instead. "I'm so, so sorry."

That was when he understood that she hadn't taken him to her bed to say *yes* to his proposal. She hadn't even kissed him thinking that *yes* was a possibility. She'd done it to say farewell.

His throat felt tight; his lungs seemed to hurt. "Why?"

Don't, he wanted to say. *Don't go. Whatever it is, don't go.*

She drew her knees close, wrapping her arms around them when she could have been wrapping herself around him. She didn't look at him. "There is something I believe about marriage," she finally said. "When you take a vow, you promise to honor and obey and—"

"You know it won't be like that between us," he said swiftly. "Whatever it is you think, we can fix it."

She looked over at him. "No. But you promise that it will last through sickness and health, through richer and poorer. Skip the actual words of the ceremony. What it all comes down to is that when you marry, you vow that you will put the other person first."

His heart, already wretchedly low, sank further.

"If you could," she said quietly, "if you could take the past back, as easily as you wound up a spool of thread, would you keep quiet about what you'd discovered about Anthony?"

He wanted to say he would. Oh, damn, he wanted to. If he'd kept quiet, if he'd said nothing at all, if he'd simply sat to one side like a useless lump and kept his discoveries to himself, her father would have gone free. She would have had her Season and he would have married her and they would be up to their ears in children at this moment, and oh, God, how he wanted that. He wanted it so much he could taste it.

But.

But he would have had to remain silent. Every day that he woke up, he would have known that her brother—his best friend—was a traitor. He would never have been able to let that knowledge go. What if Anthony had done something that threatened *his* family? His children? It would have been like a blade of ice between them. He would always have known that what he had with Judith was stolen.

Lies and falsehoods made a poor basis for a marriage.

"No," he finally said. "No. I wouldn't."

She nodded. "I don't blame you for it. Not anymore." She gave him a sad smile. "You could hardly do anything else. But I believe that when you marry, you must be able to put the other person first."

"In the past…"

"Not the past." She looked away. "That's the thing, Christian. You will never be first for me. I must think of Benedict, of Theresa. I don't even know where Camilla is. My family must always come first."

"I know. I don't care."

"What if Benedict decides one day that Anthony was right, and he too…" She shook her head. "What then?"

He had no answer, none that she would want to hear.

He tried another tack. "Judith, no man could meet your criteria."

"I don't expect anyone could," Judith said quietly.

Hence the reason she'd allowed this to go so far. He understood it all too well, now. He'd been her one taste of the forbidden fruit.

A slow coil of anger began to burn deep inside him. Nobody ever asked the damned fruit if it wanted to be forbidden.

Judith stood. "Marriage means something to me. It means that I promise to put you before all others. I love you, Christian—I love you too much to make that promise knowing that it is false."

"And too little," Christian said, "to make it true." Her eyes met his. She didn't answer.

She didn't have to. That much was clear.

She stood in front of him, her skin bare. He wanted to hold her so closely that she couldn't walk away. But his arms had never been able to stave off reality.

It hurt. God, it hurt. It was like waking from a golden dream only to discover that it was all a lie.

Judith reached for her gown.

"Let me help," he said.

When a dream ended, there were only two choices. You could burrow under the covers and try to recapture it, replaying the fragments of false memory over and over, pretending it had actually happened. Or you could be a man and face the day, however cold it was.

So he did up the buttons of her gown. He found his trousers, his coat. And when she said it was time for him to leave, he went.

It didn't matter.

That was what Christian told himself as he stood at the window of his office, the curtains open wide, looking down at the park. Behind him, his man rustled papers.

"A curious list you've given me," Mr. Lawrence said. "What is this list again?"

Christian had been holding his secrets close. "Just some people I should like to talk with. Have you discovered their whereabouts?"

"I have."

"Then let me hear it."

Once, he had told himself that all he wanted was Anthony's journals. He'd wanted to make a list of the men Anthony thought deserved justice, to see what he could do. Now that Christian had seen the names, he suspected that what he could do would not be satisfying.

Nothing would feel satisfying if Judith couldn't forgive him. He'd told himself that he wasn't doing any of this with the prospect of reward. That all he wanted was to right past wrongs.

And look—the Worths were well. He'd helped her in her search for Camilla. He'd sent out advertisements. He'd assisted her in ascertaining the truth about her solicitor, and the money had been returned to her family.

The Worths were well. His dreams were losing their power. Oh, he still had them—but with every step he'd taken forward, he was learning to fall back asleep again. What else could he ask for?

Her, his heart whispered.

"Of the thirty-six men you identified," Mr. Lawrence said behind him, "I have information regarding twenty-nine."

"Go on," Christian said. "I'm listening."

He was. It was no surprise that he'd fallen in love with Judith again. He'd never fallen out of love with her, and over the years, she'd become...more. More beautiful. More capable. More sure. More of everything he respected. She'd become so much that she scarcely had need of him.

"First," said Mr. Lawrence, "Mr. Alan Wilding, late of Wilding and Wilding Transportation—now bankrupt. Second, Mr. Jeffrey Clawson, living in Bristol under reduced circumstances."

Lists. Lists were soothing, even now. Maybe he could make a list of ways to forget Judith, something numbered from one to ten. *One.* He could... Um.

Um about covered all his ideas. He'd have to populate items two through ten with similar throat-clearing. *Ah,* perhaps. *Ahem.* Everything except *agh*—that was reserved for legal chicanery.

"Three. Lord Palmerston, deceased some months past. Four, Mr. Lyle Wilson, bankrupt and a suicide."

Christian was trying to make an impossible list. He was never going to forget Judith, no more than he could forget his sums or his childhood. All he could do was move past her.

"Five. Mr. William Shoreditch."

"Let me guess," Christian said. "He's living in some sort of reduced circumstances."

"Debtor's prison," Mr. Lawrence said.

Strange. More than strange.

Christian turned back to him. He *had* been paying attention after all. "Are any of these men still in trade?"

Mr. Lawrence frowned. "Five or six."

Strange did not cover it.

The hair on Christian's arms prickled. For a moment, a snippet of one of his old dreams came back to him—a remarkably vivid image of him reaching over the deck of a ship. Of grasping what he thought was Anthony's hand. Of looking into his own face.

He exhaled. "How likely is that, do you think?"

"I couldn't say, sir, having conducted no extensive surveys. But it seems somewhat improbable. What is this a list of again?"

"Just some men," he said. "Men who were known to be involved in trade with a company that has asked me to invest." Christian held out a hand. "There's no need to continue. Clearly, investment would not be a good idea."

Mr. Lawrence smiled and handed over the papers. "I should say not."

This is not a good idea. If Christian had any sense, he'd stop here. He would ask himself no more questions. He would burn the list and never think about it again.

But it was…unusual. So many of them had been ruined, bankrupted, or otherwise imperiled. It was…no, not *unusual*. Unlikely. Unimaginable.

Unbelievable, even.

It was almost as if someone had the same list, and was systematically ruining…

His breath caught. It was *exactly* as if someone had the same list, and was systematically seeking vengeance on the worst players.

Judith hadn't the means, and she hadn't realized Anthony's journals would allow anyone to construct such a list. Only one other person could have known these names.

"Agh." Christian's knees suddenly felt weak.

Mr. Lawrence cleared his throat. "My lord?"

For a moment, Christian could see himself in a dream, looking at Anthony.

Who are you? Anthony asked.

Christian didn't know. He felt himself reaching for his own hand. Grabbing hold. Wondering whether he should keep holding on, or if he should let go.

He'd ruined everything once, but he hadn't any choice in the matter. He didn't want to have to do it again. But what else was he to do?

Then he remembered Judith—her smile, when he coaxed a laugh from her. Her clockwork mice. That annoyed shake of her head when her sister burned scones. The way she'd looked at him when she sent him away for good.

He thought of Judith, and reason came back to him in a great gasp.

"Are you well, my lord?" Mr. Lawrence frowned at him.

Christian nodded to himself. He was. He finally was. He could see it all now.

One. He needed to talk to his mother.

Two. "Draft a note to Lady Judith," he said. "Tell her I must speak with her. It's urgent."

Chapter Twenty-Five

illian. Mother."

It had taken Christian an hour to convene this counsel in his parlor, another fifteen minutes to manage the niceties of tea (for those who partook) and sandwiches and lemonade (for him).

"Thank you for coming on such short notice."

His cousin reached out and squeezed his hand. "We're worried about you, Christian. You did so much for me when I came out. How could you imagine I would do anything else?"

"I didn't." He smiled at her. "Still. Thank you. I know I've been difficult recently. I asked you both here because I need your help, and because I need to tell you something."

They both leaned forward attentively.

"Oh, thank God." His mother smiled. "Do you mean to tell me you've changed your mind about my physician? I'll send for him—"

"No." Christian set down his glass of lemonade. "Mother. I apologize. I have done you a disservice."

"You have?" She frowned at him. "I have no recollection."

"I have." He reached out across the table and took her hand. "For the last decades of my life, I've allowed you to believe a falsehood. A comfortable falsehood, I thought, but a falsehood nonetheless."

"You're only twenty-eight. What kind of a secret..." She trailed off.

"Laudanum." He allowed the word to settle into the conversation, waited for her face to slowly change to a mask of confusion. "I don't refuse it because it makes me muzzy-headed, because it gives me vivid dreams, or even because I dislike the taste. I refuse it because I developed an addiction to it when I was young. It was so severe that when I was at Eton, I took a dose that nearly killed me. I stopped breathing."

She inhaled and tried to pull her hand away. Christian held on tightly.

"When I was...imbibing, I would set my day by my doses. It took over everything I was, everything I wanted. There is no safe dose, not for me."

His mother set down a trembling teacup. "I'm... I have no idea what to say, Christian. No idea what to think. Words can't begin to describe how I feel. I'm so sorry."

"No. Don't be sorry." He reached out and took her shaking hand.

"You must know, I never intended..."

"I know. I know, Mama. I know. You did it because you loved me. You did it to save me. And you did. It's why I never wanted you to know—not because I don't trust you, but because I never wanted you to doubt that I loved you. You never gave up on me." He slid his arm around her and held her close. "I love you. Thank you. But...it's enough. I'm done telling you comfortable falsehoods."

His mother laughed shakily. "No, no. Don't go so far, Christian. All of British society is built on comfortable falsehoods. What else will we have to talk about?"

"Well." He smiled. "Here's one thing. I hope I'll be marrying Judith Worth, and if I do… Well, let's say there will be no room in my life for comfortable falsehoods. Or, possibly, British society."

Possibly even more. Lillian had been quiet the entire time. She looked over at him. "Judith Worth? The daughter of the unfortunate Earl of Linney? *That* Judith Worth?"

"Yes. *That* Judith Worth."

His cousin inhaled. "Christian. You know she'll never be accepted in society. Her father—her brother—"

"I know," Christian said. "I don't care about society, and quite frankly, I think she'll be too busy with her own concerns to care, either. I care about my family. If she says yes, will you accept her?"

The moments seemed to pass, infinitely long. His mother looked down. Lillian set her teacup on the table and adjusted the sleeves of her gown.

Finally, she looked up. "Will she make you happy?"

"The happiest."

Lillian gave him a firm nod. "You idiot. What part of *I will do anything to see you as happy as I am* did you not understand?"

"No part," Christian said. "None at all."

"Then go ask her. What are you waiting for?"

"This." He put his arms around both of them and squeezed. "Just this."

hristian had asked Judith to meet him in Hyde Park the next day.

She had arrived before he did. He saw her as she came close, standing on the bank of the Serpentine. Her hands were clasped behind her back and she paced up and down. Occasionally she'd reach up and touch her bonnet, adjusting the brim.

She watched the waterfowl drift past, a pair of swans gliding in tandem. Her hands squeezed together. The sheer hunger in her gaze as she contemplated them nearly knocked him back a pace. She was hurting, too.

A low, insistent sense of longing filled him. He touched the hat on his head as he came up to her. She turned to him. Her eyes were wide and dark and oh, just a little hurt. As if she'd been wounded.

She had come. That was what he held on to. She had come. She inhaled as he stepped toward her, tilting her head up to look at him.

He smiled at her. "Oy, Fred," he said. "How's the algae?"

Judith's eyes narrowed. "No. You will not get me to play your male swan lover. Not now. Not in Hyde Park, of all places. I'm trying to forget you, not—"

He held a finger close to her lips and she stilled, looking up at him. "Then listen to me. I made a list, and lists solve everything. They really do."

She let out a desperate laugh. "They don't. They really don't."

"This one does." Christian gave her his best cocky smile. "Listen and learn. One, you don't trust me."

She flinched.

"And I don't blame you." He dropped his voice. "I know what I did. I know what you think. I wouldn't trust me either, were I you. I know what happened with your brother. Trust needs to be earned, not expected."

She didn't step away from him at that mention of Anthony.

"That brings me to two." He leaned down so he could look her in the eyes. "The only way you will learn to trust me again is if I am trustworthy. Nothing else will serve."

"You are." But her eyes looked down as she spoke, avoiding his gaze. "You are, Christian. It's only—it's simply that…"

"I know what it is." Christian hoped she understood the warmth in his voice for the caress he wanted it to be. "It's the next item on my list. Item *C:* Anthony is alive."

She stilled. Even her breath ceased. Her head tilted back and she looked at him with wide eyes.

"Don't fear," he told her. "Don't fear. Whatever worries you have, we can get through this."

She shook her head. "No. Before that. You said one, two, *C*. Something is wrong. Dreadfully wrong." She fumbled off one glove and reached a hand up to his forehead. "You don't look like you're running a fever."

He caught her hand in his. He could feel her wrist against his thumb. He imagined he could sense her pulse, gently beating.

"No. And that's not the only thing I've done wrong, Judith. I've kept quiet about a great many things—so many I didn't realize it until now. I've told too many falsehoods in the name of comfort without even realizing that was what I was doing. I chose my comfort eight years ago, over yours and your family's. I chose my mother's comfort over the truth about her medicine. There are too many ways…" He shook his head. "If I am going to move forward, it seems only fair that I should learn to shut my mouth about your brother."

"But—"

He squeezed her hand in his. "What would I say anyway? I don't know anything about him now. No matter what I do, what I choose, the world will stay imperfect. I can't solve all the problems of the British empire today. All I can do is choose where my loyalties lie. And that brings me to the fact that I've been reciting my list out of order."

"Out of order? You? Impossible." She didn't pull away.

He nodded. "My lists have been out of order all these years. Would you know that all this time, I believed lists started at one? I was wrong. Lists start at zero, and I've been skipping the beginning my entire life."

Her hand turned in his—not to escape, but so her fingers could interlace with his. "What is zero, then?"

"Item zero," Christian said. "It's you, Judith."

She let out a long, slow exhale.

"Nothing ever made sense because I was trying to sort everything into place from one to ten. That was the mistake. You are the start of every list I've ever made. You are the beginning, the zeroth item, the unspoken predicate of my heart. You can't put me first; I know that."

Her eyes were wide and shining. "Christian."

"You can't put yourself first," he said. "You have a younger sister collecting cats, another one who is still missing. You have another brother who is off in the world. I know you can't put yourself first. So let me do it for you."

She let out a long, shuddering breath. "Christian. When I walked away from you, I... I knew I shouldn't. I wanted to do anything else. I'm sorry. I should have trusted you."

"Trust me now." He pulled her close. "If trust was low, it's because the world has given you no reason to trust. Let me change that."

"You can't change the world." But she looked up into his eyes.

"Maybe not all of it," he said. "There are parts of it we will never put right." He slid his fingers down her wrist to her elbow. "I can't promise you perfection. There is too much wrong. But there are also little things that will go right, and I can promise you those. There will be perfect sunsets. Perfect kittens."

"Perfect sandwiches," she put in.

"Perfect walks," he told her. "Perfect arias at the opera."

"Perfect bread."

"This world will take a great deal of work," he said. "But... We can start in on that together. And while we're sorting through all the imperfections, we can find more little things to make perfect. Perfect strawberries, for instance."

"Perfect...marriages?" She smiled tremulously up at him.

"Yes." He slid his arm around her waist. "But before that, might I suggest perfect kisses?"

"Yes." She stepped close to him and tilted her face up to his. "Yes. Please."

Epilogue

Fourteen months later

Judith woke in bed.

It was early autumn, just cold enough for a fire. She could detect heat against her face and the faint odor of burning wood. Even more faint was the scent of bread wafting from the kitchens below.

It was nothing to the heat of Christian's hand on her hip. He was awake and touching her lightly. He'd promised her little notes of perfection, and he'd delivered.

Another hand touched her shoulder and he slid closer. So close she could feel his body against hers.

"Good morning," he whispered. His stubbled chin rasped against her shoulder.

"Good morning."

"I got up early just so I could toss all the cats out of the room," he whispered to her.

"Mmm. No cats?"

"No cats. No commotion."

Judith's sleep-fogged brain finally began to wake. "Oh dear. No commotion. What do you suppose Theresa is up to?"

"Nothing she won't still be doing in twenty minutes," Christian said with a smile. "Here. Let me wake you properly."

He pulled the covers back. The air was cool against her nightrail, but only for a moment. He slid next to her, cocooning her in his arms. His lips found hers.

"Mmm. You had mint tea sent up."

"I did." He kissed her again, minty and sweet, and she gave herself over to him. To the feel of his fingers running down her body. Stroking her arms, the crook of her elbow.

His mouth trailed kisses down her chin.

"I love you," she said.

"Good." His hand slid up her ribs to circle one of her breasts. "My nefarious plan is working."

"Oh, no." She could scarcely muster up what sounded like mock fear. "What nefarious plan have I fallen prey to?"

"It goes like this. One, I steal your capacity to reason." His thumb brushed over her nipple and a spark of desire awoke, coiling deep between her thighs in response.

"I like one." Judith breathed out. "Let's keep on with one for a while."

He ducked his head and took her nipple in his mouth. "Like this?"

"Yes." It came out strangled. She reached out and pulled him on top of her—not that it took any pulling worth speaking of. He settled on top of her body, holding her in place, licking, his hips pressing hard into her.

Her hands slid under his night shirt. "Two," she said breathlessly. "What's two?"

"No two, not if you can still think," Christian said with a wicked gleam in his eye.

"I can't think. I promise."

He raised an eyebrow at her. "Don't lie to me, Judith. You're thinking *right now.*"

Judith considered this. "Unfair. I don't stop thinking just because you made a stupid list. When I get lustful, I don't need all the blood in my brain to go anywhere else. Your list is physiologically impossible. I shouldn't be denied number two because of it. You need to edit."

"Two," Christian said smoothly. "Edit item number one. Let's just make it so that you enjoy yourself instead."

"Accepted. As long as you get to enjoy me, too."

He kissed her again, this time longer. His hands flirted with the bottom of her nightrail, sliding it up her thighs.

"Mmm."

"I like that," he said. "Mmm is close to mindlessness. And you said it couldn't be done."

"You said you edited."

"Mmm." He kissed her again, and she smiled.

"Three," she said. "If I don't stop *you* from thinking, clearly we'll never get anywhere." She pushed on his chest and he rolled away. Not for long. She straddled him, setting his hands on her chest. Feeling his body beneath her, all hard muscle. "Victory," she proclaimed.

He smiled up at her. "Sweet, sweet defeat."

It took them a moment to guide him inside her. She was wet and ready; he was hard and wanting. He growled in his throat as she sank onto him. God, it was good. So good.

There was no more talking as he urged her on, his hands finding her hips. There were no more numbers as she gave herself up to him, to the feel of their joining.

For a little space at the end, there was even no thinking at all. But Christian didn't need to know that.

He waited until they'd finished. And kissed. Until he'd played with her hair, until they'd reluctantly agreed that breakfast downstairs was a necessity. He called his valet into the dressing room; she made do with her maid.

Her maid was settling slippers on Judith's feet when Christian came to stand beside her.

"Oh, one last thing. I forgot to mention *why* I had a nefarious plan in the first place. Now that you're feeling favorably inclined to me, maybe I should mention that I told Theresa yesterday she could have another seven cats?"

"What?" She stared at him in horror. "You didn't. I can't believe you."

A grin took over his face.

"Oh." She narrowed her eyes at him. "I see. You *literally* didn't. I shouldn't believe you." Her hand slipped to her side, to the bed behind her. "You may have won *this* battle, Lord Ashford, but there are still numbers left on your list. I wouldn't be so cocksure, were I you."

"Are there?" He waggled an eyebrow at her. "What will you do with number five, Lady Ashford?"

Her fingers closed on a nearby pillow.

"Five…" She let her voice fall to a throaty whisper, and she motioned him to lean in. "Five, I suppose, is…"

She whipped the pillow up, smacking him in the face with it. "Death to cat liars!"

"Not the pillow!" He held up an arm. "Anything but the pillow."

She smacked him again—but as she hit him, one of the seams burst. Feathers spattered everywhere, exploding over them. They cascaded to the ground in a snow of down.

She stared at him and then very slowly, brushed feathers off her gown. "I didn't think I hit you *that* hard."

"You didn't." He brushed off his shoulders. "You know what this means, don't you?"

"No...?" But she realized it a moment before he opened his mouth again. "*No.* Don't say—"

"Who is England's greatest chicken-killer?"

"—It." She finished.

He leaned over and brushed white down off her shoulder. "You are," he said softly. "You are. I'll see you downstairs. You have feathers in your hair; you might want to do something about that."

After the Epilogue

The bread was perfect. The kippers were perfect. The number of cats in the household was…oh very well, it was nineteen, but the cat population had been growing at a relatively small rate month-by-month, and Judith would take what she could.

She almost didn't notice the knock on the front door. She almost didn't pay attention to the rumble of voices out front.

But then she heard the voice. *That* voice. She didn't recognize it, not really. Still, it sounded achingly familiar. As if she should have known it, but did not.

"No," a woman said. "You have to let me in. I don't need to go round the back. I only wish to have a word with Lady Judith. I *must.*"

"Lady Ashford," she heard their butler say. "She's Lady Ashford. Don't speak of her in such familiar tones."

Judith pulled her hand from Christian's, and before he could say a word, darted into the hall. "Wait!"

The woman standing in the front entrance was missing shoes. She wore a dingy gown, the hem ragged and dripping in mud.

Still, Judith knew her. Those eyes. That chin. Her nose. All the years hadn't changed her sister in any of the essentials.

"Camilla?" Judith's voice broke. It had been so, so long. They'd looked. They'd advertised. She'd refused to lose hope, no matter how options had dwindled as the months passed.

She'd been *right* not to lose hope. Her sister was here. Theresa followed right behind her. "*Camilla?*"

Judith threw her arms around her sister. "Where have you been?"

"Never mind." Christian was there. "Come in. We have food and towels."

Camilla looked into Judith's eyes. "Judith, I need your help."

"Anything."

Camilla took a deep breath. "I'm married."

In typical Worth family fashion, everyone spoke at once.

"What?"

"To whom?"

"When?"

"Do you love him?" The last was Judith.

Camilla's chin wobbled a moment. But it was just for a moment. When she spoke again, her voice was firm. "It hardly matters," she said. "You see, I want—no, I *need*— an annulment. And you're the only one who can help me."

Thank you!

Thank you for reading *Once Upon a Marquess*. I hope you enjoyed it.

So what happens with everyone else in the Worth family?

Once Upon a Marquess is the first book in the Worth Saga—a series about the Worth family that will span years and continents. Obviously, there's a lot of story left to tell for Benedict, Camilla, Theresa, and Anthony—along with some others you haven't yet met.

If you want to know when the next book in the Worth Saga will be out, please sign up for my new release e-mail list at www.courtneymilan.com.

What can you tell me about the next books?

Next up is *Her Every Wish*, a novella about Daisy Whitlaw (Judith's best friend) and Crash. (Crash doesn't have a last name.) It will be out in mid-January so make sure to either sign up for my new release list or to preorder it, although preorders won't be available everywhere.

What do you mean *others you haven't yet met?*

There are seven full-length books in the series. The Worth Saga is, of course, a series about the Worth family. But it's also a series about an organization (which you'll discover in Book 3, *The Devil Comes Courting*) and another family (which you'll meet for the first time in Book 2, *After the Wedding*). And, as with all my series, there will be a handful of novellas that explore side characters.

After that (as I am sure you have already guessed) is Camilla's story, *After the Wedding*.

You can read excerpts from these books right after this page.

When will all these books release?

I'm not a fast writer, unfortunately, and I'm extremely bad at predicting when I'm going to finish a book. At my best guess, maybe late in 2016 for Camilla's book? Add question marks to the end of any date I ever give you. Add lots of question marks. If you want to get an email when my books become available, you can sign up for my new release e-mail list at www.courtneymilan.com. Or you can follow me on twitter at @courtneymilan, or like my Facebook page at http://facebook.com/courtneymilanauthor.

I don't want to wait that long! What can I do in the meantime?

I have three other finished historical romance series (as well as a handful of stories that aren't in any series). If you're new to my books, I suggest starting with *The Duchess War*. It's free on most platforms right now. It's the first book in the Brothers Sinister series, and it's about Robert Blaisdell, the Duke of Clermont, who doesn't want to be a duke, and Minnie the shy wallflower who doesn't want to be a duchess. Don't listen to me. I'm terrible at describing my own books.

If you haven't tried it yet, I also have a contemporary romance series. *Trade Me* is the first book in the series. It has all the things you know and love about Courtney Milan books (humor, angst, and lengthy author's notes about things I couldn't stop researching), but there are bonus smartwatches. Come for the technology; stay for foul-mouthed billionaires and jokes about insider trading.

If you've already read all my books, I have a list of recommendations for other authors on my website at http://www.courtneymilan.com.

Her Every Wish: Excerpt

Crash has never let the circumstances of his birth, or his lack of a last name, bother him. His associations may be unsavory, but money, friends, and infamy open far more interesting doors than respect ever could. His sole regret? Once lovely, sweet Daisy Whitlaw learned the truth about how he made his fortune, she cut him off.

Daisy's father is dead, her mother is in ill health, and her available funds have dwindled to a memory. When the local parish announces a charity bequest to help young people start a trade, it's her last chance. So what if the grants are intended for men? If she's good enough, she might bluff her way into a future.

When Crash offers to help her prevail, she knows he is up to no good. But with her life in the balance, she's desperate enough to risk the one thing she hasn't yet lost: her heart.

From Chapter One

"Daisy," Crash called behind her.

The snow had changed from delicate white lace to the disgusting, dingy slush of well-trodden streets. Icy water seeped through the seams of her shoes. A cold wind tugged at her, and she cinched her scarf around her neck. She didn't look back. She wasn't foolish.

"Daisy."

She wouldn't turn. That little skirling breeze coming up behind her would make her eyes water, and she was not, she absolutely was *not*, going to let Crash see her cry. Not even if her tears were wind-induced.

But Crash had never been deterred by…well, anything, Daisy suspected. Certainly not anything so mild as someone purposefully failing to hear him. He came jogging up to her, settling to a walk at her side.

"Daisy," he said. "You rushed off far too soon."

She made the mistake of looking at him just as he cast a glance in her direction. He was a man who had mastered the speaking glance. *This* one could have been an epic saga. It was the unshakeable look that a farm lad gave to his sweetheart when she was sentenced to be fed to a dragon. *Don't worry*, it promised. *I'll save you. I've a plan.*

It was the kind of look that would have that blushing farm girl spreading her legs for her love in the barn the night before she was condemned to die. She'd give up her virginity, her trust, her love, her future in one trembling hour. When she bid her swain farewell through tears and kisses, she would believe in her soul that he was going to kill the beast. She'd believe he would save her right up until the moment the dragon crunched her between its teeth.

Even now, even knowing Crash as she did, a flush of heat blossomed along the back of her neck at that look.

Daisy's mind knew all about Crash, even if her body pretended ignorance. She'd already given him everything. She'd had that trembling hour. Eighteen months later,

Daisy had no virginity, no trust, no love, and her future was chockfull of dragons.

"Aha," Crash said, coming to a temporary halt. He snapped his fingers. "Right. Of course. I forgot. I'm to address you as Miss Whitlaw now."

He gave her a mocking smile, arranged the cloth at his neck that passed for something like a cravat, and shifted his tone. When he spoke again, he sounded almost proper—the way Daisy's mother sounded at her most querulous. The way Daisy spoke, when she wanted people to take her seriously.

"My dear Miss Whitlaw," he said in a distinctive, plummy-sounding voice, "I know you've little desire to speak with me at the moment. But I have a business proposition to put before you."

"You may recall," Daisy said severely, "that I do not care for your line of business."

That smile on his face flickered. "My line of business is the business of making people happy."

Ha. "Yes," she said. "A great *many* people."

"A great many people," he agreed, instead of getting angry at her implication like a normal person would. "I'm here to offer my services."

"I had your services once," Daisy snapped. "I don't need them any longer."

"A good thing," Crash said with a slow grin. "The sort of services I offer don't come any longer—or thicker—or harder than I have on offer."

Her cheeks flamed in memory. "Crash. *Please* don't say things like that."

He shrugged. "It's simple. I saw what happened back there. They're planning to make a joke of you, you know. All they want is to laugh at you."

"I know," Daisy said through clenched teeth.

"You should give up now."

"I know." Her teeth ground against each other.

"But you won't."

He knew that, too. His knowing things about her had fooled her thoroughly. She'd thought she was special. She had thought he actually cared. She'd been such an idiot.

"And since you won't give up," he said, "then you cannot leave them with one single thing to laugh at. You know that's how it works, yes?"

"I know," she whispered.

"You will have to be brilliant." He looked at her. "You won't be able to hesitate. You'll have to make them believe that nobody will be able to survive without your chop house. That means..." He paused, a little overdramatically. "You will have to practice."

"I know all these things," Daisy growled.

"You'll need an audience to test yourself against." Crash continued as if she hadn't spoken. "Not your friend the marchioness, nor your mother, nor the girls who work in your flower shop. You need to practice in front of someone who you hate. Someone who makes your stomach curdle. Someone who will ask questions while you want to smash his face in. If you can impress *that* man, you can impress anyone."

She looked over at him.

He took off his hat and gave her a flourishing bow. "I am, as ever, at your service."

Want to know what happens? *Her Every Wish* will be available in mid-January of 2016.

Visit http:/www.courtneymilan.com to find out more.

After the Wedding: Excerpt

From Chapter One

Lady Camilla Worth had dreamed of marriage ever since she was twelve years of age.

It didn't have to be marriage. It didn't have to be romantic. Sometimes she imagined that one of the girls whose acquaintance she made—however briefly—would become her devoted friend, and they would swear a lifelong loyalty to one another. She'd daydreamed when she lived in Leeds about becoming a companion—no, an almost-granddaughter—to an elderly woman who lived three houses down.

"What would I ever do without you, Camilla?" old Mrs. Marsdell would say as Camilla wormed her way into her heart.

But Old Mrs. Marsdell never stopped frowning at her suspiciously, and Camilla had been packed up and shunted off to another family long before she'd had a chance to charm anyone.

That was all she had ever wanted. One person, just one, who promised not to leave her. She didn't need love. She didn't need wealth. After nine times packing her bags and boarding trains, braving swaying carts, or even once, walking seven miles with her aging valise in tow… After nine separate families, she would have settled for tolerance and a promise that she would always have a place to stay.

So of course she hoped for marriage. Not the way she might have as a child, dreaming of white knights and houses to look over and china and linen to purchase. She hoped for it in the most basic possible terms.

All she wanted was for someone to choose her.

Hoping for so little, she had believed that surely she could not be disappointed.

It just went to show. Fate had a sense of humor, and she was a capricious bitch.

For here Camilla stood on her wedding day. Wedding night, really. Her gown was not white, as Victoria's had been. In fact, she was still wearing the apron from the scullery. She had no waiting trousseau, no idea what sort of home—if any—awaited her. And she'd still managed to miss out on her dreams.

Her groom's face was hidden in the shadows; late as this wedding was, on this particular night, a few candles lit in the nave did more to cast shadows than shed illumination. He adjusted his cuffs, gleaming white against the brown of his skin, and folded his arms in disapproval. She couldn't see his eyes in the darkness, but his eyebrows made grim lines of unhappy resignation.

It might even have been romantic—for versions of *romantic* that conflated *foolhardy* with *fun*—to marry a man she had known for only three days. And what she knew of the groom was not terrible. He'd been kind to her. He had made her laugh. He had even—once—touched her hand and made her heart flutter.

It might have been romantic, but for one tiny little thing.

"Adrian Hunter," Bishop Cantrell was saying. "Do you take Camilla Worth to be your wife? Will you love her, comfort her, honor and protect her, and forsaking all others, be faithful to her as long as you both shall live?"

She would have overlooked the gown, the trousseau, anything. Anything but...

"No," said her groom. "I do not consent to this."

That one tiny little thing. Like everyone else in the world, her intended didn't want her.

Behind him, Rector Daniels lifted the pistol. His hands gleamed white on the barrel in the candle light, like maggots writhing on tarnished steel.

"It doesn't matter what you say," the man said. "You will agree and you will sign the book, damn your eyes."

"I do this under duress." His words came out clipped and harsh. "I do not consent."

Camilla shouldn't even call him her intended. *Intent* on his part was woefully lacking.

"I'm sorry," Camilla whispered.

He didn't hear her. Maybe he didn't care.

She wouldn't have minded if he didn't love her. She didn't want white lace and wedding cake. But this wasn't a marriage, not really. She was being wrapped up like an unwanted package again and sent on to the next unsuspecting soul.

After being passed on—and on—and on—and on— after all these years, she had no illusions about the outcome in this case.

The candlelight made Mr. Hunter's features seem even darker than they had in the sun. In the sun, after all, he'd smiled at her.

He didn't smile now.

There it was. Camilla was getting married, and her husband didn't want her.

Her lungs felt too small. Her hands were shaking. Her corset wasn't even laced tightly, but still she couldn't seem to breathe. Little green spots appeared before her eyes. Dancing, whirling.

Don't faint, Camilla, she admonished herself. *Don't faint. If you faint, he might leave you behind, and then where will you be?*

She didn't faint. She breathed. She said yes, and the spots went away. She managed not to swoon on her way to sign the register. She did everything except look at the unwilling groom whose life had so forcibly been tied to her own.

She followed him out into the cold winter evening. There would be no celebration, no dinner. Behind her back, she heard the clink of coins as the bishop turned to Mr. Hunter.

"There's an inn a mile away," the man said. "They might allow you to take rooms for the night. Don't expect that I'll give you a character reference."

Mr. Hunter made no response. He just started walking down the road.

That was how Camilla left the tenth family that had taken her in: on foot, at eleven at night, with a chill in the air and the moon high overhead. She had to half-skip to keep up with her new…husband? Should she call him a husband?

His long legs ate away at the ground. He didn't look at her.

But halfway to the inn, he stopped. At first, she thought he might finally address her. Instead, he let his own satchel fall to the ground. He looked up at the moon.

His hands made fists at his side. "Fuck." He spoke softly enough that she likely wasn't supposed to hear that epithet.

"Mr. Hunter?"

He turned to her. She still couldn't see his eyes, but she could feel them on her. He'd lost his position and gained a wife, all in the space of a few hours. She didn't imagine that he was happy with her.

He exhaled. "I suppose this…is what it is. We'll figure this mess out in the morning."

The morning. After the wedding came the wedding night. Camilla wasn't naïve. She just wasn't ready.

How had her life come to this?

Ah, yes. It had started three days ago, when Bishop Cantrell had arrived on her doorstep with Mr. Hunter in tow…

After the Wedding will be out in late 2016.

Other Books by Courtney

The Worth Saga
Once Upon a Marquess
Her Every Wish
After the Wedding
The Devil Comes Courting
The Return of the Scoundrel
The Kissing Hour
A Tale of Two Viscounts
The Once and Future Earl

The Cyclone Series
Trade Me
Hold Me
Find Me
What Lies Between Me and You
Keep Me

The Brothers Sinister Series
The Governess Affair
The Duchess War
A Kiss for Midwinter
The Heiress Effect
The Countess Conspiracy
The Suffragette Scandal
Talk Sweetly to Me

The Turner Series
Unveiled
Unlocked
Unclaimed
Unraveled

Not in any series
A Right Honorable Gentleman
What Happened at Midnight
The Lady Always Wins

The Carhart Series
This Wicked Gift
Proof by Seduction
Trial by Desire

Author's Note

When I first had the idea for this book, I knew I wanted Judith's father to have been convicted of *something* in the House of Lords. The problem was, I wasn't sure how that would be possible.

Trials in the House of Lords were usually a complete farce. The closest trial in time to Judith's father was the Earl of Cardigan's trial in 1841 for dueling. To call that trial a complete sham would be stretching things. Basically, the Earl of Cardigan was seen dueling. There was no question he was involved in a duel.

The indictment, however, stated that he was dueling with Harvey Garnet Phipps Tuckett, while the evidence presented at trial called the man Captain Harvey Tuckett. The House of Lords unanimously agreed that there wasn't evidence to support the indictment (!!) (if you know anything at all about the standards for when evidence supports an indictment, you are likely also thinking !!!!) because how was anyone to know that Captain Harvey Tuckett was the same person as Harvey Garnet Phipps Tuckett?

In the meantime, the prosecutor for the Crown was ripping his hair out and not so gently suggesting that it was allowable to draw reasonable inferences. Needless to say, the history of trial in the House of Lords is one where lords are given every benefit of every unreasonable doubt. The only exceptions were cases of treason, and those where someone had done something that threatened noble prerogatives.

I suspect, given the amount of money that was being made on the opium trade, that Judith's father would have really been convicted.

In case you're wondering why Anthony still has a title, when his father was convicted of treason, by the time 1866 came around, the concept known as "corruption of the blood" no longer existed. Corruption of the blood sounds a lot cooler than it actually is.

The idea behind the concept is this: For the life of the current earl, the earldom belongs to the earl. Once he dies, it belongs to that earl's eldest son, and so on and so on. So, in a sense (and if you want to know exactly what that sense is, you can go to law school and learn about future interests, although I *really* don't advise it purely to satisfy a question of curiosity), an earldom is property that you can chop up in time: the earl owns it only for this life, and the remainder belongs to his sons. Corruption of the blood is a legal concept that says that once a person has committed a sufficiently foul crime, he can lose not only *his* property, but can extinguish the remainder that otherwise would have gone to his son.

It no longer existed as of 1866.

For those wondering why Anthony wasn't tried in the House of Lords, it was because his father was still alive. Trials in the House of Lords took longer—they had to give the Lords time to assemble. While Anthony had a courtesy title of viscount, the courtesy title did not give him the right to trial in the Lords. So when the evidence came out, Anthony would have been tried and convicted first. Back then, trials happened quickly.

By the time 1858 rolled around, a sentence of transportation didn't automatically mean a trip to Australia. In fact, the law was changed in 1857 to reflect what was a growing reality: most convicts sentenced to transportation served their entire sentences in England. The former penal colonies were increasingly settled by people who had no interest in taking more convicts, and many of the former ships sat in the Thames (or elsewhere) and housed convicts like massive floating prisons.

If prisoners were chosen to be actually transported at random, the chances that Anthony would have been shipped to Australia would have been very small. Prisoners, however, weren't chosen at random, and so I imagine that Anthony would have been whisked from trial to transportation.

There weren't that many convict ships to begin with, so I've had to make a few alterations from the historical record. The only ship that made the convict run to Western Australia in the fall of 1858 was the Edwin Fox. I've added a different, fictional ship—one that would have sailed in November of 1858 from Plymouth, headed for Fremantle. This was somewhat late in the season for a voyage to Australia; going that late risked running into bad weather.

I'm not going to say too much about the opium wars, because…well, we'll see them again. I will say that the event that technically precipitated the second opium war was basically one hundred percent pretext. Britain had been trying (and failing) to legalize the opium trade by diplomatic means. China seized a ship that was maybe

British. I say "maybe British" because one, the Chinese seized it because it was on a list of pirate ships, and two, its registration as a British ship was expired at the time it was seized. Also, three, of the twelve workers on board the ship, all were Chinese.

Britain demanded that the ship and all its workers be released. The Chinese government agreed to release nine of them, but initially insisted on keeping three who were pirates. Britain refused to accept custody of the nine sailors, and in retaliation, seized a ship that they believed was owned by the Chinese government. (It wasn't.) Blustering ensued, with the end result that China released the entire crew, but didn't provide the full apology that Britain wanted, and so British forces attacked. Thus started the second opium war.

Nobody would have gone to war over this incident unless they really, really wanted to do so.

More details can be found in *The Opium Wars* by W. Travis Hanes and Frank Sanello.

There are three other things I should mention briefly about events in this book. First, when Christian describes the revenge he gets on his classmates at Eton, he mentions that they board up a room. I didn't invent this prank; I read about it in a volume of *Legends of Caltech* many years ago. Second, you may be wondering how Theresa's Kindly Elf Bread works. The process is called no-knead bread, and yes, it really doesn't require kneading. Ken Forkish's *Flour Water Salt Yeast* describes this in detail, or you can just read this New York Times recipe: http://cooking.nytimes.com/recipes/11376-no-knead-bread.

Finally, that thing about literally holding tongues… I didn't invent that. I'm not sure which of my family members did (although my suspicion falls on my older brother) but I learned at a very early age to never stick out my tongue if anyone had a towel in their hand. A valuable life lesson, I'm sure.

One last super-tiny thing, which I mention only to put a sticky note on this discussion for later author's notes.

In The Brothers Sinister series, I mentioned in the author's note for the first book that I was making a few tiny changes to the history of science. And, well, yeah, if you know what happened, sorry not sorry. At this point I've pretty much made it canon that the Brothers Sinister universe diverged strongly from ours—so much so that in The Brothers Sinister universe, women obtained the right to vote in 1895. (If you haven't read the crossover short story that establishes this, Adam Reynolds of Cyclone Technologies time-travels back to meet Frederica Marshall-Clark. It's on my website.)

With that as background, I point out six tiny little words in this book. They occur when Christian is discussing the men on Anthony's List with Mr. Lawrence. Those words are: *Lord Palmerston, deceased some months past.*

You should not pay attention to these words. Yes, Lord Palmerston is a real person. Yes, he was the Foreign Secretary during the First Opium War and the Prime Minister of England during the second. But Lord Palmerston really did die of a fever in 1865, less than a year before this book starts. So it's surely just a coincidence that he's on Anthony's list and happens to be dead.

If it weren't a coincidence, the entire political landscape of the Worth Saga universe might be up for grabs. Would I do that to you?

Acknowledgments

This was a really hard book to get through. Thank you to all the numerous people who helped me do so—my geniuses, Tessa, Carey, Brenna, Leigh, who listened to me talk (complain) about this book and told me it was too complicated and didn't laugh too hard when I said I would make it work, even though they knew I would admit they were right four months later. All the Diasporans who heard me claim that this would be the month I would finish this book…thank you for pretending to believe me. Northwest Pixies, thank you for your support and our yearly retreat, where I began to work on this. Peeners, thanks for letting me vent. And special thanks to my beautiful raptors, Alisha, Bree, Rebekah, Alyssa, and Mala, who remind me daily that faces are high in protein. I would never have made it through this book without all of you to cheer me on. Mr. Milan, Pele, and Silver were always supportive. Okay, Silver was not *actually* supportive, but since he is about fifteen cats' worth of cat, he was at least useful.

The initial version of the acknowledgment referred to my chickens as useless. Then they sustained an attack by the neighbors' dogs, and now I'm worried that life is imitating chicken-killing art. So I apologize for that, chickens. Take your time with the eggs. No rush.

Thank you to Lindsey Faber for pushing me as hard as I wanted to be pushed, Martha Trachtenberg for putting up with basically infinite delays, Rawles Lumumba for everything. Finally, thanks for swift, amazing work from Wendy Chan, the Passionate Proofreader, and Sadye Scott-Hainchek at The Fussy Librarian. Thanks also to Kristin Nelson, Lori Bennett, and everyone at NLA for their support.

Finally, Melissa, thank you for calmly, sweetly prodding me to do everything I need to do, even when it takes me something like three months to do it. Also, you may have noticed that one time we took a walk and saw geese, and I started narrating goose thoughts as Bill and Fred? That kind of turned into a thing. So.

As those of you who have been reading my books for a while may have noticed, this one took a long time to write. (A really long time.) I started in August of 2014 and here we are. I'm not a particularly speedy writer, and even for me, this book was a doozy. I'm sorry. Thank you so much for your patience, and I hope the wait was worth it.